D1474665

THE UNION

Book 1 in The Union Series

T.H. HERNANDEZ

To Ernie, for believing in me

I wonder if I would've spent so much time agonizing over my future if I'd known I'd be dead so soon. Something tells me I would have done a lot of things differently. If I'd known, maybe I would have done everything differently.

When I try to breathe in deeply, wrenching pain stops me short. Every inch of my body is consumed by a bottomless ache, including my lungs.

It's been days since I've had anything to eat, but I no longer feel hungry.

I lift my head, sending a sharp twinge through my skull. My grimace stretches my bottom lip until it cracks and bleeds. The burned coppery taste of blood hits my tongue, making me retch.

I curl into a ball, trying to hide from the pain, but there is no escaping. The packed dirt, small jagged rocks that scrape my cheek, and the putrid odor of decaying leaves all remind me of where I am.

Despair flows from my soul, drowning every last remnant of hope. I begin to cry, but without enough fluid left in my body to produce tears and a throat so ravaged no sound comes out, my body heaves with dry silent sobs until I am empty.

The emptiness eventually gives way to an unexpected calm. I lift my hand over my head and study the tiny rivers of dried blood crisscrossing my palm before it floats to my chest like one of the many brown and lifeless leaves that surround me.

With a resigned sigh, I close my eyes, no longer afraid it might mean never opening them again. In just a short time, I've gone through the five stages of grief and have arrived at acceptance.

What I know of death comes from entertainment. Movie deaths are noisy and dramatic, filled with action and brutal emotion. By contrast, mine will be silent and serene.

I wonder if they'll ever find my body out here or if my family will be left to always wonder what happened to me.

In my last moments of life, I try to piece together the events that brought me here. It all started that evening in May when I took Barklyn for a walk in the park to clear my head. Back when my biggest concern was the lack of any plans for my future.

Now I know my future.

My life ends here.

Alone.

In the Ruins.

BOOK 1 - THE UNION

100 Years After the Second U.S. Civil War

"It is not in the stars to hold our destiny but in ourselves."
—William Shakespeare

1

My Biggest Concern

*I*t's no big deal, just the rest of my life. Before the war, people had more time to sort out their futures – four more years of school – but now? Now, I'm almost out of time.

I drop my tablet with my history notes onto the bed and blow out a slow breath, sending crazy red curls flying in a dozen directions. The late afternoon sun cuts a bright swath across my room. Outside the window, desalinated ocean water gurgles along the channel. But neither the cheerful sun nor the sounds of the manmade stream do anything to improve my mood.

With a dramatic sigh, I roll off my bed and pad over to my door, yanking it door open. I bound down the curved staircase into the great room where my mom is sitting at the kitchen counter, reading. Katie and Rachel are sprawled across the cream-colored velour couch watching some idiotic tween show.

Barklyn leaps down from where he'd been curled up between my twin half-sisters and bounds over to me, tongue out, head cocked to the side, expectantly.

I grab his leash. "I'm going for a walk," I call to my mom.

She glances up from her tablet, her crystal green eyes taking in my attire. "Like that?"

I glance down at my jeans and faded Epic Vinyl T-shirt. "Sure. I'm just taking Barklyn for a walk."

"Evan, I wish you'd pay a little more attention to how you dress when you go out."

I roll my eyes so hard, I nearly fall over.

"I refuse to be a walking billboard for M Clothing."

"No one is asking you to, but could you at least put on a shirt without holes?"

The holes aren't the problem, but she'll never admit it. I hate this shirt and only wear it to annoy her. Mission accomplished.

When I don't make a move to change, she waves me off with a huff. "Joe will be home in an hour. Be back by then for dinner."

"Fine."

I let myself out the front door and walk down the path, dodging a drone delivering a package to our neighbor. Taking my favorite shortcut, I cross through the cobblestone plaza, past the weeping greenhouses, and swing open the iron gate leading to the park.

Tall trees on either side of the path reach out tangled fingers and pull at one another, creating a leafy canopy. Late spring flowers fill the air with aromas of lavender and orange. The only sound is my feet slapping against my flip-flops.

Barklyn pulls at his leash until I unclip him, allowing him to zip across the clearing, a blur of brown and white fur. He spots a group of pigeons and lowers his head before launching himself at them. The terrorized birds scatter in a burst of beating wings and flustered coos.

My self-induced pity party comes to an end when a gorgeous husky wanders into the park followed by his equally gorgeous owner, Bryce Vaughn.

My central nervous system spirals into a frenzy. Bryce's skin is the color of cappuccino and his slate gray eyes are like the winter sky. And if that combination wasn't striking enough to turn my legs to jelly, the dimples that appear when he smiles make my heart forget how to beat.

I whistle for Barklyn and he bounds over to me, giving up on the birds. But the high-pitched noise also catches Bryce's attention, and he turns and waves. Oh, dear god, he's coming over here. To talk to me. And I'm wearing my rattiest shirt, the one that advertises my bio-dad's band. Spiting my mother suddenly seems like a stupid idea.

I snap on Barklyn's leash and steel myself, turning to face him. Bryce is currently dating Alivia Benton, Queen Bee of Moores Academy and my arch nemesis. But when his eyes meet mine, my lungs stall, and all thoughts of Alivia evaporate.

"Hey, Evan." His smooth, sexy voice causes my pulse to do funny things.

"Bryce." I only manage a one-word response. I am not one of *those* girls. I don't get stupid around boys. Well, not other boys, but this one is an enigma.

His hands are shoved into the front pockets of his jeans. "Do you live nearby?"

"Yeah, over there." I point in the general direction of our apartment.

"What brings you to the park this evening?"

"I needed a break from studying for my history final."

"I took it this morning. It's not too hard."

I eye him. "Maybe, but I suck at remembering dates."

He smiles. "It's just a matter of finding a way to connect the date and the event."

A breeze sails across the park, sending pieces of hair into my eyes. I twist my head to get them out of my face, using my hand to shove one of the more offensive curls behind my ear. "Like?"

"I make up poems the way we did in the lower grades. Like, 'In 1492, Columbus sailed the ocean blue.' I came up with a bunch of new ones, like 'In February 2065, the war ended with more dead than alive.'"

"Clever, and yet oddly morose."

He pulls his hands out of his pockets, shifting his feet. "The secret is to make them as twisted as possible."

I struggle to pay attention to what he's saying instead of staring at those perfect, kissable lips.

"...but what I really want to do is mix my love of history and literature. Write about the people who founded the Union. It must have been so cool to live back then."

I imagine what his lips would feel like pressed against mine and smile.

"What?" He asks, a spark of amusement in his eyes.

Crap, crap, crap. He caught me ogling his mouth. Color creeps into my cheeks. "You seem so...I don't know, excited, I guess, about your vocation."

"What's yours?"

My gaze drops to my toes and I wiggle them. "I haven't declared yet."

"Lots of teens take the summer after graduation to figure it out."

I sigh and glance up. "I'm probably gonna end up at M Clothing anyway. My stepdad wants me work for him. Hell, he expects it."

"That's an amazing opportunity." His gaze drops to my T-shirt, likely wondering why a fashion slob would go into the business. "Tons of kids at school would love to work there."

No doubt his girlfriend is one of them. She was a child model for M Clothing until Joe fired her for tormenting me. "Yeah, I suppose."

"You should do what you love, Evan. Find out what that is and don't settle for less."

The way he says my name makes little swirly happy feelings dance in my stomach. Barklyn pulls at his leash, smelling something out of range. I reach down and unhook him so he can investigate. "Go on, Barklyn." He darts off followed by Bryce's dog.

Bryce raises his eyebrows. "Barklyn?"

I roll my eyes at the stupid name. "Yeah. My mom's idea. She combined Brooklyn from Old New York, with bark because, well, he's a dog... She does that. Combines stuff to come up with weird names. Like mine."

A smile tips up the corners of his mouth. "She named you after Evansville, Indiana?"

I laugh. "Funny, but no. She named me after my grandmother, Eve, and my grandfather, Nathan."

His smile broadens, revealing his dimples. "It suits you. It's beautiful and unique."

I arch an eyebrow. Is he flirting with me? This conversation just detoured into dangerous territory. It's safe to dream about Bryce, but in the real world, he has a girlfriend. And she *hates* me. If she finds out her boyfriend is flirting with me, I am so dead.

I whistle for Barklyn and snap on his leash. "I should be getting back."

Bryce throws me a casual wave. "Maybe I'll see you and Barklyn here again sometime."

I turn and walk to the steps but can't resist a quick glance over my shoulder.

He's watching me go, his devastating smile lighting up his face. "See you tomorrow, Evansville."

2

Tomorrow

I wake with a start and realize I overslept. Throwing off my sheet with a loud groan, I stumble out of bed. Barklyn lifts his head from the foot of my bed and yawns. After watching me for a few seconds, he rolls to his side and closes his eyes.

I shuffle down the hall to the bathroom, my sisters' voices rising in anger from the kitchen below. Apparently they can't agree on which boy band has the hottest lead singer.

After a quick shower, I return to my room and dress in a pair of faded jeans. I grab a T-shirt from my drawer, but my gaze shifts from the shirt in my hand to my closet. My mom keeps it stocked with the latest fashions from M Clothing. I normally prefer comfort over style, but this morning I'm second-guessing my fashion philosophy.

A white ruffled swing tank from my stepdad's spring collection catches my eye. I slip it on and check myself in the mirror. My flip-flops look too casual, and I cross the hall to rifle through my mom's shoes, finding a pair of strappy sandals that perfectly match the top. Yay Mom.

Better, but my hair is a cringeworthy frizzed mess. With

enough time, a big round brush, and a blow dryer, I can coax my hair into soft waves, but today, I have to settle for applying some product and twirling the strands into ringlets.

A quick touch of mascara and a little lip gloss and I'm ready to go, but now it's too late to eat breakfast. I rush back to my room, jam my tablet into my shoulder bag, and fly down the stairs. After grabbing a protein bar from the counter, I kiss my mom goodbye, and race out the door.

The commuter station is overflowing with bodies, and I have to wait until the third train to board. By the time I get on, all the enclosed seating areas are full, meaning I'll have to sit in the noisy galley. I spot an open seat, but the train pulls out before I can sit and I nearly topple into the lap of the woman sitting in the next seat.

"Sorry," I mumble, dropping down next to her. I lean my head back and close my eyes. The soft hum of the electric motor is soon drowned out by the buzz of dozens of conversations, while a mixture of body odor and strong coffee pervades the car.

I do my best to block out the external stimuli and run through history dates in my head, and Bryce's rhymes come to mind. Thinking about his dimples instead of my final makes me smile. I force my thoughts back to history, working my way from Christopher Columbus through Union Formation Day.

My feet silently flip me off as I step off the train and walk across the terminal. I'm half tempted to go back home and change into my flip-flops when Colin spots me.

My best friend lopes over and throws one of his long arms over my shoulder, his shaggy brown hair falling into his dark eyes. "Hey, looking good today, EvTay."

Colin is fascinated by all things twenty-first century, from music and movies to fashion and food, and especially pop culture. Mashing up first and last names is his ultimate tribute, and a fad that died out long before the first shot was fired in the Second Civil War.

We make our way from the train station to Lisa's apartment.

She flings the door open when Colin knocks and takes in my attire. Her blond eyebrows notch up, but she wisely keeps her thoughts to herself. She knows me well enough to understand there's a reason I spent more time getting ready this morning, but the look I shoot her keeps her from asking me about it.

The three of us head to the congested sidewalk, bumping shoulders with other pedestrians. We pass shops and restaurants with dark wood exteriors and brick facades that create the illusion of a pre-war Manhattan neighborhood.

Lisa chatters about her summer plans on the three-block walk to school. She's been accepted into the internship of her dreams at a trendy restaurant in the Western Province. "I lined up an apartment, and I'm going to spend the summer out west. I'm gonna miss you guys, though." She grabs my arm, pulling me to a sudden stop. "I have the *best* idea. Come with me. Stay at my place. Ev, you can sort out your...future...." she waves her hand in front of my face, "...while lying on the beach. Maybe indulge in a summer romance. You could use a little boy action."

"No way. My mom's head would explode if I take off for the summer. Anyway, I'm not interested in dating right now."

"Fine, just look then." She rolls her dark brown eyes. "I don't get you, it's not like you have to sleep with a guy to date him. Besides, no one gets pregnant by accident anymore."

"You mean no one besides my mom."

She crosses her arms over her chest and levels her gaze at me. "You're not going to end up like your mom."

"Your mom's life isn't so bad," Colin says.

I turn to face him, eyes narrowed. "If you tell me my mom's hot one more time, I'll smack you into next week. That's just creepy."

Colin flushes bright red. "No...I mean...for having been a teen mom, she's got a pretty good life. You guys live on the top level. Most people would kill for that."

"She gave up everything she wanted because of some guy, and then he dumped her the second she got pregnant," I huff out. "That's not gonna be me."

"I'm not saying you should follow in her footsteps," Colin mumbles. "But you could pick a worse role model."

I try hard not to roll my eyes.

"Getting back to your plan...I don't think I can go. I think I'm going to work for Joe. At least over the summer."

Lisa halts and spins me to face her. "You already know you're gonna hate it. Three more months working there won't change anything. Plus, I can tell by your tone you haven't really decided."

I pull my arm loose and resume walking. "He's counting on me. I haven't told him I don't want to."

"Just because you haven't told him, doesn't mean he doesn't know," Lisa says. "He'd have to be blind not to see it."

I blow out a puff of air and change the subject. "I talked to Eddie last night. He's not coming for graduation, surprise, surprise. Apparently, my evil stepmommy is trying to get sole custody of the half-sibs. He's afraid if he leaves, she'll claim abandonment or something. He's sending me a ticket to visit him over the summer. Maybe I'll go for a week or two next month. I can spend a few days with him, then hang out with you guys."

Lisa waves her hand in front of my face in exaggerated fashion, like a mini fan blade. "You don't want to work for Joe. What are you going to do after summer? You'll never leave. You'll end up working at M Clothing until you die."

"Geez, Lis," Colin says. "That's kinda harsh."

Lisa shakes her head. "It's reality, and if she doesn't make some tough choices now, she'll end up even more miserable than she already is."

I stop and put my hands on my hips. "Hey, I'm standing right here. I can hear you."

"Good," she says with a satisfied smile.

3

Change of Subject

*T*he moment we push through the front doors, laughter, clanging of metal lockers, and voices flood me. Various body sprays, perfumes, and aftershave scents mix in a dizzying array. We climb the wide main staircase to the second floor. Lisa and Colin go left and I head right, stopping for a moment to glance out the floor-to-ceiling glass walls that allow me to see all the way to the ocean on a clear day. Today heavy clouds mask my view.

I turn and spot Bryce leaning against the wall talking with his jock friends. He's wearing loose jeans and a faded navy T-shirt that makes his eyes look more blue than gray. His head turns, as if he senses me coming, and he directs his intoxicating smile my way.

I give him a quick smile in return and can't resist glancing over my shoulder after I pass. Bryce is watching me, still grinning, his dimples sending my heart spinning on its axis.

BAM. My head slams into something solid and a sharp pain shoots through my skull. I take an unsteady step back, my feet sliding out from under me, and land ass-first on the tile.

Muffled giggles and all-out raucous laughter surround me. I

close my eyes and pray for the floor to open up and swallow me. Instead, my mortification is compounded when a smooth, brown hand reaches down to me. With a heavy sigh, I lift my gaze to meet Bryce's, finding sympathy, not humor, in his eyes. He pulls me up, his fingers lingering longer than necessary, making my pulse quicken.

"You gotta watch out for those doors, they've been known to kill people."

My face darkens and I mumble, "Thanks."

Bryce reaches out and tucks a curl behind my ear. The gesture is intimate and unexpected. "Are you okay?"

His eyes lock onto mine, sucking me in. I could drown on those babies. Being this close to him, his hand still holding mine, heats the air around me, and I struggle to keep my breathing even. My surroundings disappear and voices blur as I'm pulled into the vortex of Bryce.

I swallow hard. "Yeah, I'm fine. Just...embarrassed."

The continuous hum of voices around us halts and everything snaps back into focus. When I glimpse Alivia out of the corner of my eye, the lingering heat from Bryce's proximity freezes over. She stands with one hand on her bony hip and narrows her icy blue eyes at us. I yank my hand back and duck under his arm, dashing down the hall to my first class before the daggers from her eyes can impale me. Without looking around, I slip into my seat and snap my tablet into the docking station. Tears flood my eyes, blurring the display.

"Good morning, students," Mr. Caldwell says as he enters the classroom seconds after the bell rings. "Everything on today's final was covered in class. If you paid attention and studied, you will pass. Click the 'Caldwell-History' app and tap the 'Final' icon."

I do as instructed, temporarily restricting access to my other apps. After finishing ahead of most of my classmates, I press *Submit*, returning control of my tablet to me. I pull out my tiny wireless ear buds, pop them in, and launch my music app.

A deep bass thrums in my ears as I try to block the events of this morning from my mind. When class is over, I stuff my tablet in my shoulder bag and escape before anyone can talk to me. I keep my head down, avoiding eye contact, nearly bumping into Lisa and Colin.

"Evan, what happened? Everyone's talking about it," Lisa says.

Oh no. "Uhh, I made an ass of myself in front of half the school."

Colin pulls me around to face him. "I don't know what you're talking about, but everyone else is talking about how Alivia busted you and Bryce flirting."

"It wasn't like that…not exactly."

We turn and head down the main staircase toward our next class, and catch a few kids staring at me when we pass.

Colin drapes his arm across my shoulder. "Word on the street is Bryce was playing with your hair."

"Oh, my god!" I bury my face in my hands. This isn't good.

"What's the deal with you and Bryce?" Lisa asks.

"Nothing. I slipped in the hallway and he offered me a hand up. That's all."

She glances down at my shoes, then back up at my face before studying my hair. "So then what's with the makeup and your hair?" She flicks one of my curls.

I jerk my head away from her hand. "Nothing."

Lisa pulls to a stop and grabs my arm, forcing me to face her. "I thought we were friends. The kind of friends who tell each other everything."

"There's nothing to tell."

Lisa snorts. "Are you trying to piss me off?"

I sigh. "No. I just…you know how long I've been crushing on him. Then last night at the park he was there with his dog, and we talked. But that's all. Just talked. I don't know, though, there was something more, you know?"

Lisa nods, as if this is not a surprise to her at all. "Why didn't you mention it this morning?"

I shrug. "I didn't want it to be another me swooning over Bryce moment so you and Colin could roll your eyes again."

"Oh, Ev..." She pats my head like I'm a two-year-old.

I jerk out of her reach. "It doesn't matter. He's with Alivia, and she's going to hate me even more. I wish she'd get over Joe firing her. That was like five years ago. She models for all kinds of companies now."

"That is *so* not what this is about."

"Of course it is. She's made me her personal punching bag ever since the whole 'Eddie McIntyre is my real dad' thing."

"How can you be so smart and so dumb at the same time? Come here." Lisa grabs my wrist and pulls me into the girls bathroom.

My shoes click on the tile, echoing off the bare walls as she pushes me up to the counter. She takes my face between her hands and points me at the mirror. Colin stands behind us, and I try to twist around to make sure no one else is in here, but Lisa holds me firmly in place.

"Look." She lets go of my face and moves to stand next to me "You're beautiful, Ev. Alivia hates you because she's jealous."

"Hardly. I know I'm not ugly, but come on, Alivia's tall and model thin with that flawless complexion. Even zits are afraid of her."

As if on cue, the door opens and Alivia enters, her eyes red and her skin a little blotchy, like she's been crying. Her expression hardens when she spots us. "I always thought you were secretly a girl, *Colleen*."

"You got me *Ohhhh-livia*." Colin says.

He heads toward the door and Alivia calls after him, "It's Uh-livia with an A, not Oh-livia with an O." I roll my eyes. We've heard that about a thousand times. She catches my eye-roll. "At least I don't have a boy's name."

"Stunningly original, Alivia," I reply.

Lisa turns to me. "I'm going to class. Coming?"

"Yeah, I need to pee first. Be there in a few."

"You sure?" she mouths, eyeing Alivia over my shoulder.

I nod and lock myself in the stall while Lisa's shoes clack across the tile on her way out.

4

Alivia

The bathroom door opens and closes, and I'm pretty sure Alivia left. At least until Montreal says, "Liv, there you are. I just heard–"

I assume her abrupt silence is the result of one of Alivia's death stares. Alivia clearly doesn't want me to overhear whatever Montreal was about to say. Animated whispers follow, then someone enters the stall to my left.

I contemplate staying in here until they leave, but decide that's too chickenshit. Taking a deep breath, I open the stall door. Alivia and Montreal lean against the counter in front of me, arms crossed. Montreal's cat eyes are narrowed, staring me down.

I take a step toward the sink, assuming they'll move aside, but a sharp pain ricochets through my skull, making me stagger to the right before regaining my footing.

Gia stands next to the open stall door on my left, a satisfied smirk on her face. "I hear you like doors upside the head."

A horrific ache replaces the initial sting, and I fight back tears of pain and shock. "What's your problem?"

"Like you don't know," Gia says.

"No. I don't." Although I *do* know it has something to do with Bryce.

Movement in the mirror alerts me to what's coming, but I can't react fast enough to stop it. Gia grabs my hair and yanks my head down.

"Ow!"

Before I can right myself, Gia slams her knee into my face. The pain is blinding, and light flashes behind my eyes. A warm trickle of blood seeps from my nose, and I wipe it with the back of my hand. The sight of bright crimson on the back of my hand makes the room tilt, or maybe she hit me even harder than I thought.

I shake it off and stand up just in time for Montreal to kick me in the stomach, sending me flying into the stall. My butt connects with the ground seconds before my head jerks back, striking the porcelain edge of the toilet. A bursting shot of mind-numbing pain races through my skull.

"You think you're such hot shit because your dad's a rock star. But you're *nothing*," Montreal says. "You're the redheaded stepchild no one wants."

Her words hit closer to home than I care to admit, but they also snap me out of my daze. Pumped with adrenaline, I pull myself up and ball my fists, throwing a punch at Montreal's face with my full weight. A sickening crack accompanies the searing pain in my knuckles and nausea rolls through me.

"You're a slob with frizzy hair and a big rack. Guys are only looking at your boobs," Alivia says.

"Jealous you don't have anything for them to look at?" I ask before lunging, knocking her to the floor.

"Bitch," she screams.

I hold her down while she flails beneath me, screaming like a crazed animal. Montreal and Gia kick me, and I yelp when one of their pointed shoes connects with a rib. Squirming, I attempt to dodge their feet while hanging onto Alivia.

A hand grabs my hair and pulls my head back, allowing Alivia to wiggle out from under me. Alivia bends down until her face is next to mine. "If you *ever* talk to my boyfriend again, this will feel like a day at the spa compared to what I'll do to you."

I spit a mixture of saliva and blood in her face. "Bring it on, OH-livia."

Whoever is holding my hair lets go and my head falls to the floor. Alivia's boot connects with my temple and everything fades to black.

"Evan...Evan, wake up."

A hand gently rocks my shoulder and something cool presses against my cheek. It's a struggle to lift my eyelids, but when I finally pry them open, trendy purple sneakers come into focus. *Lisa.*

With a groan, I try to push up, but excruciating pain convinces me not to bother. I drop back down, closing my eyes. It's nice down here.

"Colin, go get help. Hurry!"

Someone lifts me and my ribs scream in protest. "Sorry," comes a whisper. I take a shallow breath and surrender to the darkness.

My eyes fly open and I blink to clear my vision. When the room stops spinning, I recognize the white walls and antiseptic stench of the school's health office. Clive, the school nurse, is waving something under my nose.

Lisa stands behind him, her twisted face relaxing. "Oh, thank god. What happened?"

Everything comes rushing back to me. My voice cracks and a sudden bout of nausea overtakes me. Clive thrusts a bin in front of me, and I lose what's left of my breakfast bar.

"Alivia," I whisper, laying back on the cot as the room tilts under me.

"Alivia? Alivia did this to you?" Lisa's screech bores through my skull and splits my head in two.

"Not alone."

"I called for an ambulance," Clive says. "You may have a concussion and other internal injuries." He hands me a glass with a straw in it. "Here, this will settle your stomach. Lisa, can you call her parents? Phillips Memorial is closest. They'll take her there."

Colin enters and gives me one of his crooked smiles. "That must have been one helluva door you walked into."

A short laugh escapes, but that only intensifies the pain slicing through my head. My laughter turns to tears, and soon I can't stop crying. Colin's eyebrows draw together and his mouth drops open.

Lisa pops back in a few minutes later. "The ambulance is here and your parents are on their way to the hospital."

Two paramedics arrive, and after running their scanners over me to record my vitals, they transfer me to a stretcher. I watch the lights pass overhead before turning to check out the crowd gathering in the hallway. They stare at the freakish parade going by, a couple visibly recoiling.

"How bad is it?" I ask Lisa.

She winces. "You look fabulous. But you know in a puffy-eyed, blotchy faced, beat-the-crap-out-of sort of way."

Two cracked ribs, a couple of broken bones in my hand, a concussion, and a crapload of bruises. My face got the worst of it though. It resembles an eggplant that's been thrown against a brick wall a few times.

Mom, Joe and the girls left to get dinner when the police arrived to take my statement. Now the police are gone and I'm alone for the first time since I was admitted.

Lisa said Bryce dumped Alivia and for some reason only Alivia can understand, she blames me. Although knowing her, this is less about Bryce and more about her image. What's most bizarre about all this is she just ruined any chance of a long-term modeling career. Even her daddy can't get her out of this mess. Why would she risk everything over a personal vendetta from five years ago?

"Thanks for taking care of my niece." My uncle's voice outside my room startles me from my thoughts.

"You're welcome, Governor. She's in good hands."

If Uncle David is here, things are about to go from nasty to downright ugly.

5

Downright Ugly

*U*ncle David enters my room followed by his security detail. The men in black stop in front of the door and face us. My uncle scrapes a chair across the floor from the window to the side of my bed.

He takes a seat, his gaze meeting mine. "Hi, Pumpkin, how are you doing?" I'm impressed he doesn't flinch at the sight of me.

"Eh, I'm gonna live."

"Hey, this is me you're talking to."

I glance at the two guys by the door. "I'm okay. Really."

He turns to his detail. "Give us a minute." They nod and step outside the room, resuming their stance, this time facing the hall. My uncle levels his gaze at me. "Tell me what happened."

I recount everything I remember, my voice somehow remaining steady.

"All three girls are in custody," he says when I finish. "But they're saying you started the fight."

"What?" The steadiness abandons me as anger and bitterness coil through. "That's not true. You have to believe me."

"Of course I do, but you landed one hell of a punch." He gives me a small smile. "It makes their story more plausible."

Kicking the crap out of me wasn't enough, now they're blaming me, too. The unfairness is a slap across my swollen face.

"Evan, I know this is hard." He hands me a tissue to wipe my nose. I inhale a shaky breath, sinking back into my pillow. "If the case goes to trial, there's not much I can do with the upcoming re-election. Alivia's father told me he's considering backing my opponent. I don't hold any leverage at the moment, but I may be able to broker a deal. A public trial for his daughter is the last thing Mayor Benton wants."

The Union's political system was supposed to cut down on government corruption, but this feels pretty damn corrupt.

"What kind of a deal?" I ask.

"One without a trial. Alivia and the other girls will do some community service."

This is unbelievable. Everything always works out for her, like she sweats glitter and farts rainbows. Suddenly the pieces click into place. "I was trying to figure out why she'd destroy her future over something so petty, but I get it now. She always knew she'd get away with it."

Uncle David sighs and rubs his face with his hands. "I understand if you don't want to let this go, but there's a lot to consider with a trial. Think it through and let me know what you decide. I'll support you either way." He stands and straightens his tie. "Are your parents here?"

"Yeah. They went down to the cafeteria to get dinner."

"I need to talk to your dad before I head back to the office. I'll see you soon."

"Thanks for everything."

He gives me a tight smile. "I just wish my everything could've been more." His security detail opens the door, and he walks out,/ leaving me alone with my thoughts.

I don't want Alivia to get away with this, but I'm not sure I have the strength to fight all of them. Letting her win is wrong on every level, but going to trial, testifying, listening to her lies? That might be more than I can handle.

Somewhere in all the thinking, the pain medication kicks in and I doze off.

"Hey, Evansville." A smooth, sexy voice pulls me from my drug-induced sleep.

Today has gone from the worst day ever to my own personal hell. When it becomes apparent he's not leaving, I stop feigning sleep and pry open one eye. "Hey."

Bryce stands near the door, his hands stuffed into the front pockets of his jeans. I raise my bed to a seated position and stare at him, waiting for him to tell me what he's doing here.

"I wanted to make sure you're okay." Bryce walks over to sit on the edge of the bed and stares down at the pale green blanket, tracing his finger over the pattern. When he lifts his head, his gaze holds mine with intensity. "I need to apologize."

I'm at a loss for words, unsure why he's apologizing because Alivia took the A-Train to crazy town.

He shifts and takes a deep breath. "I broke up with Alivia last night. We weren't serious or anything and I'm leaving after graduation next week." He shakes his head. "She jumped to conclusions when she saw me talking to you this morning."

The door opens and Lisa barrels in, Colin trailing behind her. "Oops. Didn't mean to interrupt."

"I should be going," Bryce says, standing and moving toward the door. His steel-colored eyes never waver from mine until he turns and walks out.

My head spins and I'm not sure if it's from the concussion or Bryce. I stare at the door, trying to figure out what just happened while Lisa and Colin chatter, only bits of their conversation filtering into my consciousness.

While they talk, the events of the past twenty-four hours spiral in my head. Bryce's words at the park about not settling for a career I don't want, working for Joe, getting my ass handed to me in the bathroom, my uncle's proposed deal. They slide and move until they suddenly line up, like pieces of one of those sliding picture puzzle games.

"Evan?" Lisa's pinched features make it clear she's annoyed I'm not paying attention to her.

"Can you get my parents for me? I need to talk to them."

She furrows her brow, but just shrugs and says, "Okay."

After she leaves, Colin sits on the edge of my bed. "They really did a number on you."

"Yeah. It feels like I was plowed by a train."

He shakes his head, but Lisa returns with my mom and Joe before either of us can say more. Colin and Lisa hug me goodbye with promises of visiting again tomorrow.

Alone with my parents, my eyes flick between them. My body is relaxed, my limbs heavy. It might be the drugs, but I'm not nervous. I take that as a sign this is the right decision. I haven't been this sure about anything in a long time, if ever.

I take a deep breath and exhale. "I know what I want to do. Eddie is sending me a ticket to visit him and the kids." My mom bristles at my bio-dad's name, and I hurry on before she can shoot me down. "I want to upgrade to an L-Train ticket and go to the Western Province with Lisa and Colin. I want to take the summer to figure out what to do with my life."

"I'm sorry, but no," my mom says.

Tucking in my top lip, I count my breaths. I need to act like the mature almost-adult I am if I want her to consider my idea. "Why not?"

"With the divorce and all…it's just the wrong time." Her jaw clenches and she works hard to keep her voice even. "He can come here if he wants to see you."

"He always comes here. Besides, he can't. He's worried Ashlynn will fight him for custody if he leaves now."

My mom tries and fails to hide a smile. She's never been a fan of my stepmom, but now it appears they're both on the same side of the "Eddie is a tool" argument.

My best chance might be to get Joe on my side. I shift my gaze to his dark eyes. "I know you want me to work for you, but it's not what I want. Katie and Rachel are dying to take over the business someday, and they'll love every minute of it." I let out a soft sigh, knowing this is hard for him to hear. "I adore you, Joe. You've always treated me as your own daughter, but the truth is Katie and Rachel share your DNA and are more like you because of it."

The pain in his eyes comes close to destroying my resolve. The last thing I want to do is hurt him, but I need him to understand. "You're the only real father I've ever known, but sometimes even biological kids aren't like their parents. Look at me and Mom. In some ways, I'm no more like her than I'm like you." I pause, gathering my thoughts, desperate to say the words that will make him see. "I have to find what drives me, not take over what drives you."

His eyes soften and I give him a small smile before turning back to my mom. Her face is set in a determined scowl. I may have swayed Joe, but my mom is a special kind of stubborn. We need to be alone if I'm going to use the nuclear option.

I turn back to Joe. "Is Uncle David still here? I need to talk to him about something, too." He kisses the top of my head before going off in search of his brother.

With a deep breath, I start my assault. "Please, Mom. I have to do this."

"You're too young to go off by yourself."

I stifle a groan. "I won't be on my own. Lisa and Colin will be with me. And I'm not too young – I'll be eighteen in four months."

"And until then, you're my responsibility." Her tone isn't unkind, but there is an air of finality to it.

The remnants of hope slip through my fingers, and I reach out to grab them. "I can't stay here. I'm smothering. I've never even been out of the Eastern Province. How am I supposed to figure anything out living this stifled existence?"

She rolls her eyes. "Aren't you being a little dramatic, Evan?"

Probably, but I'll never admit it. "This is so unfair. You treat me like a child, like I'm going to make the same mistakes you did if you give me even an inch of freedom."

Her eyes flash with anger, but her voice remains calm. "I'm sorry you feel that way." She stands, smoothing the blanket. "I did the best I could."

The rigidity of her shoulders and her flat tone tell me I've lost, I'll be stuck here forever. I take one last desperate stab at claiming my own future, hating that she's left me no choice but to play the wounded child card. "You *owe* me. I've spent the last five years playing catch-up on who I am, but I still need to discover so much about myself."

She pauses at the door, her body stiffening. I don't enjoy throwing this in her face, but it's true. Sure, Eddie chose a budding music career over family responsibilities, but she made the twisted decision to tell me my father was dead and then lured Joe into going along with the lie. While it's not her fault Eddie was a dead-beat dad, it *is* her fault she kept the truth from me for twelve years. If Eddie hadn't had a sudden attack of guilt a few years back, I still wouldn't have a clue.

I used to blame myself, thinking I did something wrong. It took four years of therapy to accept I'm the only one who isn't to blame in all of this, but I still battle with identity and abandonment issues on a regular basis.

Mom sinks down on the bed next to me, tears welling up in her beautiful green eyes. "I know." She lets out a shaky sigh. "It was just you and me until I met Joe. I can't seem to remember my life without you."

I soften a little toward her, but now is not the time to get mushy. "Mom, I'm not leaving forever, but I need to find my own place in the world."

She chews her lip, one of the few mannerisms I get from her. "This is so sudden, Evan. I'm worried that after what happened, you're running away."

"I'll admit I'm happy to get away from all the drama here, but I feel more like I'm running toward something." I reach out and place my hand on hers. "There's so much more of the Union for me to experience, so many options to explore. I know I can figure out what I'm supposed to do with my life if I just look in the right place."

Her gaze drops to our hands for several long moments. She shakes her head. "I'm sorry, Evie, it's just not a good idea."

I close my eyes against the threatening tears, refusing to cry in front of her. Mom leans forward and kisses my head, but I jerk away. She sighs and the bed shifts as she gets up.

After I hear the door close, I open my eyes and let my anger beat back the tears. This is so unfair, I've never had a say in anything in my life.

When I turn eighteen in September, I'm leaving here and never coming back. I don't know where I'll go or what I'll do, but I am so done with this shit.

My door opens a few minutes later, and I turn to see my mom standing just inside the door, her shoulders sagging. "You can go. Find whatever it is you're searching for." She lets out a shuddering breath. "We'll upgrade your ticket."

A rush of relief runs through me. I can't believe what just happened. I'm afraid to say something for fear she'll change her mind. Finally, I whisper, "Thanks, Mom." But after she leaves my room again, I can't wipe the goofy grin off my face.

6

Running Toward Something

The stack of clothes on my bed, chosen by my mother, are completely impractical. I toss the lot into my dresser and choose more suitable items along with an assortment of comfortable footwear.

After packing, I dress in a pair of jeans and tank top, throwing an oversized white T-shirt over it, and manipulating my hair into a loose braid.

Five weeks after the attack, there are no visible scars. After being released from the hospital, I opted to take the rest of my exams remotely. I didn't feel like putting up with the stares, whispers, and endless questions about what happened.

Talking Lisa and Colin into switching to the L-Train was easy. The hard part was telling my uncle to make the deal with Alivia's dad. I hate that she's getting off with nothing more than a slap on the wrist, but I chose to do what's right for me for a change. And right now, that's getting the hell out of here. A trial would've meant staying put for another four months with no guarantee a jury would even believe me.

My pride and unwillingness to let Alivia get the best of me

have driven far too many of my decisions. It's long past time to clip the strings of anger, bitterness, and resentment and just...let go.

The high-speed A-Trains run on elevated rails on the top level of the Union; their purpose is fast and efficient travel. The L-Trains, on the other hand, are modern-day cruise ships, gliding along ground level near the coast. They stop numerous times in each province, allowing passengers to disembark and sightsee.

The terminal is a crazy mess of people waiting to catch the train or pick up arriving friends or family. Two little kids run past followed by their harried parents, attempting to herd luggage and children alike.

My family is here to see me off, even Barklyn. He sits at my heel, taking everything in. Outwardly, he seems calm but I think he senses something's up.

Lisa and her parents join us, which ramps up the anxiety in our group. Mom grips my hand a little tighter, the way a child holds on to the string of a balloon.

We make small talk until the Jennings show up a few minutes later. Barklyn lets out a yip and runs up to Colin, who bends down to ruffle the fur on his head.

My heart is racing by the time the train finally rounds the bend and comes into view. I catch my breath at the absolute enormity of it. I've only seen them from a distance, but up close it's a behe-moth — the width of at least three A-Trains and twice as tall. While small windows dot the sides of A-Trains, this L-Train is almost entirely windows. The tinted glass begins a foot from the bottom and curves up and over the top.

It slides to a stop and I move to get in line. Mom pulls me into a tight embrace, crushing me to her until I worry she'll never let go. Joe pries her from me and gives me one of his abbreviated hugs. "Call us when you get to Lisa's, let us know you arrived in one piece." He slips me a wad of cash. "For incidentals...or whatever."

"I will, and thanks, Joe." I wrap my arms around him and fight sudden, unexpected tears. We may not be related by blood, but he'll always be my dad.

Standing on the platform with my family for maybe the last time for a while, I can't help but think about my life with them. I get why my mom didn't give me Eddie's last name, but I always wondered why Joe didn't legally adopt me. The one time I asked, I got a vague answer, and after I found out the truth of my paternity, anger took the place of curiosity.

I'm a part of my family and they're a part of me. But I can't ignore the fact that I'm Evan Taylor. Not Evan Minelli or even Evan McIntyre. This trip might be about finding my future, but it's also about finding out who I really am.

I say quick goodbyes to my sisters. We've never been particularly close — I've always been an outsider in their twindom — but now that I'm leaving, any chance at being closer is probably fading.

Mom walks back over and takes my face in her hands. "I love you, Evie. I'm going to miss you, but I am so proud of you."

"Thanks, Mom. I love you, too."

I give Barklyn one last pat on his fuzzy head and queue up. With a cleansing breath, I step onto the train and place my finger on a biometric scanner, confirming my identity. A uniformed porter with a broad smile and a name tag that says "James" greets me.

James takes my bag and leads me down a hallway through four cars before reaching a room on the right. He scans my fingerprint again and sends a signal to the PrintPad next to the door. When I press my finger on it, it beeps and James pushes the door open.

My room for the next ten days is as luxurious as it is small. Plush taupe and white furniture sits in the center of the space. Tinted glass wraps two-thirds of the way over the top and is covered with heavy damask drapes. An intricate crystal chandelier hangs in the middle of the room, suspended by a solid pole.

I push the drapes aside and peer out at the coastline in the distance.

"Housekeeping will be by this evening to turn down your bed," James says. I whip around, but it suddenly occurs to me there's no bed. He smiles. "If you should need to rest before then, press this." He slides his finger on the control panel embedded into one of the armchairs and taps an icon titled "bed". He steps to the side as the furniture grouping slides across the floor and a bed unfolds from the wall. He lifts the cushions from the couch. "The pillows are in here."

I tear my eyes away from the magical bed long enough to thank and tip James. My smile grows when I turn around and take in my temporary residence. After putting my bed away with another tap on the screen, I work on unpacking until a knock interrupts me.

Lisa stands on the other side of the door, her dark eyes shining. "Did you see the bed?"

"Yep! Coolest bed ever. Where's your room?"

"A couple of doors down. Colin's across the hall. Let's go see what he's up to."

Colin yanks the door open with a broad smile. "This train is wicked."

Lisa plops down in one of the armchairs and puts her feet up on the coffee table. "What should we do first?"

"I want to check this out." Colin points to a map on his display wall, indicating an area in the middle of the train. I walk over and take a closer look. The A-Train is forty-five cars long with thirty devoted to sleeping and another fifteen housing restaurants, bars, and other assorted entertainment.

We step into the hall and get our bearings. We're in the fifth car, which means we have to walk through ten more sleeping cars before reaching the entertainment zone.

There are only two doors on either side of the hallway instead of the five the sleeping cars have. Lettering on the doors indicate they lead to restaurants, a coffee shop, bars, nightclubs, shops, and even a gym. The last entertainment car has a small movie theater on one side and a recreation room on the other.

The smooth floor in the rec room illuminates a patch of light wherever it meets a shoe. It's a pulsing array of colors with everyone walking among the video game displays, air hockey, foosball, pool tables, and even a string of antique skee ball games. Between the thumping bass, electronic game sounds, and the smacking of wooden pool and skee balls, the place is a steaming pit of sensory overload.

Once my eyes adjust to the lower light, I spot an insanely attractive guy with messy blond hair standing at one of the foosball tables. He glances up when we near, revealing eyes as blue as the summer sky. He directs a sexy half-smile at Lisa. I turn to see if she's noticed and based on the way she's glowing, she has.

He looks past us and calls out, "Hey, Mike, over here."

We make room for Mike to pass, and my heart skids to a stop as I come face to face with Bryce Vaughn.

7

Bryce Vaughn

*B*ryce halts, his eyes locking onto mine as his brows draw together. He's the last person I expected to see on this train, and I'm not entirely sure how I feel about it. He's still the most beautiful boy I've ever seen, but whatever attraction I felt for him is all jumbled up with Alivia's boot to my head and two cracked ribs. Someone should clue my body in though, because it's responding in direct conflict with my brain.

"Hey, Bryce," Lisa says. "I thought you were going to the Northwest after graduation."

"I am. Decided to take the scenic route." He inclines his head toward Jack. "Come on, I want you to meet a friend of mine." We follow him to the foosball table. "Jack, this is Evan, Lisa, and Colin. Guys, this is my friend, Jack."

We exchange pleasantries, but Jack appears to be anything but pleased to meet us. Awkward silence hovers over our little group until it becomes a living thing.

"It's good to see you again, Bryce," I say, then grab Lisa's arm and drag her with me into the corridor.

Lisa's eyes bug out as she glances over my shoulder. I swivel to find Bryce followed us. Lisa and Colin suddenly find the movie schedule on the other side of the hall fascinating.

"Evan, do you want to get dinner tonight?"

I tear my gaze away from my traitorous friends and turn back to Bryce. "Uhh..." Why am I hesitating? Isn't this what I always wanted? Or did I only want what I couldn't have? Part of me likes the idea of going out with Alivia's ex, even if she never finds out about it. My own personal payback.

He flashes his dimples and gives me a pleading look.

"Sure," I say.

"Cool. Pick you up at seven?"

"Sounds good."

"See you then, Evansville." He heads back into the rec room, an explosion of sound pummeling us before the door closes again.

"Well, well, well," Lisa says, a trace of smugness lacing those words.

"Don't even start," I warn.

On the way back to our rooms, we stop at a café with a dark green door and gilt lettering spelling out Alice's Coffee. Inside are rows of booths that look like sculpted hedges setting atop a black and white checkered floor. In the corner of each booth is a topiary tree with twinkling lights. A hostess dressed as the White Rabbit leads us to a booth and the Queen of Hearts takes our order.

"What do you think of Bryce's friend, Jack?" Lisa asks while we wait for our drinks.

"I think he's a douche," Colin says.

Lisa spins in her seat and pins Colin with a glare. She may be the only person on Earth who doesn't know how Colin feels about her.

"He's hot, I say. But he did seem friendlier before he realized we knew Bryce."

"Did anyone else notice Jack called him Mike?" Colin asks.

"I could have sworn that's what he said, too," Lisa says.

"Maybe that's a nickname or something," I say.

"Right," Colin says. "Like everyone knows Mike is a nickname for Bryce."

I roll my eyes. We finish our coffee and head back to our rooms where Lisa helps me pick out something to wear for my date. Nothing I packed is really first-date worthy.

"Oh, I have just the thing," she says, tugging me down the hall to her room. She pulls a pretty little black dress with white polka dots and long flared sheer sleeves from her closet. It's flirty, without being too flirty. Good for a first date with a guy you're interested in, but aren't sure how much, and don't want him to know if you are or not. That's asking a lot of a dress.

The overhead speaker beeps and a voice says, "We'll be pulling out of the station in thirty minutes. Thirty minutes until departure."

Butterflies scramble in my stomach. I'm *actually* leaving the Eastern Province.

Half an hour later, as we slowly glide forward, Lisa and I stand at the window in my room, watching the station recede from view. A smile stretches my face until my cheeks ache.. "This is it, the beginning of my life."

Lisa puts an arm around me. "I'm so glad you decided to come with us, Ev."

The train gains speed and I watch the coast whiz past for a few minutes in a giddy state of euphoria. Everything is about to change. I plop down on my couch and examine my feet. Days of wearing flip-flops has left them calloused. "Let's go get pedicures," I say.

"Now you're speaking *my* language."

I shake my hands, trying to calm my racing heart. "I haven't been on a date since Cade Stewart in grade eleven."

"Oh, he was hot. Whatever happened with him?" Lisa asks, coaxing a few of the more uncooperative curls out of my face.

"He tried to jam his tongue down my throat after he walked me home."

"Eww, creepy. I hate when the cute ones are creepy." She sets the spray bottle down and turns me around to face her. "You look really good, Ev. You should wear makeup more often."

I check out my reflection and take in her handiwork. She managed to tame the crazy that is my hair, and applied just the right amount of eye shadow and mascara to make my eyes pop.

"You're stunning," she says quietly. "Okay, I'd better go before he gets here. I'm dragging Colin to dinner whether he wants to go or not." She gives me a quick hug. "Have fun."

At seven o'clock on the dot, a knock makes my heart skip a beat. With one last glance in the mirror, I inhale deeply and open the door.

Bryce stands on the other side in a pair of khakis and a fitted white T-shirt that hugs his muscles under a charcoal blazer. His warm gray eyes travel down to my feet and back up to my face. "You look incredible, Evan."

"Thank you."

He holds the door for me and falls in step beside me as we head toward the entertainment cars. "Do you like Japanese? I hear the sushi is fantastic."

"Yeah, that sounds good."

He stops at a bright red door with a brass handle in the shape of a fish. Inside, we're greeted by low background music, the soft hum of voices, and the clanking of dinnerware. Most of the tables are occupied and only a few stools are available at the sushi bar. The cheerful restaurant is a mixture of lime green and teal uphol-stered chairs, chrome accents, and pendant lights resembling Cali-fornia rolls.

The hostess greets us with a warm smile. "Welcome to Side Car Sushi. Do you prefer a table or a seat at the bar?"

"Table," Bryce says with his full-dimpled smile.

She beams. Apparently, twenty-something girls aren't immune to his charm either. She leads us over to the window and waits for us to sit before touching the edge of the table. It illuminates, displaying the menu.

We order an assortment of sushi and attempt to make stilted small talk until our food arrives. But over dinner, we end up talking about school.

"Do you remember the discussion we had about Maxwell's *The Undoing of Sentience?*"

"How could I not?" I say with a laugh.

"You said Bidwell didn't need to sacrifice himself to achieve the greater good—"

"Because the ultimate goal would've been achieved without it, and it was pointless."

"We had a discussion about the merits of that logic."

"If you want to call it a discussion, it was more like a fight."

"All I said was he would've compromised his principles if he'd done anything differently."

I point my chopsticks at him. "It was the way you said it. And I stand by my argument that as long as he achieved his goal, it didn't matter what the rest of the world thought of his principles."

He grins. "You were rather forceful in that belief as I recall. I'll admit I'd never looked at it in those terms. But once I did, I viewed all the themes from that angle and decided you were right. Maxwell may never have intended it that way, but it changed everything about the book for me."

"In a good or bad way?"

"Definitely good. I always hated that book before, but now I can see it as something else. A metaphor for the choices we make and how they not only affect us, but everyone around us." His eyes hold mine with an intensity that curls my toes. "And that was when I first realized you were someone to pay attention to."

And yet he went out with Alivia...interesting. "So, I thought you were leaving after graduation," I say, changing the subject. "That was a month ago."

"I was. I mean, I did. I went back home to the Northeastern Province and hung out with friends. Jack decided to come with me to the Northwest and talked me into taking the L-Train." He pauses to eat a piece of sushi. "What about you? Does this mean you're not going to work for your stepdad?"

"I thought about what you said and realized you were right."

He gives me another dimpled smile and grabs a roll with his chopsticks. We slip into comfortable conversation while we eat, talking between bites. Neither of us is in a hurry to leave and we end up lingering at our table long after our dishes have been cleared. Soon we're getting the stink-eye from the hostess.

On our stroll back to the room, my feet decide they've had enough of the heels I borrowed from Lisa. I bend down and remove my sandals, hooking the backs over my fingers.

"Can I ask you something?" I say.

"Sure."

"How long have you known what you wanted to do with your life?"

"Since I was a kid. I can't remember a time I didn't want to be a writer."

I sigh, wondering what it would be like to have that kind of vision for my life.

As we approach my room, nerves flutter through me. Is he going to just say goodnight, kiss me, or pull a Cade Stewart maneuver? When we get to my door, I turn to face him, butterflies scrambling in my belly. My eyes rise to meet his gray ones, my breath stalling.

Bryce places one hand on my hip and the other on the door above my head. My eyes drift lower, stopping at his perfect lips. Seconds tick by, and the warmth from his body so close to mine does ridiculous things to my circulatory system. Maybe he's waiting for me to make the first move. I tear my gaze from his mouth and meet his stare, uncertainty dancing in those baby grays.

I nervously pull my bottom lip between my teeth. He finally lowers his face, soft lips brushing across mine. I sigh and lean back against the door as our mouths move against each other in a slow rhythmic motion.

Holy crap, I'm kissing Bryce Vaughn and it's even better than I imagined. And I've imagined it a lot. I reach behind his neck, pulling his face a little closer, my shoes still dangling from the fingertips of my other hand.

His fingers curl around my hip and our kiss intensifies, igniting sparks in my veins. Nothing else exists except us and this moment until he pulls back, his eyes lingering on mine.

He grins. "See you tomorrow, Evansville."

My breathing is shallow and rapid as I watch him walk down the corridor. When he reaches the vestibule, he glances back over his shoulder and waves before the doors open and he disappears behind them.

I enter my room, my entire body tingling. That kiss was...was nothing like the clumsy experimental kissing I used to do with Avi, the son of my uncle's chief of staff, nor anything like the mouth probe I got from Cade Stewart. A kiss that's a zero on the creepy scale and leaves me wanting more is probably as close to perfect as I can get.

Someone came in to turn down my bed while I was gone. I change and plop down on my back, my mind replaying the events of today. A date with a hot guy and tomorrow I'm going to set foot in someplace other than the Eastern Province for the first time in my life. A smile stretches across my face. I may not know what I want to do with my life, yet, but a whole new set of experiences awaits me on the other side of my dreams.

8

New Experiences

Colin stabs his quiche with a fork. "So how was the date?"

"Good," I say, deliberately underselling it.

Lisa notches an eyebrow. "Just good?"

I shrug.

"Uh-uh. Spill."

As much as I try, I can't hide my grin. "Okay, fine, it was actually pretty amazing."

"Can you imagine if Alivia knew?"

I snort. "I know, right?"

"So, did you go out with him just to spite her?" Colin asks. "Cause that's not cool."

"Of course not. You know I've been crushing on him for half a year. But the fact that Alivia would be royally pissed off if she knew only makes it that much more delicious."

He rolls his eyes and stuffs the rest of his breakfast into his mouth, swallowing in one oversized gulp. On the walk back to our rooms, we run into Jack and Bryce in the corridor. Bryce gives me a dimpled smile. "Good morning."

A sudden bout of awkwardness overcomes me, but I shake it off and murmur a response.

"Hey, we're heading into the province today. You guys wanna come with us?"

The thought of spending the day with Bryce is intriguing and I glance at my friends to gauge their reaction.

Lisa eyes Jack like he's the last piece of dessert on the train. "Love to."

Colin makes a face, as if he just sucked a lemon. He's quiet for a long time before answering, his voice devoid of any emotion. "Sure, why not."

Bryce reaches out and squeezes my hand. "Cool. See you later."

The three of us head back to our rooms where Colin sulks and Lisa is more animated than normal. We pull into the Southeastern Province just before noon and meet the guys. Jack falls in step beside Lisa and the two begin a session of heavy flirting.

A dark cloud forms and hovers over Colin's head. I let out an exaggerated sigh and glance up at Bryce. "I'll be right back." I drop back and lean in close to Colin. "Tell her before it's too late," I say out of the side of my mouth.

"I don't know what you're talking about."

"Bullshit. I know you're into Lisa, but she's clueless. If you don't' tell her how you feel, she's gonna find someone who will."

He makes a face and I can't tell if that means he's thinking about it or not, but he just shakes his head.

"Fine," I hiss. "That's your choice. But you don't get to be a jackass because you're too afraid to man up and be honest with her." He rolls his eyes and I huff before catching back up to Bryce.

We exit the depot and the Southeastern Province comes into view. I suck in a sharp breath at the sight. A rich patchwork of stucco walls adorned with cheerful shutters greets me. Window boxes spill bright flowering vines. Ivy stretches long limbs up the sides of buildings before climbing over roofs.

From where we stand near the beach, the Union sprawls before me, growing higher as it moves farther inland, like the ancient hillside cities we read about in world history. We head toward the borough and hike up two flights of stairs to an open-air market overflowing with vendors selling fresh produce, craft beers, and baked goods. A musical trio plays contemporary jazz that echoes off the stone walls surrounding us.

I stop at a booth and select a small clay pot for my mom, painted to resemble the local architecture. The artisan scans my fingerprint into the PrintPay system before wrapping my purchase.

"I'm hungry," Colin announces.

It occurs to me that it's long past lunchtime now and Colin can't go more than a few hours between meals. Considering his mood, I'm surprised he lasted this long without blowing a fuse. He's definitely not himself.

"Ooo, check out that place," Lisa says pointing at café nestled into the buildings just outside the marketplace. "I've always wanted to try one of Adam LeFevre's restaurants. I hear his seafood specialties are to die for."

I glance over at Jack. "Lisa's going to be a chef, so she knows her food."

"She'll get no argument from me then. Let's go."

We're seated on the patio where Colin wedges himself between Lisa and Jack. Lisa leans forward to peer around Colin. "So Jack, how do you know Bryce?"

Jack grins. "We grew up together."

"Why does he call you Mike?" Colin asks.

Bryce picks up his menu and studies it before answering. "My first name is Michael. My middle name is Bryce. Jack's known me as Mike since we were kids."

"So, why don't we know you as Mike?" Lisa asks.

"When I was in grade 8, there were three Mike's in my class, so my teacher assigned middle names to two of us and it just stuck."

"That's boring," Colin said. "I was hoping for something more interesting."

Our waitress arrives to take our order and after she leaves, the conversation turns to everyone's future plans. Since I don't have any, my eyes sweep the courtyard, landing on a man sitting alone two tables over, staring at us.

He's older than my mom, maybe early forties, with a tall fore-head, long nose, and deep-set hooded eyes. He catches me looking at him and nods before taking a sip from his mug. Our food arrives and when I glance over again, the hooded-eye man is gone.

"What should we do after lunch?" Lisa asks, stabbing her crab cake salad with a fork.

Jack and Bryce exchange a look before Bryce clears his throat. "I-I forgot Jack has family in the area, and we're going to visit them." He turns to me. "Sorry. I know I invited you to join me. I just forgot about this. I'll make it up to you, though. I promise."

Although I'm mildly disappointed, I don't want him to know. "No worries. You have nine days to make good on that."

He grins. "How about dinner tomorrow?"

"I need to check with my social calendar." I turn to Lisa and Colin, raising my eyebrows. They both shrug. We've got nothing planned. "Okay, you're on, but I expect something epic."

His smile broadens to include his dimples. "Hmmm, I better start thinking then."

The guys say their goodbyes and take off. With Jack gone, Colin's more upbeat. He leads the way into the heart of the borough where we explore the rest of the afternoon.

I throw on a pair of designer jeans and a ruffled, layered tank for my dinner date with Bryce. He arrives a little before seven in heather gray T-shirt that does sinful things to his eyes. Dark stubble grazes his jaw and faint shadows under his eyes mar his otherwise perfect skin.

Over pasta in the café, he asks about my summer plans, which leads to a discussion about Eddie and if I'm going to see him. We end up spending the entire meal talking about me and my jacked-up family drama.

We leave the restaurant and walk toward the back of the train. Bryce pushes open the door to the pool car where a low rectangular basin of water, about a foot deep, sits in the center, surrounded by lounge chairs, umbrellas, and palm trees. We claim two chairs away from other passengers.

"We talked about me all through dinner," I say. "It's your turn to spill. Tell me about your family."

"I'm pretty boring. I have three sisters. They're older and on their own so they stayed behind when we moved to the Eastern Province. I have a dog, Bella, who you met, and both of my parents are engineers."

"What kind of engineers?"

"Structural. They design lightweight composite materials so the Union can continue building upwards."

"That's not so boring."

He shrugs. "Compared to you...your life made magazine covers."

I cringe at the memory. After the very public revelation that my father is lead singer of Epic Vinyl, reporters camped out in front of our apartment for days trying to get a picture of the mysterious redhead the rocker abandoned more than a decade earlier.

"What else do you want to know?" he asks.

"Why did you move?"

"My parents' jobs."

"Okay, maybe your life *is* kinda boring."

He chuckles, but before he can respond, Jack appears in front of us, his fingers curling in and out in agitated fashion. "What's up?" Bryce asks him.

Jack inclines his head toward the corridor.

"I'll be right back," Bryce says to me.

The guys walk over near the doors and begin a heated discussion. The ambient noise prevents me from overhearing them, but a lot of animated gesturing is taking place. While they to argue, I glance around the car and notice the same hooded-eyed man from lunch watching at me from across the pool. I startle, but suddenly it makes sense. He's obviously a passenger on the train. He must have recognized us yesterday. I smile and wave. He waves back and walks out of the car, glancing at Bryce and Jack as he leaves.

A few moments later, Jack storms out, leaving Bryce staring at the floor. He shakes his head and returns to me, reaching down a hand to pull me up.

"Sorry."

"What was that all about?"

We exit the pool car and start back toward my room. "This was supposed to be a guys' trip." He shrugs. "He's not happy that I'm spending all my time with you."

"I'm not sure what to say."

He stops and turns me to face him. "I *want* to spend time with you."

"But Jack's your friend and you guys planned this trip together."

"Jack and I have spent most of our lives together. You and I only have eight more days." He reaches down and takes my hand. When we reach my door, he grips my hand tighter, as if he's unwilling to let me go. He backs me up against the door and kisses me until nothing else exists. No people walking by, no rocking of the train, just me and this boy, and his mouth hot on mine.

I sigh and my lips part. Bryce pulls me closer, his tongue brushing mine. My hands wrap behind his neck and we stay locked together, our mouths exploring one another's, for what could be mere minutes or hours.

Someone clears their throat, alerting me that we're no longer alone. I open my eyes to find Jack standing behind Bryce.

Bryce's head drops. "I'm sorry, I have to go." He leans in and kisses me again, his lips lingering long enough to let me know he doesn't want to leave and enough that Jack clears his throat again. With a heavy sigh, Bryce pulls his face from mine. "See you later."

"Uh-huh," is all I manage to say in response before letting myself into my room.

9

Later

The next few days fly by as only vacation can. Bryce and I spend as much time together as we can squeeze in. In some ways, this feels like one of those old-fashioned summer romance movies Colin is so fond of. Hot, fast, intense, but doomed to end five days from now when we go our separate ways.

We stopped at the southern tip of the peninsula in the Southeast the other day. Lisa, Colin, and I spent the day lying on the powdery white beaches and dipping our toes into the balmy ocean waters.

Yesterday was our first stop in the South and the borough we explored was a musician's nirvana. Colin was in his element as we club hopped, listening to modern music, classical, and everything in between. One band even allowed Colin to sit in and play guitar on a song. He comes alive when he's playing his music. That whole lack of confidence thing disappears and he becomes a different guy —a guy girls can't take their eyes off.

Our next stop isn't until tomorrow, so Lisa, Colin, and I lounge in the pool car, eyes closed, pretending we're still on the beach. The piped-in wave sounds and salty-air aromas help complete the fantasy.

"So..." Lisa interrupts a long stretch of drowsy silence. "If you could change one thing about Union life, what would you choose?"

Colin groans. "Stop, Lisa. We're on vacation. No more school."

"No," I say. "It's an interesting question. I'd make community service mandatory."

Colin opens one eye and looks at me, incredulous.

"I'm serious. I'm not against people paying taxes, but I'm tired of the wealthy buying their way out of their entire commitment, as if they're too important to be a part of society. I'd change it so they could only pay five percent in income taxes instead of ten and have them do two hours of community service each week."

"Right, like that would ever happen." Colin laughs. "Can you imagine Montreal Anderson scrubbing hospital toilets?"

"It'd do her a world of good. Volunteering creates a better understanding of what other people's lives are like." I roll to my back and prop myself up on my elbows. "She wouldn't have to scrub hospital toilets, but I'll bet she'd be a lot nicer if she spent some time with sick kids or the elderly."

Lisa gives me a thoughtful look. "I see what you're saying. Everyone should contribute time as well as money. I mean if they can."

"Exactly. Force them to see beyond their own narrow scope of Union life."

After another hour of lazing around the pool car, we head back to our rooms to change for dinner. Food is followed by a movie and then across the corridor to the rec room. Sometime after midnight, Bryce find us and pulls me in for a quick kiss before joining us in a game of darts. Lisa, Colin, and I are wicked good. With all the hours hanging out in clubs waiting to see Colin's band, we spent our time learning to play then refining our skills at the dartboard.

Jack arrives in the middle of our third game, and I groan inwardly, sure he's here to drag Bryce off again. Much to my surprise, he hangs out with us instead.

"You think you can teach me how do that flipping throw you do?" Jack asks, Lisa, his smile tipping up one corner of his mouth.

Colin scowls and stalks off to play skee ball.

Lisa beams and stands behind Jack, shifting his shoulder with her hands. Her trick isn't really so much about accuracy as it is showing off, so while Jack gets the hang of flipping the dart, it never hits the board.

After Bryce and I soundly defeat Lisa and Jack, Jack grabs Bryce's sleeve and drags him to the corner. Bryce's body is tense, his hands shoved into the front pockets of his jeans. But there is no wild gesturing this time.

A few minutes later, Jack leaves and Bryce returns to me. "I need to talk to you about something. Can you meet me for breakfast in the morning?"

"Yeah...is something wrong?"

His face relaxes and he shoots me a quick grin. "Naw. Not wrong. I...we'll talk in the morning." He kisses me briefly before going after Jack.

Colin rejoins us, all moody and sullen, but quickly warms up as we play air hockey and shoot some pool. Before long, it's nearly four in the morning.

I'm not sure what time I'm having breakfast with Bryce, so I call it a night, or more accurately, a morning, and head back to my room.

I startle awake a little before seven and tumble out of bed, stumbling into the bathroom to brush my teeth. Rushing to dress, I yank on a pair of jeans and a top and I run my fingers through my hair, trying to get it to cooperate. A knock disrupts my process, and I stuff my feet into my flip-flops on my way to open the door.

Before I can say anything, Bryce's arms are around me, his lips landing on mine, and I melt like ice cream on a hot summer day. I wonder if I'll ever get used to this rush whenever he kisses me. I hope not.

He takes my hand and leads me into the corridor, closing the door behind us. We walk to the café without speaking. After ordering, we take our drinks and scones over to a table by the windows. Bryce takes a sip of coffee and set his mug down, then picks up my hands, running his thumb absently over my knuckles.

After a minute goes by without him saying anything, I lower my head and peer up into his eyes. "You wanted to talk about something?"

He lifts his head and the sadness swimming in his gray eyes sends anxiety to gnaw a hole through my stomach. "I had my whole life planned out. Knew where I was going and what I was going to do." He pauses and licks his lips. "I'm crazy about you, Evansville. You're all I can think about."

I open my mouth, but nothing comes out. I'm not sure what I was expecting him to say, but not this. On the one hand, this fits with our whirlwind vacation romance, but on the other, it's too intense, too soon.

A shadow crosses the table and I glance up to see Jack. Annoyance burns through my chest, building to something much stronger. I press my lips together to keep from saying something I'll regret.

"We need to go. Now." Jack turns to me, his shoulders dropping as he scratches the back of his head. "I'm sorry, Evan. This is important or I wouldn't be here."

Bryce scowls. "Can you give us a minute?"

Jack nods and walks out of the café but waits just outside the door.

Bryce stands and pulls me up, his hands circling my waist. He kisses me slow and deep, leaving me breathless. In the restaurant, with all these people around.

When he speaks, his voice is soft, but hoarse, as if he's in pain. "I-I think I'm in love with you." Then he releases me without another word and walks out to join Jack.

I stand in stunned silence, my fingers reaching up to touch the lips he just plundered. Bryce Vaughn is in *love* with me?

We barely know each other, but my heart races whenever he's near, I count the minutes until I'll see him again, and I smile more when we're together. Maybe this is what it's like to be in love.

This revelation settles over me like a soft, billowing sheet and I realize I'm smiling. I wonder how long I've been smiling.

We pull into the depot shortly after noon. Lisa and Colin were slow to drag themselves out of their rooms this morning, but they met me for lunch and now we're heading out to explore.

The buildings here are missing the bright colors and whimsicality of the Southeastern Province and the formality of the Eastern. What they lack in color, they make up for in rustic charm. They're constructed of natural materials, giving them an earthy vibe. Most are adorned with window boxes, hanging planters, and arbors covered in climbing vines, creating an alluring combination of raw beauty.

I breathe in deeply, letting the clear air fill my lungs, a small smile tugging at my lips.

"Why are you so chipper today?" Lisa asks, narrowing her eyes in my direction. "Aren't you tired? We were out so late, or early, or...whatever." She flicks her hand.

I weigh the pros and cons of spilling what happened this morning with Bryce, but I'm going to burst if I don't tell someone. "Bryce said he's in love with me."

Colin raises his bushy eyebrows and Lisa squeals, crushing me in a hug. "How did he tell you? Was it romantic?"

"I don't know. Kinda, but also kinda odd, like he was conflicted about it." I replay our brief interaction.

"Maybe he wants to stay in the Western Province with you," Colin says.

"I don't want him to give up his dream for me. That's weird, right? Who rearranges their life for someone after only a week?"

"You could go with him," Lisa says. "After you spend the summer with me, I mean."

"Are you kidding? My parents would completely unravel." I run my hand through my hair and let out a sigh. "This is all happening way too fast. No one is moving anywhere for anyone. We need to see what happens over the next few days. I don't want him to stay in the Western Province for me and I'm not going to move up to the Northwest for him."

"Ev..." Lisa ducks under a low branch while Colin and I walk around it. "You set out on this trip to find your place. How do you know it's not up in the Northwest if you don't go?"

To my surprise Colin doesn't tell her she's crazy. "You could stay with me up there. I already have a place lined up for the end of summer."

"And do what?"

"Come with me to the conservatory."

"No. You know I'm not going to go into music."

"Look, I know you have issues with your dad—"

"Eddie. Not my dad. He may have spawned me, but that was where his involvement ended."

"Whatever. But with your heritage, you'd get into the program."

"Okay, first, I don't want a music career and second, like I'd ever name drop my sperm donor to get ahead."

"Fine. Just don't rule it out until you think about it."

"Yeah, thought about it. No."

Disappointment colors his features but he lets the subject drop. What surprises me most about this whole conversation is that neither one of them asked me if I'm in love with Bryce, as if it doesn't matter or it's a foregone conclusion that I am. No matter what I feel for him, I won't drop everything to move somewhere for a guy. That's crazy. That's my mom. She would have done anything for Eddie if only he'd wanted her. I refuse to be that girl.

"The two provinces aren't that far apart. I can visit Bryce, or he can visit me. Plus, we can video chat and text. He's not going to alter his life over a girl he barely knows."

We walk up a short flight of stairs and down a narrow alley to a wisteria-covered footbridge, making our way to the other side of the shopping district. Luckily, they drop the subject of me and Bryce drop for now.

After winding our way through the borough, stopping in shops, and sipping iced coffee at a sidewalk cafe, we stumble upon a restaurant with tables on a wooden deck overlooking the ocean four levels below us. Potted trees covered in small white lights create a twinkling canopy as dusk approaches. After placing our orders, I excuse myself to use the restroom, the hostess pointing around the corner.

As I wash my hands, I study my reflection in the mirror. The humidity hear turns my red curls into a frizzy mess. I run my wet hands over them, attempting to tame them before heading back to rejoin my friends.

I take two steps before an arm is thrown around my waist from behind and someone jerks me backward into the shadows between the buildings.

Shock leaves me immobile for a few precious seconds. Then I suck in a breath, reading for a scream. A large, rough hand clamps across my mouth before even a whisper escapes.

Terror slides down my spine while my mind whirls, attempting to make sense of what's happening. I twist to break the hold of the arm around me, but he's too strong. My nails claw at the hand over my mouth in vain.

I kick back with my foot back, seeking a shin, a knee, or his groin, but the jerk lifts me off the ground so the little leverage I had is gone.

"We can do this the easy way or the hard way," a gravelly male voice hisses in my ear. "Personally, I don't care but I promise you want the easy way."

His voice slices through me, like tiny razor blades. I'm pretty sure I don't want this any way, easy or not. While my brain struggles with my next move, instinct takes over and I thrust myself forward. My left foot hits the ground and I bring my right one up, driving it onto his instep with all my strength.

He howls before unfurling a string of profanity and loosens his grip on my waist. It's just enough for me to twist around and stare into closely-spaced beady eyes set into a long face. My hands reach for his face, ready to claw his eyes out, when I see the man standing behind him — the man with the hooded eyes.

"Here, use this," the hooded eyes man says, handing a cloth to the man holding me.

Beady Eyes places the rag over my nose and mouth. I wrench my head to keep away from the sweet acidic odor. Terror crawls through me, stealing my ability to think. The instinct that magically appeared before, abandons me now.

Lightheadedness spills into the corners of my brain and I hold my breath, but it's too late. As I try to fight the heaviness climbing my limbs, my eyelids slip closed.

BOOK 2 - THE RUINS

"Man can live about forty days without food, about three days without water, about eight minutes without air, but only for one second without hope."
—Charles Darwin

10

Darkness

*M*y eyes flutter open to complete darkness, my brain cloudy. My shoulders ache and my arms are numb from sleeping on them. When I try to sit up, the moments before I blacked out come rushing back, filling me with dread.

My hands are tied behind my back, so the best I can do is roll to my side. I strain into the darkness to make sense of my surroundings. I'm inside something that's moving. It's too dark to make out anything, so I rely on my ears. A train. But not the L-Train, nor a commuter train. Maybe a cargo. My pulse throbs behind my eyelids and I fight the urge to vomit.

Shit, shit, shit. Tears fill my eyes, but I can't afford to cry. I need to figure a way out of this mess. Lisa and Colin must have looked for me when I didn't come back. That only provides small comfort though, since I have no idea where I am or how they'd find me.

None of this makes any sense. The only kidnappings in the Union are due to custody disputes. Maybe Eddie had me kidnapped. Except that's completely crazy. If he was going to do that, why wait until I'm almost an adult and already on my way to see him?

This must be about money. A ransom or something. That seems so fantastic though, like straight out of a movie. There was that one kid who disappeared a couple of years ago, but it turned out he'd just run away.

Maybe it's got something to do with my Uncle David. As one of only seven governors, he has an incredible amount of power. Only the Prime Minister has more. Unfortunately, it's the only thing that makes sense. If I have any hope of surviving, he might have to give them what they want.

Whatever they used to knock me out is fogging up my brain, but as it clears, I realize we're no longer moving. To my right, a door slides open, filling the space with harsh light. I squint as Beady Eyes approaches with a scruffy man wearing a menacing sneer.

My heart hammers in my chest as they reach my side, Beady Eyes yanking me to my feet by my arm. I stumble, which makes him tug me harder. The scruffy man shoves me from behind and if Beady Eyes wasn't holding on to me, I'd have face-planted.

They guide me across what I now recognize is a boxcar. Since cargo trains run on all levels of the Union, we could be literally anywhere right now.

They drag me off the train into a dim corridor, rusty water bleeding through cracks, staining the concrete. Somewhere along the way, I lost one of my flip-flops. Their boots clop on the hard floors, echoing off the walls, while my one bare foot slaps against the ground and my other slaps against my footwear.

We stop at a freight elevator and Beady Eyes shoves me inside. I'm numb as we descend, as if this is happening to someone else and I'm merely a witness. The doors open and we enter another corridor before stopping at a small manhole cover. Beady Eyes lifts the heavy metal lid to reveal a murky shaft with steel rungs leading down. He goes first, then Sneer Face nudges my shoulder.

I turn to look at him, wondering if he's going to just throw me down.

"Whatcha waiting for?" he snarls.

"I need my hands."

With a sigh, he steps forward and peers down the shaft before pulling a knife from the back of his waistband. He drags the back edge of the blade down my cheek, making me shudder.

"Don't try anything. This knife'll cut a lot more than rope."

I suck in my breath and swallow hard as he moves to my back and saws the ropes, releasing my bound limbs. Blood rushes back into my hands and I rub the ridges in my wrists. I flex my fingers a few times to get some feeling in them before I step onto the first rung, fully aware Beady Eyes is down below and Sneer Face is behind me, boxing me in. Nowhere to run. Yet.

My remaining flip-flop slips on the second rung, careening to the ground where Beady Eyes kicks it aside. Once Sneer Face joins us at the bottom, we hike through the drainage pipe until Beady Eyes stops next to a narrow crack in the wall. It's barely wide enough for a person to squeeze through, but that's what Beady Eyes does. When he disappears, Sneer Face shoves me and I pivot sideways, entering the opening. My breath stalls in my lungs and I feel as if the walls are crushing me. I close my eyes as beads of sweat dot my forehead. I can't do this.

"We haven't got all night," Beady Eyes calls.

Holding my breath, I tell myself I'm not in a confined space and inch forward. A few more steps and a slight breeze flutters across my face. A few more and Beady Eyes yanks me out.

Out. Outside the safety of the Union walls, where nothing has survived in a hundred years. The barren Ruins, uninhabited, poisoned, wretched. My bare soles drag against dry earth and a new level of unease rolls through me. These two idiots don't seem to be too worried about all the toxins, but they don't seem very bright either. Maybe they slept through history class.

I stumble on rocks, the contaminated ground harsh beneath my bare feet. Hours later, we're deep in the Ruins and I have yet to feel any effects of dangers I've been warned about. Maybe it builds up over a period of days or weeks rather than hours.

My feet ache from walking so far without shoes, every rock, stick, and various sharp objects taking their toll.

"Move it," Beady Eyes growls, shoving my shoulder with his palm.

Sneer Face must realize that pushing isn't enough, because he takes off his boots and peels off his grubby socks before tossing them at me. "Put 'em on."

My lips curl back and I shy away from the foul-smelling things. No way I'm I touching them, let alone wearing them.

Sneer Face leans over, his face inches from mine. "Put the damn socks on. Now."

Hell, they can't be any worse than what I've been walking on. I drop to the ground and pull them on. They're so long, I can fold them over on themselves, creating a double layer of padding.

We walk on for another couple of hours before we stop at the edge of an old road. The pavement is buckled and cracked from the extreme temperatures of the early twenty-first century and the civil war that followed.

Minutes go by without anyone speaking. I have no idea what we're waiting for, but now seems like a good time for some answers.

"What do you want from me?" I don't get a response, not that I really thought I would. My need to know what's going on is too powerful to contain. "What do you want with me?" I ask louder.

Sneer Face narrows his eyes and laughs. "You're a means to an end. Think of yourself as serving the greater good. You Unis love that shit."

"I don't understand."

"You don't need to understand. Just be quiet and if your boyfriend cooperates, you'll get to go home," Beady Eyes says.

"Bryce? What does he have to do with this?"

"He's sticking his nose where it don't belong. By now, he's too busy looking for you to be worried about things he shouldn't."

11

Means to an End

*T*wo bright lights cut through the darkness, bouncing up and down along the tortured road before the vehicle they're attached to pulls to a stop in front of us. The Union was designed for pedestrians and mass transit. The only vehicles on the other side of the wall belong to the government. So where did these guys get their hands on one?

The driver lowers a darkened window and the man with the hooded eyes stares back at me, flashing a smug smile. I bite back a scream as Beady Eyes opens the back door, shoving me in before climbing in next to me.

"What are you going to do with me?" I ask Hooded Eyes, who seems to be their ringleader.

He glances over his shoulder. "That's up to your boyfriend."

"What does he have to do with this?"

"He has an unhealthy fascination with my business interests."

What business interests? And why would Bryce care? This made more sense when I thought it was about my uncle. Then the government vehicle would fit, but this...I got nothing. Tears of frustration fill my eyes, but I don't want these guys to see me cry. I turn my face to the window and bite my lip to keep it from trembling.

Maybe Jack's weirdness had nothing to do with a guys trip, but whatever it is Bryce is involved with. All the little things about Bryce start to tick away in my head — the fact that he was leaving town right after graduation but didn't, his name, his odd behavior in the café the other morning... How long ago was that? It feels like days, but might have been yesterday or even this morning.

The sun is dawning when we pull up to a small house. Before the Union, people lived in detached homes instead of apartments as we do now. This place looks ancient, as if it's been here since the mountains in the distance formed.

Hooded Eyes yanks open my door and I climb out without looking at him. He nudges me up crumbling concrete steps leading to the front door. My hands shake and I curl them into fists to hide my terror.

The house is a dingy white, more stained than not. Large chunks of the stucco have fallen away, revealing the brick infrastructure beneath. Cracked red tiles dot the roof and at least half are missing. More houses in a similar state of disrepair march up and down either side of the street, some with caved in roofs, others nothing more than crumbled remains, only a chimney still standing.

The air is pungent and the ground is scattered with scrubby-looking weeds and tall brown grass. Cactus and some cartoonish trees litter the landscape, like something straight out of one of those old Westerns Colin makes me watch.

Hooded Eyes ushers me across the broken sidewalk at the top of the steps to the porch and opens the door, pushing me inside.

We enter a small living room with a beat-up couch along one wall. A weathered piece of wood perched atop two cinder blocks sits in front of the couch. To the right is a round, rusted table and four wooden crates up on ends like stools.

Beyond the table is a doorway leading into what I assume is a kitchen. A guy with black hair and dark eyes walks through it and stops, staring at me for a moment. He tears his eyes away from me, or rather my chest, and nods at Beady Eyes. "Rush, I need to talk to you."

Hooded Eyes turns to Sneer Face. "Take her to the back room."

"Do ya want me to tie her up?"

"Naw, she's a Uni. Even if she managed to escape, she won't last more than a day out there."

Sneer Face grabs my arm and drags me down a hall, shoving me into a bedroom at the end. He closes and locks the door behind me. As soon as his footsteps recede, I rush over and try to open the door, but it won't budge.

The room is small and empty except for a hideously stained mattress in one corner. A narrow walk-in closet in the corner is also bare, even the rods are gone. Nothing to use as a weapon.

Short windows are set up high, requiring me to stand on my toes to peer out. More houses sit out there, and beyond them is more grass, cactus, and weeds. Far in the distance are hills and a small mountain. I lean against the wall and slide down to the floor. Hooded Eyes is right, even if I escaped, I wouldn't survive the first twenty-four hours.

The hopelessness of the situation sinks in, and before I can stop myself, I'm crying. I hate that I'm crying because it's not productive, but I can't seem to come up with anything productive to do, which makes me cry harder.

Sometime later, the dark-haired guy opens the door and tosses a water bottle at me. I duck and it hits the floor, but to my amazement, doesn't break. The bottle looks like glass, but when I pick it up it's pliable and crinkles in my hand. Plastic. There's not much plastic in the Union. It fell out of favor along with petroleum after the war. What little plastic we use is made from polymers and imported from Europe.

He flips me a protein bar and I reach out to catch it. After he closes and locks the door again, I open the water and take a long pull then unwrap and take a bite of the bar. It tastes like sawdust and catches in my throat, making me choke. I rinse it down with more water and finish it off before leaning my head back.

I blow a piece of hair out of my face and get up, searching for a way out. I can't trust my survival to a guy I barely know. If Bryce doesn't do what they want, I'm not sure what these guys will do with me, but I'm guessing it's nothing good. I stand on my toes to look out the window again. It's too small for me to fit through, and even if I managed to get out of here, I don't know how far I am from the Union, or even in which direction it is.

Boredom sets in and I spend my time tracking the path of the shadows across the room until early afternoon. I have to pee but no one's checked on me in hours. I yell and bang on the door until heavy boots approach, stopping on the other side of the door. When it opens, the dark-eyed guy stares at me, head tilted. His expression is almost kind, giving me a small flicker of hope.

"I need to use the bathroom."

He cracks the door wider and jerks his thumb toward a door on the left. After closing the door, I'm overtaken by the stench of ammonia mixed with the gag-inducing smell of human feces. The toilet is nothing more than a metal can with a worn seat perched atop. I breathe through my mouth, hovering over the can to take care of my business.

When I'm done, I survey my surroundings as quickly as possible, trying not to inhale. There's one tiny window, a grungy shower stall, and a sink that hasn't seen water in forever. The cabinet underneath is empty, and on the wall where a mirror should be only bits of adhesive remain. Too bad, mirror shards would make an effective stabbing implement.

My gaze flies back to the window. I could break it and get a jagged piece of glass. Stretching as far as I can, my fingers land a good two inches below the sill. There's nothing for me to stand on to get closer.

Outside the door, I hear the dark-eyed guy shifting. I can't stay in here forever. When I open the door a moment later, he's not waiting to escort me back to my cell. He's not in the hall or in the bedroom. Weighing my options, I head toward the living room.

At the end of the hall on the right is a room filled with pallets of water bottles similar to the one he gave me, a variety of alcohol, clothes, condoms, tampons, and sugar. Where did all this come from and what the hell are they doing with it?

Around the corner is another bedroom filled with even more pallets full of stuff. A small bathroom is to my left, and the right leads to the dining room where Rush, Dark Eyes, and Sneer Face are sitting at the table playing cards. They look up briefly when I enter, but otherwise pay me no attention.

I glance at the couch with its sagging center and dark stains and opt to remain standing.

Dark Eyes gives me a small grin. "You wanna play?"

This could be an opportunity to build some sort of alliance with him. If I'm going to get out of this alive, I might need someone on my side.

I force a smile. "Sure. What are you playing?"

"Poker," Rush says.

They're playing a version I'm not familiar with, but they give me the basic rules and deal me in. I learn Sneer Face is Hopp and Dark Eyes is Dantel.

Hopp goes into the kitchen and returns with four cans, handing one to me. I take a sip and choke it out. "What's this?"

Hopp smirks. "Beer."

I've had beer in the Union, not a lot but some. This tastes like carbonated spit. I try laughing along with them like we're all part of the same happy gang, and I'm not their hostage.

I only take occasional sips of beer to keep my head clear, but Dantel chugs them like he's in a drinking contest or something. Hopp and Rush exchange a look every time Dantel goes to get another one.

Evening approaches and the sky is beginning to darken when the car pulls up out front.

"Walker's back," Hopp says, panic lacing his words.

Rush grabs my arm and drags me to the back room. They're clearly afraid of this Walker, which means I'm terrified of him.

12

Dangerous Alliance

The bedroom door creaks, startling me from a fitful sleep. It's too dark to make out anything except a silhouette across the room. I sit up and rub my arm, sore from where I dozed off on the hard floor. Squinting into the darkness, I determine it must be Dantel, based on size and shape.

He stumbles and rights himself. Shit, he's drunk. I stand as he approaches, unsure why he's here.

"We're alone. Let's have some fun, baby." His words slur together.

Oh, hell no. I'm not interested in the kind of fun he has in mind. My heart kicks up the pace and I scan the room for options. He moves toward me, unbuckling his belt while I move away, attempting to stay out of his reach, until I've backed myself into the corner.

Dantel leans in, putting both hands on my waist. His breath is stale, reeking of booze and something potent and musky, like a skunk. He crushes his lips to mine, stuffing his fat tongue in my mouth. The taste of beer is overpowering and I turn my head, fighting the urge to be sick.

"Don't be like that. You're so pretty." He reaches out and pets the side of my head.

Fear and bile mix in my stomach and seconds later his mouth is on mine again, hungry and demanding as he gropes me. All over. I shrug my shoulders back and push his pawing hands away from me, but he's insistent.

My brain reels and something clicks inside, flipping me into preservation mode. I take his bottom lip between my teeth and bite down until the salty metallic tang of blood hits my tongue. Shocked, he jerks back enough for me to connect my knee solidly with his precious baby-making parts.

"Son of a b—" He keels over, groaning.

While he attempts to recover, I dart down the hall and through the dining room to the front door.

It's locked.

My hand shakes so much I only fumble with the deadbolt.

Dantel stumbles toward me just as the lock turns and I yank the door open. My foot doesn't even reach the porch before he grabs my arm and hauls me back.

I jerk my shoulder to free myself, grasping the door frame with my other hand. He's too strong, though, and my palm too sweaty. It slips against the rotting wood, pieces of chipped paint clinging to my skin. Dantel carries me like I'm nothing more than a bag of mulch, eyes blazing with rage as he throws me on the couch. Straddling my waist, he pins me with his weight as he pulls off his belt and wraps it around my wrists, binding me.

This can't be happening. Terror unfurls in my stomach as he unbuttons his jeans. Tears stream down my face, but I refuse to give up as long as I remain conscious. With newfound resolve, I fling myself forward, slamming my head into his nose. He roars and his hands fly to his face. I shake off my own pain and wiggle out from under him before dashing out the door.

Without a concrete plan, I run blindly down the sidewalk and cut around to the back of the house, my heart battering my ribs. A dark shadow staggers after me, struggling to stay upright. My foot slips on loose dirt and I stumble forward, landing hard on the ground. I scramble to get up, my bound hands thrashing.

Dantel swerves left, yelling a garbled mess of words. As he closes in, fear trickles through my veins. My already sore wrists rub against one another, creating friction as I wiggle my hands, trying to get the belt off. I free one hand and roll over, pushing myself up.

Dantel reaches for me, but I twist out of his grasp so all he gets is a fistful of my hair. He yanks me back and panic claws up my chest, gaining a foothold. I kick back and connect my heel with his shin. He swears and lets go.

My pulse thundering violently, I turn and run. The socks provide only minimal protection, but I push through the pain. Dantel's ragged breaths are too close still. I dig deep and find a burst of speed, enough to pull away from him. When I glance back, he's bent at the waist, his back heaving, but I don't back off.

When my lungs burn and every breath scrapes my throat, I slow my pace but never stop. By dawn, I'm in the foothills. I avoid the worn footpath, opting to wade through the brush instead. The trek is steep and branches claw at my arms and legs. Before long I'm winded and my feet ache, but still I press on.

The sun climbs high, inflaming the earth around me. The sweet dusty smell of the desert surrounds me and a grimy layer of dirt and sweat plasters my skin. The hot wind feels like opening an oven door and sends pieces of hair into my face that cling to the sticky coating.

The day wears on and the climb becomes steeper until I'm forced to stop for a short rest. I twist and knot my stupid hair on my head to keep it off my neck. A nap calls to me with promises of relief, but I'm still not far enough away from the house.

The sun continues its relentless assent, turning the air from blistering to scorching. The muscles in my calves scream in protest before cramping. My throat is drier than the ground I stumble across, my stomach has long since given up on food, and I'm scared as hell.

When I reach the top, I pull up in the shade of a large boulder and sit, resting my head on the rock. My eyes close and vivid images bombard me in that place between waking and dreaming.

A rattling sound startles me, and my eyes fly open, scanning the area. A beige snake with black markings is coiled a few feet from me with its head and long neck up.

Neither the snake nor I move as blood rushes through my ears. My brain is encouraging me to run at the same time instinct tells me not to. The snake and I stare at each other, and for several long moments, the only movement is the snake's quivering tail.

I blow out a short breath. "I won't beat you senseless with a rock if you don't bite me. Deal?"

It doesn't answer, only flicking that stupid tail the way my sisters' cats do when they believe they've been annoyed beyond reason. Fighting the urge to bolt, I scoot away crab-style, putting the boulder between us. When I'm on the other side, I scramble up, turn and run, my left foot slipping on a loose stone as I go.

As the day drags on, a weird sensation flows over and under my skin, like I'm on a vibrating platform. It occurs to me it's been awhile since I've needed to wipe sweat off my brow, although it's hotter now than ever.

Overwhelming thirst dominates my thoughts and I glance around for signs of water, but all I see are dirt, stones, and plants. Breathing is harder now, which is odd because I'm heading down-hill. The sun burns my pale skin, but the only shade is near the larger rocks. Since a rock is where I met my little snake friend, I avoid all of them.

My brain churns through the run-in with the snake, something nibbling away in the dark corners my mind. During a short break, I take in my surroundings and it hits me what it is about the snake that bothers me. We were told the Ruins are uninhabitable, but the snake proves at least something besides desert plants can live here. And if it's here, it's eating something else that lives here.

Scanning the ground for evidence of life, I spot scattered holes and a lizard sunning itself. The Union said it would take hundreds of years for the Ruins to support life again, but life managed to take hold despite what we did out here. This gives me hope, and with a burst of renewed energy, I stand and continue on.

By the time darkness falls, my head weighs a hundred pounds and my limbs are buzzing. I rest my head against the trunk of a strange looking spiky-leafed tree, closing my eyes for only a moment to catch my breath.

The next thing I'm aware of, it's nearing dawn. I push myself up on jelly arms, consumed with manic thoughts of water. My pace is much slower than yesterday when I resume my trek.

Once the sun rises, I can make out trees in the distance. Real ones with actual leaves, which means there must be water nearby. I'm not sure Ruins water is safe to drink, but I do know I'm going to die if I don't drink something.

Even though I've been walking for hours, the trees don't appear any closer. My legs have taken on a sponge-like quality and I stumble, but manage to stay upright. If I fall, I may never get up again.

When I finally arrive at the nearest tree, there's no water. How is that possible? Despair overtakes me and I drop down, pounding my fists on the wasted ground. I stuff a soft green leaf in my mouth, seeking moisture, but I'm so parched, I gag on the pieces, which tears my throat like shards of broken glass.

My head spins as roll to my back and struggle to form rational thoughts, but there's nothing rational about this. I left home to find my place in the world, is this really where my search was supposed to lead me? It's more like a cruel joke. If I was on a date with destiny, it just took a bizarre turn into a twisted ending I never saw coming.

If only I hadn't gone to the park that night, none of this would've happened. I begin to cry. For my family and friends who will never know what happened to me, and for myself. I'm not ready to die; I'm only seventeen.

I can't help wondering if I would have spent so much time

agonizing over my future if I'd known I'd be dead so soon. If I'd known, maybe I'd have done everything differently.

Now I know my future.

My life ends here.

Alone.

In the Ruins.

13

Irrational Thoughts

*M*y mom stands below me, watching as I glide above the earth. Worry lines crease her brow, but I smile and tell her I'm okay. Lisa and Colin call for me, lifting rocks and peeking beneath them. I yell down to them, but they continue their search as if they didn't hear.

Bryce appears before me, arms crossed, a sneer on his face. He lets out a half laugh. "You actually believed I loved you. You're so gullible, it was almost too easy." His face twists and morphs into Walker's.

Belt in hand, Dantel approaches and reaches for me.

A small voice asks, "Is she dead?"

Is who dead? I struggle to open my eyes, but I think someone glued them shut.

Another voice answers, "I'm not sure... No, she's still breathing."

"Who is she?"

"I don't know. I don't think she's from around here. Have you ever seen hair that color?"

I want to ask them who they're talking about, but my lips won't move. The effort to speak wears me out and I drift into a world without color, or light, without dreams, or fears.

A cool breeze ruffles my hair and the sharp call of a bird cuts through the silence. I start to ask Lisa and Colin how they found me, but they tumble away, like small shells sucked out by the tide.

Water fills my mouth, choking me. Water!

A lilting female voice says, "Not so fast, you'll make yourself sick."

I turn toward the voice but I can't see. Something is over my eyes. Terror floods me, and I try to sit up, but I don't have the energy.

"Ben, can you go check on the broth?" the voice asks.

I pull back from her, trying to make sense of where I am and what's happening.

"You're dehydrated. We need to be careful to balance your electrolytes."

Oh, good, I'm in a hospital. She knows what she's doing. My thoughts become heavy, like feet dragging through deep mud. A cold, sticky substance is rubbed onto my sunburned lips, and I flinch.

"Sorry," she whispers. Small footsteps stop next to the bed. "Thank you, Ben."

A straw is placed in my mouth and I take a sip, gagging when the rancid taste hits my tongue.

She laughs. "It's awful, I know. Take small sips."

I start to ask who she is and where I am, but she shoves the straw back between my lips, forcing me to drink more.

"Get some rest. We'll talk later, but...you're safe for now."

For now? Like I might not be safe later? Footsteps recede and soon I'm drifting somewhere between consciousness and delirium.

When I wake, my eyes are no longer covered. Sitting up, I take in my surroundings. This isn't like any hospital room I've ever seen. The walls are white plaster and stone, curving into a domed ceiling with a round window at the top, bathing the room in soft, natural light. No fancy machines sit beside my bed, and speaking of the bed, it's just a regular mattress on a rustic wood frame. My skin tingles as I realize this is all very wrong.

A high-back wooden chair and a small table with a chipped ceramic cup of wildflowers sits next to the bed. Across the room is a beat-up chest of drawers with several missing drawer pulls, and simple white drapes hang above the windows.

A stunningly beautiful girl, who looks to be about my age, enters the room with a glass of water. Her flawless skin is the color of caramel and her long, dark hair is braided into dozens of tiny cornrows adorned with beads. She's dressed in denim shorts, a tank top, and high-top boots — no scrubs.

A beautiful smile warms her face, making her pale brown eyes crinkle at the corners. She hands me the glass. "Hello, I'm Sonia."

It's the same melodic voice I heard earlier. My voice cracks and breaks when I attempt to say my name. I take a sip and try again. "I'm Evan." It comes out hoarse, not sounding like me at all. "Where am I?"

"We call it Green Canyon and that's as good a name as any."

What the hell kind of answer is that?

Her eyes crinkle again. "We'll talk more later. Right now, I need to treat your burns."

A blonde girl of fifteen or sixteen enters carrying an aloe vera plant and hands it to Sonia. Her long hair is collected into a single braid reaching to her waist. She has a smattering of freckles across her nose and large, wide-spaced blue eyes.

Sonia smiles at her. "Thank you, Ally."

Ally gives me a sideways glance and a half smile before sitting cross-legged on the floor next to the bed. Sonia snaps off a leaf and rubs the soothing gel to the sunburned areas of my shoulders, arms, and face.

"Where are your shoes?" Sonia asks.

"I lost them."

She stares at me as if I just told her I'd misplaced my head and not my flip-flops, but she doesn't say anything more about them as she applies a sticky paste to the bottoms of my feet.

When she's finished, she stands. "Excuse me. I'll be right back." She walks out, leaving me alone with Ally.

I check the condition of my feet. They don't seem too bad. "What's that stuff she put on me?"

Ally chews the inside of her cheek. "You're not from around here are you?"

Well that was non-sequitur. I want to ask about my family and friends, how they found me, and what happened to my kidnappers, but before I can pick one, Sonia returns with three guys and yet another girl. This girl is attitude personified and her royal blue eyes bore into mine, making me squirm.

A tall guy exuding confidence steps forward. He's over six feet, incredibly good looking in a natural, rough-around-the-edges sort of way, and is about two days beyond needing a shave, but somehow it works on him. Raking a hand through his short wavy brown hair, his dark eyes travel over my face.

Finally, he smiles and reaches out to shake my hand. "Hi. I'm Lucien." His voice is deep and resonant, and more than a little sexy.

I take his hand and I'm surprised by how rough it is beneath mine. "I'm Evan," I say with a very non-sexy croak.

He gestures toward a guy who looks remarkably like him with the exception of his eyes, which are lighter in color. "This is my brother, Cyrus." Then he nods at the tallest of them, a boy with dark skin and a smile that consumes his entire face. "That's Marcus." Lucien takes Miss Attitude's hand and pulls her to him, wrapping an arm around her waist. "And this is Draya."

Draya appraises me with her cold eyes but doesn't say a word. She's the only one who hasn't smiled. The dynamic of this group is not professional, like they're friends or family rather than colleagues.

Draya turns to Sonia and Ally. "Can you step out for a few minutes?"

Unease rolls through me as the other two girls leave.

Lucien grabs the chair from beside the bed and flips it around, setting it across from me. He sits with his arms crossed over the back and studies me. "How did you get here?"

"Um, I don't know. The last thing I remember was being out in the Ruins. I assume someone rescued me. That wasn't you?"

Instead of answering my question, he asks me another. "Where do you think you are?"

"I'm not sure. Don't you know?"

I study the faces in the room but can't decipher what any of them are thinking, except Draya. A small, amused smile plays at the corners of her mouth.

My face must betray my growing uncertainty, because Lucien says, "We're not going to hurt you, I promise. I'm just trying to piece together what you're doing out here."

Out here? Wait, what? I'm still in the Ruins and haven't been rescued at all. Realization crawls over my skin like tiny bugs. I'm not home, I'm not safe, and these people aren't my rescuers. Maybe they didn't let me die in the desert, but they didn't take me home either. There are no good reasons to keep me in the Ruins, only very bad ones.

My eyes dart to the door and I wonder how quickly I can make it out of here. But after that, where would I go? Perhaps if I pretend to cooperate for now, I can try to go out one of the windows later.

"How did you get out here?" Miss Attitude demands.

"Back off, Draya," the brother says, his voice low and even. "Look at her. She's terrified." Cyrus, I think Lucien called him.

I set my jaw and stare him down, hating that I've shown them weakness.

He walks over and sits on the edge of the bed. "What can you remember?"

The gesture is far too familiar for a stranger. Anger beats back some of my fear, and I sit a little straighter and narrow my eyes. I'm fed up with being kidnapped, pawed at, and fighting for my survival.

The staring contest continues for several long moments before Cyrus stands and whispers something to his brother. Lucien then pulls Draya and the other guy from the room.

The rising wave of anger I was riding peters out now that we're alone. He's got a good seven inches on me and probably outweighs me by more than sixty pounds. The muscles in his arms flex, all corded and sinewy, leaving no doubt he can do some serious damage to me with just one of those arms.

He watches me as I process my defensive strategy, but in a completely unexpected move, takes a seat on the floor a few feet away. My eyes take in every detail, assessing my opponent. He's not like Walker's crew. He's younger and a lot cleaner, although good grooming doesn't mean he's trustworthy, but he might be my best chance to find out what's going on.

"I want some answers before I'll tell you anything," I say.

He blows a puff of air out between his lips. "Fair enough. What do you want to know?"

"Who *are* you?"

"Um..." He cocks his head to the side, as if I'd asked him the lamest question ever. "I'm Cyrus—"

"Not your name, but who you are and what you want with me."

"I don't know what you mean."

I let out a frustrated huff. "Why are you out here?"

"We live here."

My hands ball into fists. "Why are you lying to me?"

His forehead crinkles and his eyebrows draw together. "Evan...I'm not."

"I may be confused about a lot right now, but I *do* know people don't live in the Ruins."

His expression softens. "We've lived in the Ruins our whole lives. We used to live northeast of here until a tornado destroyed our town. But we were all born out here."

"What the hell is wrong with you? Why can't you just tell me what's going on? Who are you and what do you want with me?"

He scratches a thumbnail across his eyebrow. "You're not going to believe anything I tell you anyway, so why don't you tell me what you think's going on."

His condescension is infuriating, building pressure in my head, but I'll play along for now. "Fine. You're in business with Walker and you're either trying to get a ransom from my uncle or something to do with Bryce. What I can't figure out is why you haven't handed me back yet."

Anger flashes in his eyes and I realize I've pissed off a potential kidnapper. Maybe not my smartest move. He opens his mouth but no words come out. Instead he shakes his head. Silent minutes of silence pass until it becomes clear he's not going to say anything.

"How long have I been here?" I ask.

"Four days."

"*Four days*? How could I have been here *four days*?"

"You were in bad shape. Sonia gave you something to help you sleep."

The top of my scalp prickles and seething anger unfurls inside me. Walker will be here any minute and they made sure I wouldn't be any trouble until he arrived. There's nothing I can do now.

Hopeless frustration takes over and I snap. "You *drugged* me?" Before he can respond I scream, "Get out! Get out! *Get out!*"

He lets out a deep sigh as he stands and leaves the room without another word.

Rage like I've never known saturates me and I hurl the glass of water in my hand across the room. It hits the wall, shattering.

Ally flies into the room a few seconds later, eyes wide as she takes in the shards on the floor. "What happened?"

I glare at her. "It slipped."

14

Anger Management

*C*risp, clean smelling sheets rub against my cheek. My eyes snap open and I take in the white walls, the wood chair next to the bed, the broken glass on the floor, and hopelessness settles into my bones, making my limbs heavy.

I'm still here, which means Walker hasn't arrived yet. No one's been in to see me since I screamed at Cyrus last night nor have they brought me anything to eat or drink. I guess they're expecting Walker to feed me. Or maybe they just don't care. They also don't seem too worried I'm going to escape, the door isn't even closed all the way.

My legs wobble when I stand to drag the chair beneath the window and climb up to see out. It's a long way down, but not an impossible distance. Wooziness from lying in bed for days, dehydration, and not eating hits me and I sit before I fall on my ass.

Taking in my surroundings again, I'm struck by the difference between this place and the dump where Walker was holding me. The room I'm in feels solid, well maintained, and it's clean. My stomach growls, reminding me it hasn't been fed in days, maybe even a week. An old saying comes to mind — you can catch more flies with honey than vinegar. Maybe I can't escape, I've pretty much proven I can't survive on my own, and screaming and throwing things has apparently gotten my meal privileges revoked. It might be time for a new approach.

The glass shards from last night's tantrum still lie on the floor and I'm careful to avoid them as I walk past to peer out of my room. Stairs lead down to a wide hallway with four rooms leading off. The first is a bedroom with a neatly made bed, the second has a couple of bunk beds built into the walls. The other two are also bedrooms with a bed in them rather than pallets of stuff like the other house.

Another short flight of stairs at the end of the hall leads down where busy morning sounds and aromas rise, enticing me. I step gingerly on tender feet into a bright kitchen and dining area. Sonia, Ally, and several small boys are working at a long concrete counter, washing berries and placing them in bowls. Eggs cook in a cast iron skillet on a large grill, making my mouth water.

Sonia glances with a smile. "Good morning, Evan. How are you feeling?" She sounds genuinely pleased to see me, furthering my confusion.

"Okay, I guess. Sore."

She points to the boys with a spatula. "This is Ty, Will, Ben, and Connor, and you know Ally."

I'm clueless as to which name goes with which boy. They say hello before returning to their work.

Sonia holds a small broom and dustpan out to me. "Here, you can use these to sweep up the broken glass in your room."

I stare at her for a few beats. If they're holding me against my will, they can't possibly expect me to clean up around here. But I take them from her and turn to go back upstairs.

Draya calls out behind me, "Do you know how to use those? Will can show you if you need instructions."

I bite back a snarky response. "No thanks, I got it." As I walk up the stairs, I try to put these new facts into perspective. The small children are hardly miniature kidnappers. Their presence here only makes things more confusing. I'm only half paying attention as I sweep and step on a sliver of glass, lodging it in my foot. I swear loudly and sit to pull it out.

Sonia arrives a moment later with a wet towel and a clean bandage. "We'll get you shoes today. After we eat, though. Are you hungry?"

I nod and my stomach belts out its resounding agreement.

When we get back downstairs, breakfast is ready. Sonia gestures toward a chair at the end of a long table, large enough to seat ten. I mentally count the people I met so far — Sonia, Ally, Lucien, Cyrus, Draya, Marcus, and the four boys whose names I can't remember. The young kids scramble for spots on two benches flanking the table. Lucien, Marcus, and Cyrus enter the kitchen as breakfast is placed on the table and plop down on the benches. Five bodies sit on each side while I occupy the lone chair, feeling very much apart from this group.

The others dig into their meal, eating and talking about their plans for the day. "Evan needs shoes," Sonia says, then turns to me. "What size do you wear?"

Draya rolls her eyes as I croak out, "Seven."

Flavors hit my tongue with my first forkful, stopping me. I'm not sure what I expected, but this food is incredible. It's basic scrambled eggs with cheese and blackberries in cream, but the eggs are so fresh, they practically melt in my mouth. The sharp bite of the cheese adds a savory punch and the blackberries burst in my mouth, their rich juices flowing down my throat.

"Do you want some tea, Evan?" Ally asks.

"Yes, thank you." I take the offered mug, wishing it was coffee.

I study the group while I finish my breakfast. They talk and laugh like a family. The two youngest boys, both blond with bright blue eyes, regard me with interest. Whenever they catch me looking their way, they quickly glance away. One is five or six and the other isn't much older.

A lanky teen with shaggy hair that keeps falling into his dark eyes sits across from Ally. Next to him is a boy with curly hair. The younger one gives me a shy smile, a dimple appearing in his left cheek.

Maybe I misjudged them. They don't seem sinister nor do they appear to be part of a larger plot involving me, although it's the little kids that make me doubt my initial assumptions. I still don't know who they are or why they're out here.

After Lucien finishes his breakfast, he approaches me. "Take a walk with me, Evan."

I glance around the table, but no one is paying any attention to us.

"I won't bite, I promise." There's a spark of humor in his ebony eyes.

With a sigh, I get up and follow him through the living room to another staircase leading down to the front door sitting below the main level. Outside the air has a sweet, clean earthy odor with a hint of sage. We cross a wrap-around porch and beyond that is nothing but open space as far as I can see. A winding stone walkway leads away from the house like a gray river carving a path through dirt and plants. A large, flat-topped granite rock sits to the left.

We pass a chicken pen, not all that different from the ones we have back home. The hens flock to the fence, squawking as I follow Lucien into a fenced-in area with a wooden barn in the corner.

"Watch your step." Lucien points to a pile of some sort of animal droppings. He opens the door to the barn and I freeze at the sight of two full-grown cows. *Real freaking cows.* They're enormous. In the Union, we raise small livestock like chickens and goats, but large animals are raised in the area between the Southwestern Province and the Mexican border.

I'm awestruck by these beautiful creatures. Lucien pats one on her neck and whispers something to her, and I swear she responds with a low moan and a swish of her tail.

Lucien glances over his shoulder. "They won't hurt you." The cows distracted me so much I didn't realize he was leading me into a confined space with no way out. He positions a metal pail near one of the cows. "Do you want to try?"

Confusion tumbles through me. He brought me here to show me how to milk a cow? I shake my head and consider my escape options. Maybe it's the way Lucien just assumes I trust him, or how he doesn't seem to care, but I take another step into the barn.

He palms a teat in his hand and pulls down, squirting milk into the bucket. It creates a tinny sound as it strikes the pail's bottom. He grabs another and does the same, alternating hands as a steady stream of milk flows. "Tell me what you know about the history of the United States."

I scowl, wondering what kind of game he's playing.

"Humor me." A smile pulls his full lips tight, transforming his ruggedly handsome face. He's insanely good looking for a kidnapper.

I take a deep breath and think back to breakfast, and the boys, and even to what his brother told me last night. Chewing my lip I try to sort through everything. If they're waiting for Walker to come get me, why am I not locked in the room upstairs? Why drag me out to the barn to milk cows?

For the moment, I decide to play along. In my tortured voice I regurgitate what I know about our history from the Founding Fathers through the Second Civil War, and the great migration to the coasts in search of drinkable water. He finishes milking one cow as I talk and moves his stool to the other. I'm mesmerized by the movements of his hands as I share what I know of the Union formation and the past one hundred years.

When he's done with the second cow, he hands me a rake and shows me how to groom the straw on the floor of the barn. We work side by side as he tells me a story, one so horrifying it can't possibly be true.

"The facts are a little different," Lucien starts, eyeing me. "The Ruins were devastated, but not uninhabitable. Many stayed behind, close to a third of the surviving population."

I stop raking and stare at him. "That's...that's not possible."

His rake scrapes across the barn floor, the tines vibrating when they catch on something, releasing a sharp twang. "No doubt migration was the first choice of most people. Safe drinking water was scarce and the majority of the country was in ruins, but the ones who remained didn't want to give up their way of life."

I shake my head, trying to dislodge his words. This isn't true, but I still get caught up in the story. "Why would they risk their lives by staying behind?"

"Freedom. People were afraid of where the newly formed government was heading."

This is total bullshit — the abandoned homes, the crippled roads, the lack of any real civilization — they all reinforce what I learned in school. "So, what happened to everyone?" I ask, unable to mask the snark. "A third of the population after the war must've been like...fifty million."

He runs a hand through his hair. "We're still here, but we're scattered — the area outside the Union is massive. The Union didn't care about the ones who stayed behind. At least not at first. But they *did* care about the environment and believed fossil fuels caused global warming."

I resist the urge to roll my eyes. "Yeah, everyone knows that."

He shrugs. "The Union had science on their side, and even people who didn't believe in global warming couldn't deny real weather changes taking place. They just didn't agree humans were the cause. The Union saw a manmade disaster and the others chalked it up to long-term weather patterns."

"Okay, I'll buy into that. It makes sense. The Union only uses renewable energy, but that doesn't mean the rest of your story is true."

He eyes me. "Those who believed the changes were natural didn't think they could do anything to prevent it. They also thought restricting power sources was as stupid as it was danger-ous. The Union blocked access to the oil fields off the coasts, but the inland people found ways around it."

A chill crawls over my skin when I realize I'm about to find out his motive for telling me all this, and I'm pretty sure I'm not going to like it.

"The Union had the military and used it to bomb all the power stations and oil fields in the Ruins so they couldn't be used. Millions were killed in the strikes, and millions more died in the aftermath."

Anger burns in my gut. I don't know if I'm angry with him, myself, or the Union, but I decide for now to unleash it on him. "You're lying."

He rolls his lips inward, biting down on them. When he speaks again, his voice is controlled. "I wish I was....but I'm not."

"The Union would *never* do that. All human life is valuable, no one is more important than anyone else." I squeeze my head, trying to purge his words. When I glance up, he's studying me with eyes so dark they seem to swallow his pupils. "Why are you telling me this?" I whisper.

"Because you have a right to know. I assumed you did, but...the things you said to Cy last night..." He shrugs. "I was afraid you might not." His features soften, as if he feels sorry for me.

I don't want his pity. What he told me is so horrible, so unthinkable, it can't be true. But why would he lie? What does he have to gain?

I storm out of the barn, stumbling over a rock. A string of obscenities flies out of my mouth. I'm not sure where I'm going, but I need to get away from Lucien and his bullshit stories.

"Evan? Are you alright?" he calls after me.

I turn around to glare at him and realize I'm still holding the rake. I fling it to the ground and stalk off.

15

Alternate History

*T*he sounds and smells of nature that shouldn't even exist bombard me as I try to make sense of what Lucien told me. All of it flies in the face of what I know about history. Either the Union is lying or Lucien is.

They said the Ruins can't sustain life, that no one has lived out here for over a century. They lied about that, maybe they lied about everything.

My world's been ripped apart and thrown in my face like bitter confetti. The home I know doesn't exist and never really did. How am I supposed to go back when it's all a fantasy?

A rumble in my stomach reminds me how long I've been out here, and I trudge back to the house in an emotional funk, not wanting to face anyone but needing to eat. When I open the front door, raised voices echo down the stairs.

"I don't care," Draya says, her words dripping with disdain. "We saved her spoiled Union princess ass. Would it kill her to show a little gratitude? She hasn't lifted a manicured finger to help out around here, expecting us to wait on her like she's still in the Union."

"Give her a break, Dray," Sonia says. "She's still recovering. You saw her feet."

"I saw her fancy painted toes. It must be nice to live in a world where decorating your feet is a real thing."

"She's probably scared," Ally says. "How would you feel if you woke up in a house full of strangers?"

"If someone wants to drop me in utopia, I'll be happy to find out."

For the first time in my life, I'm ashamed of where I come from, of how I grew up, of my priorities up until now. Since the moment I opened my eyes out here, I've been solely focused on myself. I didn't think about how they live out here or how Union life must appear to them.

Ally glances over at me, her eyes widening. She tries to subtly gesture toward me, but it's so obvious, it's almost comical.

"Aw, looks like we've hurt her feelings," Draya says. I gotta give her credit for being as blunt to my face as she is behind my back.

Shame explodes into anger. It's not my fault I was born in the Union any more than it's her fault she wasn't. Heat floods my face, and I turn, marching back down the stairs and outside, slamming the door behind me. I stomp away from the house, alternating between tears, rage, and confusion.

The events of the past week are more than I can process, hell they're more than anyone should have to process. It's disorienting and without someone to talk this through with, I feel isolated on top of everything else.

The sun hangs low, balancing delicately on treetops, when someone calls my name. One of the brothers is coming toward me holding hiking boots in one hand and a pair of socks in the other. Pale eyes. Cyrus. I guess they're tag-teaming me now.

Relief washes over his features when he spots me. *Seriously?* After how they found me, just how stupid does he think I am? Blowing out a mouthful of air, I realize I need to make the best of this situation until I can get home.

"I got a size seven. Let me know if they don't fit," he says, handing them to me.

"Thanks." While lacing up my boots, I decide if I'm going to make the best of things, I should start by apologizing. "I'm sorry about last night. About screaming at you the way I did."

He studies me for a moment, his golden brown eyes sizing me up. I brace myself for a lecture on how I owe them for rescuing me, but all he says is, "Apology accepted."

Since he seems willing to meet me halfway, I press my luck. "Can I ask you something?"

He reaches a hand out to help me off the rock. "Sure."

"How many people live out here?" We start back to the house and I'm forced to take three steps for every two of his to keep up with his longer strides.

"If you mean the land mass outside the Union, I don't know, but in this valley, a few thousand. Why?"

"Just curious." I survey my surroundings with objectivity for the first time and I'm struck by the raw beauty, so different from the planned and cultivated Union.

Cyrus stares at me, like he wants to say something more, but he just runs a hand through his hair. "We should get inside. It's almost time to eat."

Missing lunch has taken my appetite to new levels. Dinner is some sort of fish, pan-fried with herbs and a lemon cream sauce that would make Lisa jealous. I have to stop myself from making rude "mmmm" sounds. When I finish my fish, I attack a fresh garden salad of lettuce, chopped apples and walnuts, savoring every bite, while simultaneously attempting to blend into the background.

"How was the trading post today?" Sonia asks.

"Crowded." Cyrus says between bites.

Draya cuts her eyes to him. "You're a wealth of information, as always, Cy. Anything more you'd like share? How much did we get for the cheese?"

"Enough to cover everything I picked up and then some."

"Good." Lucien says. "Georgia's at the end of her cycle. We'll need to breed her again soon."

I watch the exchange, trying to figure out the hierarchy of this group. Lucien seems to be the leader, for lack of a better word, but it's more like everyone just does what needs to be done without a defined structure.

After dinner, the older blond boy, who I now know is Will, Sonia, and Ally clear the table. I get up to help, carrying dishes into the kitchen and stacking them on the counter. The little curly-haired boy steps up onto a stool and pours a bucket of hot water into the sink, and a wave of missing home slams into me, unexpected and hard.

"You okay, Evan?" Marcus startles me out of my daydream, concern coloring his usually jovial face.

I blink, realizing I was staring into space, my hands hanging at my sides while everyone else was working. "Yeah, sorry. Homesick, I guess."

"Oh, get *over* yourself." The level of Draya's hostility catches me by surprise. "We all miss our families. We've all lost someone they care about or left someone behind. Stop acting like you're the only one."

Lucien opens his mouth to say something but Cyrus reaches out to grab his arm, stopping him. Whatever truce Cyrus and I came to earlier is clearly over.

My gaze bounces between them and my anger resurges. "What the hell is your problem? I get you don't want me here, but I didn't ask to come. I was drugged, kidnapped, nearly raped, and I almost died. You may have rescued me, but that doesn't give you the right to dump on me every five minutes. I'm done taking your shit, Draya."

She raises her chin in defiance and I stare right back, never breaking eye contact until she turns away. I snatch a towel from the counter and dry the clean dishes stacked up in the sink while Ally and Sonia put them away. We work in silence, giving me a chance to cool off. By the time we're done, I'm calm.

When I turn around, everyone is settling into their evening routine. Candles provide a warm glow throughout the living room where the younger kids are playing a game with a wooden board and painted rocks. The rest are taking seats at the dining room table with a deck of cards. After my tirade, I'm feeling a little persona non grata, so I head out the front door.

The night air is warm and pleasant with a sweet earthy odor that is richer than earlier. I glance at the chairs on the porch before spotting the large chunk of granite, and make my way over to it, hoisting myself up.

I lie on my back and close my eyes, letting the heat from the rock, baked by a day spent in the sun, penetrate my muscles. When I open my eyes, I gasp, caught off guard by the sheer number and vibrancy of the stars. I've never seen stars like these, that spill endlessly across the night sky, as if reminding me just how small and insignificant I am.

My mind wanders as I take in the artistry and beauty of my environment.

"Mind if I join you?" Cyrus's deep baritone startles me from my thoughts.

I scoot over to make room. "Be my guest."

He pulls himself up and sits beside me "What're you doing?"

"Looking at the stars. We don't see them like this back home, there's always lights interfering."

He lies next to me and looks up, but I doubt it has the same effect on him. This is his view every night.

I wonder if the others sent him out here to talk to me. Sonia's the obvious choice to broker a peace deal. Cyrus must have drawn the short straw. He seems on the verge of saying something, but when a full minute passes without him uttering a word, I close my eyes again and tune in to the desert night sounds.

"You can come inside."

When I open my eyes and turn to him, our faces are less than a foot apart, his eyes searching mine. He's so close I can smell something earthy, like warm sunshine, and something else that is all boy.

"It's pretty clear Draya would rather I didn't." I turn back to the stars. "But I like it out here. It helps me think."

"What are you thinking about?"

"How everything got so screwed up. Can you believe that the whole reason any of this happened was because I was trying to figure out where I belong?" I let out a jaded laugh. "And now I'm more lost than ever."

"Maybe it's fate."

"What? Me being here?"

He shrugs. "Yeah. You unloaded a mouthful inside, but I got the gist of it. That's a lot for just random chance."

I stare at him, his golden eyes sparkling in the moonlight, clearly believing in destiny. "I don't buy into the idea that my life is predetermined and I just have to wait for it to unfold."

He gives me a thoughtful look. "I think it's more like you have a purpose to fulfill, but it's up to you if you embrace it." He speaks with the same odd accent everyone here does, as if they're drawing out the vowels in each word.

"That's an interesting philosophy, but it seems too preposterous."

"Maybe." He smiles up at the stars. "Maybe it was just coincidence that everything happened the way it did, and that we left the Summer Fest two days earlier than planned. If we hadn't, we wouldn't have found you in time." He turns to me, an intensity in those pale eyes of his. "Maybe it's all random, but maybe you're on this earth for a reason, and being here fits into it somehow."

I roll to my side and prop my head up on my hand. "You really believe that?"

It's dark, but I swear color is creeping up his neck. "I believe everything happens for a reason, even if we don't understand it."

I've never met anyone like him before. With the way he lives, he still finds a way to put it all into perspective and find some meaning in it. I move to get up. "I should go apologize to Draya."

"She'll respect you more if you don't."

I turn back to him, pieces falling into place. When he stopped

Lucien from saying something to Draya in the kitchen, I assumed it was because he agreed with her, but maybe not. Based on our interaction last night, he may have figured I'd go all rabid dog on Draya if she pushed me hard enough. I'm not sure I totally get him, but I think I misjudged him. Maybe I misjudged Draya, too.

"What's her problem with me anyway?"

The corners of his mouth twitch up. "How much time do you have?"

I laugh for the first time since I was kidnapped, and it feels good.

He sits, pulling his legs up and resting his forearms across his knees. "She sees you as a threat."

"A *threat*? Have you seen me? I'm barely alive, hardly anything to fear."

He looks as if he's biting back another smile. "She's wary of anyone and anything from the Union. You represent what she fears and distrusts most. Give her time, she'll come around."

I doubt I'll be here long enough for that, but I can cut her some slack for now. I hop down to head inside then glance back to ask one more thing. "What time do you all get started in the morning?"

"Sunrise."

"Okay. See you then." It's time to start pulling my weight around here.

After saying good night to the others as I pass through the living room, I go upstairs to the room I'm staying in. On the chest of drawers is a stack of books that wasn't there earlier. Real books. I've only seen paper books in museums and private collections.

I pick up one and pull it to my face, inhaling deeply. It smells acidic but also like grass...with a hint of vanilla. The binding is beat up and inside the pages are yellowed and dog-eared, but otherwise it's in remarkable shape. Someone has taken very good care of it.

I crawl into bed with *Pride and Prejudice* and wonder who left them for me. This simple act of kindness, once again, forces me to reevaluate everything I thought about Lucien and his gang.

16

Pulling My Weight

*A*lthough I read late into the night, I still manage to drag myself out of bed at dawn. When I pick up my clothes, I'm hit by such a foul stench I blink back tears. I *really* need to wash them. I run a hand through my hair and my fingers catch in the tangles. And I need a shower. Bad.

Ally is in the kitchen when I get downstairs. I help her set the table then crack the eggs before going out to the garden to pick berries. After I finish, I wander over to the barn.

Lucien glances up from milking. "Good morning."

"Hi. So, I found some books last night. Do you know where they came from?"

A smile pulls at his lips. "I might."

"Are you going to tell me?"

"No. If they wanted you to know, they would've handed them to you instead of leaving them for you to find."

Now I'm even more curious. "They're in remarkable shape. Most books in the Union are in private collections. Where did they come from?"

He continues milking, his back to me. "Many are from before

the war, people value and take care of them. But you can purchase newer ones at the trading post."

"Why would someone leave them for me if they're so valued?"

"Because whoever it is trusts you to respect them. And because we assume you can read. Books are meant to be read."

I stare at his back, not sure I heard right. "You can't read?"

"Some, not much," he says matter-of-factly.

That's crazy, everyone knows how to read. "I don't understand—"

"What's not to understand?" He shrugs. "We learn what we need to survive. In most cases, reading is a luxury, not a priority."

"Then why do you have books?"

He's quiet for a few beats, and the only sound is the tinny hiss of milk hitting the pail and the gentle snorting of the cows. "They represent something we want. We all *want* to be able to read books, and lots of people can. Most of it depends on where you grow up, if your parents can read, or if you live somewhere with a school."

"But..." I pause, thinking how best to phrase this without coming off as arrogant. "Well, you just sound so, I don't know, you don't speak like someone who's illiterate."

He glances at me over his shoulder, a thoughtful expression on his handsome face. "I imagine you learn to speak the way you're spoken to."

I guess you don't need to read and write to speak well. Even with my Union education, I have a lot to learn about people in general and about the Ruins specifically. I pick up a rake to groom the straw after realizing I've been standing around while he works. "Why do some places have schools and some not?"

"After the bombings, big cities were too dangerous. People were afraid living in large groups made them targets for more Union attacks." He runs a hand through his hair and arches his back before returning to his work. "People banded together in small communities, but every time they'd get a power system up, the jets would bomb it. Eventually they stopped trying to rebuild modern societies and decided to live like early settlers."

When he's done milking, we head back to the house. "Towns tend to be small and tight-knit. If you're lucky, you find people you can trust. Those are the people you want to build a community with."

After breakfast, I look for Sonia and find her at the kitchen sink. "Hey, is there somewhere I can bathe or clean up?"

A broad smile lights up her face and she raises her left brow, nodding. "We have a shower." She leads me to her room where she sizes me up before pulling some clothes out of her dresser. Back downstairs, she grabs a plastic bucket from the kitchen before heading outside.

We pass the pen and gardens to a dirt path curving away from the house. Soon I hear the constant murmur of running water. When we round the corner, a wide rocky creek comes into view. We hike upstream and around another bend before stopping beside a small pool surrounded by jagged rock walls. On one side of the pool is a twenty-foot-high waterfall, and in this moment, I don't think I've ever seen anything more beautiful.

Sonia reaches behind one of the rocks and pulls out a long branch with a pink flag on the end, jamming it in the ground. "This will alert anyone coming along that the girls are using the shower now."

I begin to strip, feeling awkward in front of Sonia, but I guess if I'm going to take a shower in the great outdoors, I need to get over it. I dip my toe in the water and yank it back. The air around me might be hot, but the water is definitely not. Holding my breath, I tense and plunge in. Icy fingers dance across my skin, stunning me.

Sonia tosses me a bar of soap, and I wade over to the rock behind the waterfall and climb up. The soap has a clean, slightly sweet scent, not at all like the perfumed soaps of the Union. I rub the bar into the mess that is my hair and work up a good lather before rinsing off in the falls. The cold water rushing over me and igniting goose bumps across every inch of skin is nothing like the perfect one-hundred-five-degree showers I take back home, but there's something pure and natural about this.

While Sonia takes her shower, I lie on the warm rocks, letting the sun lick the remaining drops from my skin. When I'm dry, I dress in the clean clothes Sonia brought and fold up my dirty ones until I can ask about doing laundry. My hand brushes across something in the back pocket of my jeans, something I forgot I still had.

Sonia dresses and pulls a wooden pick from the bucket. "Let me help you with your hair. When we get back to the house, I'll check your feet."

"Where did you learn so much about medicine?" I ask, clawing at a particularly stubborn knot.

"From my mother."

"How long did it take to learn everything?"

"I can't remember a time I wasn't learning. I probably started as soon as I was old enough to help my mom, but there's still a lot I don't know."

We're both quiet as she picks a couple of twigs from my hair that have stubbornly stuck around post-shower. I use my fingers to untwist the tangled curls from one another. "How'd you meet everyone here?" I ask.

"I grew up with Draya, Lucien, and Cyrus. Same with Marcus." A smile fills her voice at his name. "We — Marcus, me, Lucien, Draya, and Cy — were swimming nearby when a tornado hit. The storm came up so fast we had to duck into a cave and hope for the best instead of trying to make it home. When it was over, we ran back home, but the town was...only half the buildings remained. Lucien and Cyrus's family didn't get to a storm cellar in time. We found them...their bodies about a mile away."

A fist-sized lump lodges in my throat and my heart breaks for people I barely know.

"Lucien and Cy said they couldn't stay." She pauses for a few moments and clears her throat before continuing. "I think being there was too hard...after what happened."

Draya's right, I need to get over myself. At least I still have a family to go back to.

"Marcus said he was going with them, and even though I was only fourteen, I convinced my parents to let me go, too." She stares at her hands, twisting them. "Marcus, Draya, and I packed up what we could carry and joined Lucien and Cy. We walked several weeks before we found this place."

"Have you seen your family since?"

"No." She lifts her head and gazes east. "We hike a couple of days in one direction or another to hunt or trade, and we go to Summer Festivals, but not back home. I miss my family, but I knew I wanted to be with Marcus before I even knew what it meant to be in love." A small smile graces her lips. "Once he decided to go, my decision was made for me. I'd follow him anywhere."

Wow. She left everything behind to be with Marcus. I always thought following a boy was weak and pathetic, but she makes it sound powerful.

We stand and Sonia turns me to face her, pushing a piece of hair away from my face. "We're going to help you get home, I promise."

Intense feelings of gratitude engulf me, and I remember what I found in my pocket. "I want to ask you something, but I'm not sure how, exactly."

She studies me for a long moment then sits back down, patting the ground next to her. "You can ask me anything, but I can't guarantee I'll answer your question."

"It's nothing personal, but, well, I don't want to offend you." I sit, curling one leg under me. "I already made some terrible assumptions and don't want to do it again."

"Oh." She laughs. "Well in that case, I promise I won't be offended."

Reaching into the back pocket of my dirty jeans, I pull out a wad of Union cash. It's what's left of the money Joe gave me at the train station. "I know you trade for what you need, but I was wondering if this has any value here."

Her gaze locks onto the bills in my hand, rises to meet mine, then shifts back to my hand. "Evan, where did you get that much money?"

"Uh, I just...I got it from my stepfather for incidentals and stuff. I forgot I had it."

"That's a lot of money," she whispers. "You need to put it away before anyone sees it."

"I want you to have it. It's the least I can do to repay you for all you've done."

"We can't take it, it's too much."

"Sonia, I don't need it." I put the cash in her hands. "Maybe you can use it for something."

Her eyes are bright, reflecting the smile radiating from her face. "We can buy a generator."

I can tell that's a big deal, even without her ginormous grin, but her gratitude makes me uncomfortable. "Sonia, can I ask you to do me a favor?"

"Sure."

"Don't tell anyone about the money until after I'm gone. Not even Marcus."

Her smile slips. "Why?"

"Because. How you are right now? I can't handle that from everyone else. It's not that much money to me. Some new clothes or shoes. Fun money. For you, it's, well, I don't even know what it is."

"It's all the difference in the world," she whispers.

God, I really am a princess. "So, you promise, right?"

"I promise." She reaches over and hugs me, filling me with unexpected warmth.

I'm beginning to wish I hadn't offered to help Will dig the new latrine this morning. Even though I wore gloves, fresh blisters pop up on the pads below my fingers. I hope Sonia has something I can put on them.

On my way downstairs, I poke my head into the room she shares with Marcus, but she's not in there or in the kitchen. Ben and Connor are folding laundry on the dining room table while Ty pushes dirt around the floor with a broom in his four-year-old attempt at sweeping.

"Hey, guys," I say. "Have you seen Sonia?"

"She's outside," Connor says.

"They're watching the gun show," Ben says with a roll of his dark eyes.

"The gun show?" This is new. I have yet to fire a gun, and I'm not sure I actually want to, but I can't deny I'm intrigued.

Heading out the door off the kitchen, I bounce down the stairs to the wraparound porch. A steady thwacking comes from beyond, but it doesn't sound like gunfire.

When I round the corner, Ally, Sonia, and Draya are leaning against the railing with their backs to me. Ally turns and glances over her shoulder as I approach.

"What's going on?" I ask.

"Just taking in the scenery," Sonia says.

I step closer to see what's so fascinating. "Holy...*woah*," Any additional words refuse to form in my head, much less come out of my mouth.

"Yeah," Ally says, her cheeks pinking up.

Cyrus stands with his back to us, shirt off, shorts hanging low on his hips revealing two dimples on his lower back. He swings an ax, bringing it down on a log in front of him, splitting it in two. Muscles flex and contract with each pass, and sweat runs down smooth, tanned skin.

"*Damn*," I whisper.

His biceps bulges when he brings the ax up again. He reaches for another log, places it on the chopping block and takes another swing.

"So, um…" I clear my throat. "Does this go on every day."

"Yup," Draya says.

Suddenly it occurs to me she's watching her boyfriend's shirtless brother with way too much interest. I cut my eyes to her. "I take it this is the gun show."

Sonia's grins. "Well, he does have impressive guns."

"Don't you have a boyfriend?" I ask her.

She shrugs. "Do you see him chopping firewood without his shirt on?"

"Does he know you watch him?"

"Doubtful," Draya says. "It'd go to his already inflated head."

"Whose turn is it today?" Sonia asks.

"Mine," Ally says. "But I think Evan should take it."

Three pairs of eyes turn toward me, and Draya's lips quirk up in a mischievous smile.

"Uh, turn for what?"

"To take him something to drink," Ally says. "We all rotate. Honestly, you need to see the front, and it's the only way."

"Oh, no," I say, backing away. "I'm not participating in your eye groping."

"Aww, come on, you're practically drooling. And your eyes have barely left him since you walked out here," Draya says.

"That's not the point."

"Suit yourself," Draya says, handing a glass of water to Ally.

As if I have no control over my own arm, it reaches out and snags the glass from Draya. "Fine. I'll do it."

"Thought so," Ally says under her breath.

Crossing the length of the porch to the steps, I walk down the path to where Cyrus is working. He glances up as I approach and wipes his arm across his forehead, smiling as he reaches out to take the glass.

"How do you know this is for you?" I ask.

His left eyebrow notches up. "It's not?"

"It is."

His smile broadens. "What're you up to this afternoon?" he asks, taking a sip of water.

I stare at his Adam's apple bobbing as he swallows. "I was looking for Sonia to get something to put on these," I say running my fingertips lightly over the blisters on my left hand.

"How'd you get those?"

"Digging a latrine."

He smiles. "Oh, really?"

"What?"

"Nothing." He shakes his head. "Too bad though. I could show you how to chop firewood, but you probably don't want to do that with blistered hands."

"No, probably not."

He finishes the water and hands the glass back to me. "Thanks for this."

"Apparently it was my turn."

"What?"

"Nothing." I give him the same lame non-answer he gave me. Touché. I turn to head back to the porch.

"Hey," he calls out. I glance back, my eyes locking onto his six-pack abs before gliding over sculpted chest muscles and finally meeting his eyes. "Green tea."

"H-huh?"

"Your blisters. Soak them in green tea. Apply some aloe vera and wrap them in gauze."

"Oh, thanks."

He turns back and swings the ax again, and I watch one more time as those muscles do magical things to my circulatory system.

17

Closer Than Ever

$\mathscr{I}$ can't believe how fast time has gone by out here. When I first arrived, I was itching to get home, but now...now I'm not sure what I want. With every passing day, I'm less convinced that leaving is what I need or even want to do.

When morning dawns on my last day, I dress in my own clothes and fold up the shorts and T-shirt Sonia lent me, placing them on the dresser. I knot messy curls on top of my head and sit on the edge of the bed to put on my boots, the mattress sinking beneath my weight. A bittersweet air settles over me as I realize this is the last time I'll be in this room.

Sonia, Marcus, and Cyrus are escorting me back to the Union after breakfast and I'm working to ignore the growing sensation that I'm not ready yet. My parents must be worried sick, but this place and these people own a piece of me now, too.

After stripping the sheets, I take one last look around what has been my home for the past several weeks. My time here has transformed me in ways I still don't fully understand. Maybe I still haven't found my purpose, but I believe I'm closer than ever.

With a small sigh, I turn and walk downstairs, dropping the

bedding by the back door with the rest of the laundry before entering the kitchen.

Sonia is busy making tea while Lucien and Draya talk in low tones in the corner, Lucien rubbing Draya's arms. Marcus leans against the counter, his features pinched.

In the living room, little Connor, one of Ally's brothers, is curled up with a blanket on the couch next to his sister, who appears to be crying. Something is very wrong.

Cyrus is nowhere to be seen and neither is Ally's other brother, Ty, sending prickles up my spine. I walk over to Sonia. "What's going on?"

"It's Ty." Tension colors her light brown eyes.

"What happened?"

"He's sick, very sick."

"Sick?"

"I think he has pneumonia."

"Pneumonia?"

"Oh, my god! What is your problem?" Draya snaps at me from across the kitchen. "People in the Union don't get sick?"

I pivot to face her, ready to say something cutting when I catch the fear in her eyes, choking the words off before they reach my tongue. "Yes, but not often. What can you do for him?" I ask Sonia.

"We can't do anything," Draya answers. "I'm sorry if it delays your return to your precious Union."

"You really think *that's* what I'm worried about?" Her expression is defiant before she turns away. "There's nothing you can do? No medicine you can give him?" I ask Sonia.

"We can't afford the medicine he needs." She moves to the stove as the tea kettle whistles.

"But there *is* something he can take?" Little buds of hope sprout in my chest.

"It's expensive," Lucien says.

"How much?"

Lucien rubs the back of his neck. "More than we have."

Sonia gives me an almost imperceptible shake of her head, letting me know she hasn't told anyone about the money. Which means she still has it. The little bud grows. I nod, and she reaches into her back pocket to pull out the money I gave her.

"What's that?" Draya asks.

"Cash. From the Union." I brace myself and swivel to face her. "I had it on me when I was taken. I gave it to Sonia."

"Sonia?" Marcus asks.

"I asked her to keep it secret until I was gone."

"What the hell for?" Draya demands.

"Because I didn't want it to be another 'thing' between us." I huff out a frustrated breath. "In the Union you can buy your way out of your obligations. That's not what I'm trying to do."

No one says anything, not a word, and when I turn to look at Lucien, he's staring at me with his dark, unreadable eyes.

"Is it enough for the medicine Ty needs?"

He takes the cash from Sonia, pockets a bill, and hands the rest back to her. "Yes."

After Lucien leaves, Sonia finishes the tea, stirring in some honey, and turns to go upstairs.

Ally pops up from the couch. "I'll take it to him."

"No," Sonia says. "I should go."

"He's *my* brother."

"What's the matter?" I ask, not sure why they're arguing over who's going to take him tea.

"He's highly contagious," Sonia says. "We don't want to expose anyone we don't need to."

"Then let me go."

"So now you're a martyr, too?" Draya snaps.

I close my eyes and count to three before turning to face her. "No, but I've been vaccinated against most major illnesses. That's why people in the Union rarely get sick. The odds Ty has something I'm not immune to are pretty slim. Let me do this."

Sonia hands me the cup, and I go upstairs to find Ty on the bottom of one of the bunks. My breath catches at the sight of him. He's ashen and his bluish lips are slack in sleep. I press my palm to his forehead and it feels like an inferno is raging in his skull. His chest moves up and down with exaggerated motion as he breathes, a wheeze accompanying each one. I can't do much for him while he sleeps, so I set the tea on the floor next to his bunk and return to the kitchen.

Sonia pours some hot water from the pot on the stove into a smaller bucket, adding some cooler water. "Here," she says, "wash your hands with some soap. We have to contain this as much as possible."

"How does it spread?"

"Through saliva and mucus...I think. It depends on what strain he has, but without any way to run tests, I'm basing my assumptions on what's been going around. He probably picked it up at the falls. Lots of people in the area are sick."

"He should be isolated then. I'll keep him upstairs with me." I grab some clean sheets and head up to my room to make the bed before going back down to get Ty. He's heavier than I would have guessed based on his size. He moans a little, coughs, and snuggles into me.

Even though no one gets sick much in the Union, I know enough about viruses and bacteria to realize we need to kill the germs. I head back downstairs for a bucket, soap, and rags and scrub the surfaces of all of the beds in their room.

When I return to the kitchen, Lucien is back. He places a bottle in my hand. "Give him a dropper of this twice a day. It needs to stay cool, so store it out in the springhouse." He hands me another bottle I recognize as an anti-inflammatory. "You can give him this to bring his fever down."

Ty wakes enough to swallow the medicine along with some more tea. Sonia put something in it to help him sleep and I finally understand why she drugged me when I first got here.

Ty sleeps most of the day, only waking for brief periods. Marcus and Cyrus drag another mattress up and lay it on the floor beside the bed so I can sleep next to Ty. After dinner, I'm exhausted and collapse on the mattress, falling asleep almost immediately. Ty's coughing wakes me throughout the night, and he whimpers in his sleep. It's a long, rough night.

By morning, his cheeks have a little bit of ruddiness to them, and he's awake for longer stretches at a time.

"Here, try some of this." I offer him some soup.

He takes a couple of sips, coughs again, and lies back in bed, but his eyes remain open, like he doesn't have the strength to sit up, but he's tired of sleeping.

"Do you want me to read to you?"

He nods. "Can you read the book about the family living on the island?"

I glance at the stack of books on the bedside table, but I'm not sure any of them are the one he's referring to.

"It's in my room," he says.

I bite back a smile and bounce down the stairs. Since I stripped his bed and know it's not there, I open the top drawer to the closest dresser and find *The Swiss Family Robinson* tucked inside. When I pull out the colorful book with elaborate illustrations, it's clear why this wasn't among the books in my room. Even if he can't read, there pictures tell a vivid story.

Returning to the room, I sit next to him and tuck him into my side as we read all about the Robinsons' adventures. He's asleep within twenty minutes though, although he sleeps for shorter periods of time than he did yesterday.

"How's he doing this morning?" Sonia asks, peeking her head into the room.

"Not nearly as much coughing last night." I stand and stretch.

Based on the shadows on the wall, it's early morning, before sunrise.

Sonia steps inside and moves to the bedside, placing the back of her hand against his forehead. "He's been on the medication for forty-eight hours now, so he shouldn't be contagious. I'll have Marcus move him back to his own bed and give you your room back."

"I really don't mind," I say and realize I'm going to miss the little guy, but I won't miss sleeping on the floor. Even on a mattress, it's uncomfortable.

Cyrus pokes his head in the door and glances from Sonia to me and back to Sonia again.

"What's up?" Sonia asks.

"Connor."

With a heavy sigh, she follows him downstairs. Between Marcus and Cyrus, they get Connor tucked into my bed with clean sheets and Ty back in his room.

I administer the medication and spend my day keeping an eye on Connor as the others bring tea for him and food for me to the door. Sonia pokes her head in just before dinner, dark circles marring the caramel skin beneath her eyes.

"Uh, Sonia, how are you feeling?"

She coughs. "Not so good."

"Sit," I order and run downstairs to grab another set of clean sheets, bumping into Cyrus in the kitchen.

"Hey, how's it going?" he asks.

"Sonia has it now."

I can see worry flash across his face, but he pulls it together quickly. "Okay, we're on it."

He and Marcus drag another mattress up to the room and I spend the evening taking care of my two patients. One thing I know from this experience, whatever my ultimate career is, it won't be in medicine.

Sonia's been down four days and I'm scared. I sit on the floor beside the bed, wishing she'd wake up. She coughed all night, a chest-rattling hacking that made her vomit twice. It's been a struggle to get any fluids in her because she's too weak to even sip through a straw.

Closing my eyes, I wish I believed in a higher power who I could pray to for her well-being, but instead, I try to will her back to health with the non-existent powers of my mind.

"What do I have to do to get something to eat around here?"

Relief floods through me and I spin, throwing my arms around her. "Sonia!"

I bounce downstairs feeling lighter than I have in days and get a cup of soup for her. No one is inside to share the good news with. Returning to the room, I hand her the soup and sit cross-legged on the mattress at the foot of the bed.

"How is everyone?" She asks. "What are they up to?"

"Everyone's okay. No one else has gotten sick, but I haven't seen much of them lately. Too busy taking care of you."

"Thanks, Evan. For everything."

I wave her off and glance at my nails.

"I'm tired of sleeping and doing nothing," she says.

"Do you want me to read to you? Ty has a book with pretty pictures."

"No." She laughs. "Tell me something about yourself."

"Like what?"

She taps her finger against her lips. "Do you have a boyfriend back home?"

"That's a loaded question. I thought I had one, but...hell, I have no idea."

I spend a little time explaining about Bryce and what the kidnappers said without going into too much detail.

"What do you think that means?"

I shake my head. "I don't really know, but I do know he lied to me and that's a deal breaker. Whatever we had was dead the second he told me his name was Bryce."

"So, he goes by his middle name, that's not so strange. Even out here."

"It's more than that. Whatever he's into, it got me kidnapped and nearly killed. If it was just the name, I might be able to get past it. But I always had this sense when we were together that he was holding back. I don't have a lot of relationship experience, but I can tell when someone is withholding information from me."

"And honesty is important to you." It's a statement and not a question.

"Isn't it to you?"

"Of course, but truth is complex, and sometimes all the details don't need to be shared with everyone."

"Okay, I can see that to a certain extent, but with my family situation..." Oh shoot, I just opened a box of steaming shit I'm not sure I want to get into.

"What situation is that?"

I sigh and wonder how much I want to tell her, but honesty is my thing, especially after my entire life was a lie, so I give her the Evan Taylor tabloid story of my life.

When I'm finished, she's quiet for a few moments, then lets out a slow breath of air. "Wow. Okay, I think I'm starting to understand you a little bit more."

I laugh. "Is that a good thing?"

She chuckles. "Most definitely. We like you Evan. All of us." I lift an eyebrow. "Yes, even Draya. And...well, getting to know you better only makes me like you more."

I drop my head, unsure of what to make of all this sharing, but suddenly I want to know more about her and the others here. "What about you guys. Cyrus said you were coming home from some sort of circus or something when you found me."

She laughs. "Festival, not circus. The Summer Fest. They have one every year somewhere in the area. People come from all over for a week of trading goods, gossip, and competitive spirit. It's fun and a chance to meet people beyond our small community."

"Why'd you end up leaving early?"

She studies me for a few moments. "What else did Cy tell you?"

"Nothing, why?"

"That's a story for another day." She leans back, closing her eyes, and I take that as my cue to let her get some rest.

I'm thrilled to join the others for dinner for the first time in nearly a week. Lucien shares news from the trading post. "Eight in total have died so far."

My fork stalls halfway to my mouth. "Died? From pneumonia?"

He nods. "It's the worst anyone's seen in years."

"Can't we just buy more medicine and help them?"

"I did. Today. I spent the rest of what we had. I just hope it's enough." He pauses and levels me with a dark stare. "The money's raised a lot of questions, though. Everyone's asking where it came from. I told them a traveler repaid us for our hospitality, which is true. That seems to have satisfy most of them. At least for now."

After helping Ally tuck the boys into bed, I head outside. The fresh evening air skates across my bare arms and legs as I climb atop the rock. I lie on my back, thinking about the last few days and force myself to face the truth. I'm torn between staying and leaving. At first, my reluctance to leave had to with my feelings toward the Union, but now I'm not so sure that's it.

"Mind if I come up?" I scoot over to make room for Marcus. He sits next to me with his arms resting on his knees. "How is she, really?"

"She's okay. Really."

"Thank you," he says with a slight catch in his voice. "I don't know what I would've done if..."

"I know."

At the sound of the front door opening, we both turn. Cyrus walks across the porch toward us.

"C-can I go see her now?" Marcus asks.

"Yeah, I think she'd like that."

Marcus hops down and he and Cyrus exchange a loaded glance before Marcus heads inside. Cyrus takes the spot vacated by Marcus, stretching out his legs in front of him "We'll get you home, I promise."

I lean my shoulder into his. "I know. I'm not worried." I don't want to tell him I'm not ready to leave, it'll only lead to questions I don't have answers to. We sit in comfortable silence for a while, enjoying the night and each other's company. The warmth of him beside me creates a fluttery sensation in my belly that's both familiar and foreign. Like I'm attracted to him, but I can't be. I mean, I barely know him and I'm still reeling from whatever it was Bryce and I had going on.

When I turn toward him, he's staring at me. The butterflies in my stomach amp up their craziness and I have a sudden urge to kiss him. Which is a really bad idea for a ton of reasons. I quickly look away and babble incoherently until the words "tell me about your family" fall from my mouth. Then I remember what Sonia said about the tornado killing them, and I want to die a little myself. I turn back to him, horrified. "I'm so sorry, I-I shouldn't have asked that."

"It's fine." His mouth curves into a slow, sexy smile, sending the beating wings in my gut into a frenzied dance.

I close my eyes to protect against this weirdness, no doubt brought on by lack of sleep and not the shirtless wood splitting.

"I had a great childhood. Me, Lucien and my little brother and sister, Bartholomew and Penelope, lived a pretty good life with our parents."

The next thing I'm aware of is Cyrus gently waking me. I sit up and glance at him, disoriented. "Oh, god," I mumble, running a hand through my hair. "I can't believe I fell asleep."

"After the week you had, it's understandable." A long pause fills the space between us before he continues. "I wanted to thank you for...for everything you've done."

I chance meeting his gaze, and his eyes are bright with sincerity. Before I do something stupid, I say, "You're welcome," and move to get down. "Goodnight, Cyrus."

"G'night, Evan."

I head back inside, check on Sonia, and fall into a much needed deep sleep, filled with visions of a dreamy boy with the body of a god and the soul of a poet.

18

Something New

*L*ife settles back into our normal routine while we wait for Sonia to recover. This morning, I'm going fishing for the first time in my life. Marcus, Lucien, and I hike upstream where the creek is much wider and the water flows faster and deeper. A sweet mixture of grass and something I've come to associate with fresh water in the Ruins fills the air.

Marcus holds a cricket between his thumb and forefinger. I squirm as he pushes the hook through its abdomen. "Your turn," he says, a wicked gleam in his eye.

I squint, torn between a desire not to stab myself and not wanting to watch the critter as I jab a fishhook through it. The morning is cool, but nervous sweat beads on my forehead. A slight click indicates the hook is through the outer shell and into the gooey center. I shudder, totally squigged out, and cast my line the way Lucien showed me.

As we sit on the bank waiting for a bite, Marcus asks, "What's it like living in the Union?"

I'm surprised it's taken this long for someone to ask this, so I've had plenty of time to think about how best to answer. "In some ways, it's a lot like living here. People work together to grow produce in our community gardens, and we trade with other neighborhoods at our local market, which is sort of like a trading post. One of the biggest differences, though, is people are packed in tight because land is scarce."

Lucien cocks his head, studying me. "Is it true the government is socialist?"

"I guess, but it doesn't really fit the historical definition, it's more like a modified socialism." My arm tires and I shift my pole to my other hand. "They guarantee everyone's basic needs but we still have a pretty healthy dose of capitalism. We have individual freedoms but also social responsibilities. No one starves or is denied health care." I shrug, thinking about how sick Ty was with an easily curable illness.

"I don't get how that can work," Marcus says. "How can you have both socialism and capitalism?"

"It ties back into what I was saying the other morning. Everyone is required to donate ten percent of their work hours to community service. It's only about four or five hours a week per person, but it makes a huge difference." My back starts to ache, so I sit on the bank and prop my knees up, balancing the pole between them. "People work in hospitals and schools, delivering food to police and firefighters. It works pretty well. But the wealthy who can afford it can pay ten percent of their income in taxes instead."

"Sounds pretty socialist to me," Lucien says, taking a seat on the ground next to me.

"Maybe...but most people think the benefits outweigh the negatives."

"What negatives?"

"Well, like the way you guys live here, that would never work there. You can't own a gun, so hunting is out of the question. But you don't need to hunt."

"It's a tough call," Lucien says. "There's something to be said for being able to do what you want whenever you want, even if we have to fight for our survival."

Before I can say anything more, I get a bite on my line and let out a squeal. Marcus shows me how to reel it in, then Lucien gives me my first lesson on cleaning a fish. The Union may have its faults, but right now not having to gut a fish while it stares at me with those huge eyes is currently at the top of my list of benefits.

By the time we're ready to head back, we have half a dozen fish. We walk at a leisurely pace, enjoying a lazy summer morning.

"Can I ask you something?" Lucien asks, his dark eyes intense on mine.

"Yeah." I ready myself for more questions about the evil socialist republic I come from.

"Marcus said he and Cyrus offered to take you home. Why didn't you go?"

I'm not prepared for this question and end up stammering. "I... uh...I-I'm not sure I'm ready yet." I can't put into words what I'm feeling, but I realize I've likely overstayed my welcome. "I know you didn't plan on me staying this long when—"

"Oh. Evan, no. That's not what I meant."

"I'm the only person in the house with a room to myself, I assume I displaced someone."

He grins. "That would be Cy, and I don't think he minds." "Look, Evan, you're a part of our family now and welcome to stay as long as you want." He puts an arm around me and hugs me against his side in a warm embrace.

Guilt eats away at me thinking about what my family and friends are going through back home, but I like it here. I like the people who've taken me in and treated me as one of them, the way they live, and the world they live in. I don't know what to do, but it's tearing me apart.

19

Torn Apart

*M*arcus and Cyrus invited me to join them at the trading post this morning. I tried to accept with indifference, but my giddiness gave me away. By the time we reach the falls, the air already feels like my blow dryer on high. We left just after breakfast, and we're only about ten minutes into an hour-long hike.

We follow the creek, passing more houses than I realized were out here. People wave and call out greetings. A girl around my age stands on the front porch of a small white house. She waves enthusiastically and bounds up to us. She's quite pretty with wide blue eyes and long platinum blond hair. She glances at me before turning her full charm on Cyrus.

"I haven't seen you around in a while, Cyrus. Where've you been?"

Marcus grabs my elbow and tugs me along. "Let's give them some privacy."

I don't want to give them privacy. I don't like the way she's putting her hand on his arm or the way she's leaning in, and...is she batting her eyelashes?

"Come on, he'll catch up."

Glancing over my shoulder at Cyrus and the blonde, I follow Marcus. "Who is that?" I ask before I can stop myself.

"Lucy."

"Are they—"

"Why didn't you wait for me?" Cyrus asks, jogging up to us.

Marcus shrugs, "Just giving you some room, man."

Cyrus shoots Marcus a look then glances at me briefly before taking the lead. We walk in silence until we crest a steep hill and the trading post comes into view. It's nothing like the colorful open-air markets in the Union with their dazzling umbrellas and striped awnings, but somehow it's even more spectacular. Dozens upon dozens of booths line either side of a series of narrow dirt aisles, packed so thick with shoppers, the ground is obscured below them.

I pick up the pace and rush down the hill to a large, waving banner hanging over the entrance with the word "currency" printed on it.

"There's no official currency," Marcus explains. "We'll trade these for credits to buy other things."

Maybe there's no *official* currency, but there are plenty of Mexican pesos, Union dollars, and money from the Northern Territories being exchanged.

Cyrus opens his backpack and lines up our butter, cheeses, and milk on the counter. I copy him with the stuff in my pack, and Marcus does the same.

We wait behind a dozen people until it's our turn. Women and men, all ages, dressed like everyone at the house — shorts, tank tops or T-shirts, socks and hiking boots. Children run between the throng of bodies, using them as shields in a game of tag.

When we're finally up, a scruffy man with a short beard streaked with gray, nods at us. "Hey, Cy, Marcus."

"Rick." Cyrus shakes his hand then quickly adds, "This is Evan."

Rick grunts a response, the only acknowledgment of my existence. He wipes his palms on his jeans before grabbing the first item before him. He weighs the block of cheese and glances at the board behind him that lists the names and current trade-in value of almost anything anyone could want. He does some quick calculations on a small chalkboard and shows the figure to Cyrus.

Cyrus surveys the board and says, "I think you're off by seven."

My eyes widen with newfound awe. Maybe he can't read all that well, but he just discerned the price of two dozen items and added them in his head in a matter of seconds.

Rick rechecks his math. "Yeah, you're right, sorry." He takes out a ledger, crosses off a number, and writes the new total in ink. Cyrus and Rick both sign beneath the new figure.

"What happens now?" I ask.

"We go shopping," Marcus says. "When we're done, we'll check out." A woman across the table from Rick is working with people to total their purchases. "We'll either owe more credits the next time, or have a balance."

"What about the stuff we brought?"

"It'll be divided up and available for sale in one of the booths shortly," Cyrus says, leading the way into the market.

A constant hum of voices is punctuated every so often when someone finds an unexpected treasure. Sentries, armed with rifles, are positioned every five yards or so, keeping a watchful eye.

Cyrus stops at a bakery where heavenly warm, yeasty aromas greet me. He puts two loaves of bread in his pack before making his way down the aisle and stopping to grab some clothes for one of the boys.

We turn and work our way back up the other side, passing a booth of fragrant body and hair products. They can't be made out here, they're professionally packaged and labeled. "Where do these come from?" I ask Cyrus.

He leans over and whispers in my ear. "Ask me later."

I'd kill for a jar of anti-frizz cream. I wonder how much butter and cheese one of these would take.

Cyrus must see me coveting it, because he picks up the jar and places it in my hands.

"No. I can't."

He and Marcus have another one of their silent eye conversations. I swear my twin sisters don't communicate telepathically as much as these two.

"Everyone gets a little something extra now and then. I think it's your turn. What do you say, Marcus?"

My face burns as red as my hair, but they both seem so pleased, I finally relent and take the offered product. "Thanks."

After getting some potatoes, carrots, and onions, our last stop is to pick up some chicken feed. While Marcus and Cyrus talk to the feed guy, I wander down the aisle. Near the end is a vendor selling books, one in particular catching my eye. A thought takes hold, and I check the price before running the hair product back to the booth it came from. I return to the book vendor, stuffing the one I want into my pack.

When I rejoin the guys, Cyrus introduces me to their friend. "Dag, this is Evan. She's staying with us for a while. Evan, this is Dag. We came from the same town."

Dag's bright blue eyes travel over my body as he takes my hand. "Nice to meet you, Evan. That's a beautiful name for a beautiful girl."

I resist the urge to gag on the cheesy line. He draws out his vowels even more than the others do, as if he thinks it's charming.

Cyrus pulls my hand back. "That's enough, Dag."

As Marcus leads the way to the currency booth, I glance over my shoulder at Dag, who's watching my ass. I follow Cyrus's and Marcus's example again, and empty my pack on the counter to check out. While the woman totals up our purchases, Cyrus eyes the book and quirks an eyebrow my way.

"I know I didn't ask, but I have an idea, and I put the product back." He doesn't say anything, but considering the book costs less than the jar of hair cream, it shouldn't be a problem. When we finish, there's a credit balance remaining on the account. Cyrus and Rick sign below the total and shake hands before we reload our packs and start back to the house.

"They have all these guys with guns to make sure no one steals from the trading post, but how do you know you can trust Rick?" I ask. "The ledger stays here, what's to keep him from changing the number before you come back?"

"The system relies on honesty. Cy knows how much is left, if the amount is different next time, we don't use the trading post anymore. We can trade directly any time we want and Rick knows it." Marcus shifts his pack to his other shoulder. "Rick offers convenience and honesty. One without the other isn't worth anything. He makes a small fee on every item traded and we only need to go to one location. But if we couldn't trust him, we'd cut him out of the middle."

"What's up with the book?" Cyrus asks.

"I have an idea of how I can contribute something uniquely me."

Cyrus grins and I don't know if he suspects what I'm up to or if he thinks I'm embracing my destiny — the destiny I don't even believe in.

The sun is a blazing fireball by the time we reach the halfway point, and I'm relieved when we stop in the creek to cool off. They strip down to their shorts, but I only remove my boots and socks, wading into the refreshing water fully dressed. After cooling off, I sit on a rock waiting for the guys to finish splashing and dunking each other.

It takes all my willpower not to stare at Cyrus's bare torso. I force my eyes to my own body. In just my short time here, I've developed muscles in my biceps and shoulders I didn't have before. Shocked, I check out my legs and notice my thighs and calves are also more defined. When the boys are finally done messing around, they dress and we continue our hike, feeling much cooler.

The blonde, Lucy, is out front, working in the garden wearing nothing but a tiny beige bikini that makes her appear completely nude. I struggle not to roll my eyes.

She sees us immediately, as if she's been waiting, and comes bouncing over. And I mean *bouncing*. That girl is fully aware of her physical assets and how to use them for maximum attention.

"Hi." Her voice is bright and cheery, and her flaxen hair shines in the late morning sun.

"Hey, Luc," Marcus says.

She slinks up to Cyrus and whispers something to him. They both laugh.

Disgusted, I turn to Marcus. "I'm going back to the house. I'll see you there."

Before he can answer, Cyrus calls over his shoulder, "You two go ahead. I'll catch up with you."

I stew as I stomp toward the house. I have no designs on him. Wanting to kiss a boy doesn't mean I own him. Taking over his bedroom doesn't mean we're in a relationship. Thinking of Cyrus and Lucy only pisses me off. I need to talk about something else. Anything else. "What's Dag's deal?"

"Dag? He's nothing but trouble."

"I figured that much out on my own...but you guys are friends, right?"

He shrugs. "I guess. We grew up together. But Dag was always into stuff he shouldn't have been. He's a year older than me and Cy and we thought he was cool. We were always following him around, getting into trouble."

I try to picture younger versions of Cyrus and Marcus running around the Ruins getting into trouble, wondering what "trouble" even looks like out here.

"He's got a reputation as a heartbreaker."

"He seems very sure of himself. So, did he come with you after the tornado?"

"Naw. Lucien never would've allowed that. He could always see Dag for the delinquent he is. He just showed up here one day. Said after we left, the town was too boring and pointed himself in the direction we headed and walked until he got here."

Yeah, I'm not buying it. Something tells me there's far more to Dag than meets the eye.

20

More Than Meets the Eye

*A*fter dinner, I pull out the book I picked up at the trading post and take it downstairs where the younger boys are playing in front of the couch.

"Would you like to learn how to read?"

Ben's dark eyes widen as if he can't believe what I asked. "Would I!"

Ty and Connor nod their blond heads.

"Okay. Good. Let's go outside while it's still light enough."

Ben narrows his eyes. "Wait, why are you teaching us? You're still going to read to us, aren't you?"

"Of course. But if you know how, you won't need to wait for me, or you can read stuff the others aren't interested in."

"Oh." He smiles, revealing his one dimple. "I thought maybe you were gonna leave."

This kid knows where to hit me where it hurts, but I can't lie to him. "I need to go home, Ben. My family's there. They miss me."

His big brown eyes fill with tears. "I thought we were your family."

I wrap my arms around him. "You are. Let's not worry about it now, okay? I'm not leaving yet. I promise."

He nods and I release him, turning toward Ty and Connor. Their faces are equally drawn. I had no idea they cared that much. They barely talk to me, and the only time we spend together is when I read to them in the evenings.

I push the unsettling emotions from my mind and focus on my plan, explaining about vowels, consonants, and sounds. Taking a stick, I draw the vowels in the dirt in both upper and lower case and explain how each has a long and a short sound, giving them examples of words so they can hear them in action.

They practice with their own sticks until the darkening sky makes it impossible to see and we head back inside. I sit on the couch next to the candle, Ben beside me with his curly head resting on my arm, and open up *Dr. Seuss's A, B, Cs.* I begin with the letter A and ask Ben to point out all vowels on the page he can identify. Before long, Ty and Connor lose interest and wander off.

We skip the next few pages and go to E and do the same until we get through all the vowels. Then Ben hops down and returns with *Little House in the Big Woods,* the book we're currently in the middle of. I read until Ty lets loose a jaw-splitting yawn.

Ally ushers the boys to bed and I head outside to my favorite spot. Before I even get settled on the rock, the front door closes and footsteps make their way toward me.

"Can I join you?" Cyrus's deep baritone calls up.

"Suit yourself." It comes out snippier than I intended. He was with Lucy all afternoon. I don't want to think about what they were doing that whole time, and I'm pissed that it bothers me so much.

"You all right?"

"I'm fine," I say, trying to soften my tone.

Out of the corner of my eye, I see him studying me, and when I let my gaze meet his, warmth slides over me like a fuzzy blanket on a cold winter night. I'm an idiot. Why do I always set my sights on boys who are interested in someone else? First Bryce and Alivia and now Cyrus with Lucy. Maybe I only want what I can't have. I'm sure it has to do with my daddy issues. I mean, doesn't everything?

"Are you sure nothing's wrong?"

"Yeah. Yeah. I'm...sorry. Long day, I guess. So, what's the deal with the trading post? Where do they get everything? Some of it looks like it's from the Union."

"There's a pretty sophisticated smuggling network here. They bring stuff in from up north or down south, and I've always suspected some also goes into and comes out of the Union." He lays down beside me, fixing his gaze on the night sky.

"Wait. So, they get stuff from the Northern Territories or Mexico or even the Union and bring it here to trade for what? Locally grown produce and some fresh eggs? That doesn't make sense. Why would they take such a risk for something they can get much easier almost anywhere else?"

He shrugs. "I don't know how everything works, but there's a profit to be made or they wouldn't bother."

Some of the pieces start to fall into place. Milk, butter, and cheese had the highest values of anything we traded. If it's going back into the Union, that makes sense. Dairy from cows is rare and expensive back home because of the limited land for raising livestock. But there's more to it than that. There must be. "The house where I was held had crates of products like what was at the trading post. Do you think the guys who kidnapped me are smugglers?"

"Could be. They've got to stage stuff somewhere. They could be smugglers, or mules, or distributors. But if they're warehousing products, no doubt they're involved somehow."

How does Bryce fit into all of this? That's still a huge missing piece. I let out a yawn to rival one of Ty's. "I'm beat. Thanks for inviting me this morning. I had fun."

"Anytime."

I say goodnight to Lucien and Draya on my way through the living room and go up to my room. As I'm about to climb into bed, I notice something on the chest — the jar of hair balm. One of them must have seen me put it back and grabbed it for me. It's such a simple gesture, but my heart swells a little more.

21

Simple Gestures

*A*lly sits next to me on the edge of the watering hole while Draya and Sonia finish their showers. Draya and I managed to develop a semi-civil relationship. She doesn't criticize me every chance she gets and I avoid her as much as possible. It's not ideal but it works for us.

I apply some of my new hair product, twirling the strands into ringlets as Ally watches in fascination.

"Wow, that's cool. I wish my hair would do that," she says, braiding her hair, her fingers flying in an acrobatic blur.

"Thanks, but I wish my hair was like yours."

"Mama used to say you always want what you don't have." She winds a band around the end of her braid.

The irony of this conversation is not lost on me. "Yeah, my mom said she wanted curly hair curly like mine, and I always envied her beautiful straight hair."

"Do you miss her?"

"We had our issues like most mothers and daughters, but I do miss her. A lot."

Ally drops her gaze to her hands in her lap. "I miss mine, too."

"Where is she?"

She glances over at Sonia and Draya in the water. "We lived about two hours north of here. Daddy went hunting one day and never came back. No matter what Mama tried to tell us, I knew he'd just up and left us. I guess three kids and a wife were too much for him." She pauses and leans back on her forearms, staring at nothing.

"A few years ago some guys came to our house looking for food. We barely had enough for us, but Mama gave them what she could. They wanted more and demanded our pigs, too. Mama offered one, but they insisted on all three. I think she'd had enough at that point and walked toward the kitchen where she kept the shotgun. One of them grabbed her before she got far."

She reaches down and picks up a rock, rolling it between her fingers. "Mama yelled for me and the boys to hide, so we ran outside. We heard her screaming as we crawled under the chicken coop. I left the boys and told them to keep quiet then went back to the house and peeked in the window. I saw them..." Her voice drops to a whisper. "...doing stuff to her. I screamed at them to leave her alone, and one of them told the others to grab me."

My heart beats wildly as Ally's story unfolds in vivid color. I picture everything like the worst movie I've ever seen, the kind that leaves nightmares in its wake for days after.

"I ran to the woods and climbed a tree, not wanting to lead them to the boys. They finally gave up looking for me, but I still waited until dark before I went back to the chicken coop. Connor told me Mama screamed for a long time before she got quiet. We spent the night under there.

"The next day they tied ropes around the pigs' necks and grabbed some chickens. I was sure they were going to find us but they didn't. When they left, we waited a couple of hours before crawling out. I ran to the house, and when I opened the door..."

Ally cries, heaving sobs wracking her body while I sit uselessly beside her. I reach out a shaking hand and rub her back until she composes herself. "Sorry," she says, wiping a tear.

"Don't. You have nothing to apologize for. I'm so sorry I asked. I had no idea. I really need to learn to keep my mouth shut."

She gives me a watery smile and shakes her head. "I haven't talked about this in ages. I think I needed to. Talk about it I mean." She takes a deep breath and lets it back out. "When I opened the door, she was lying on the floor. Naked. Her eyes were open but I knew she was dead. There was...so much blood...everywhere. I know what they did to her, but I didn't want the boys to see her like that. I made them wait outside while cleaned and dressed her. We buried her behind the house."

Ally lets out shuddering sigh. "I did my best to take care of the boys. I hunted and they gathered eggs and stuff..." She trails off for a long moment. "But Ty wasn't even three yet, he still needed his mama."

"How did you end up here?"

She wipes her eyes with the back of her wrist. "Cyrus, Lucien, and Marcus found us. I almost shot Cyrus's head clean off." She smiles a little. "I was out chopping wood when Cy asked if I needed help. I freaked. When I saw Lucien and Marcus behind him, I thought they were more bandits coming to take what they wanted. I ran into the house, locked the door, and told the boys to hide under the bed. I grabbed the shotgun and sat inside the door, ready to shoot anyone who tried to come in.

"Cyrus knocked but I ignored him. He knocked again before poking his head around to look in the window. I was so scared, I didn't aim, I just fired. I missed him, but not by much. Marcus and Lucien started yelling they only wanted to know I was okay. All I had to do was tell them I was fine and they'd leave."

"I didn't answer because I didn't know what to say," Ally continues. "I was only thirteen, too young to be a mother to two little boys, but I wasn't sure I could trust them either. I sat for hours, thinking about what to do. While I was trying to sort it all out, Marcus fetched Sonia. She talked to me through the door, and something about her voice or what she said got through to me." She glances up at Sonia and smiles. "When I opened the door,

Sonia took one look at me and pulled me into her arms as if she knew that was exactly what I needed."

My heart breaks apart in my chest, and I have no idea what to say.

Draya wipes her hands on her shorts. "We'd better get back and let someone else use the shower." She turns to me. "Your hair is pretty like that."

My mouth falls open as I stare at her in stunned silence.

A knock comes as we're finishing the dinner dishes. I'm learning neighbors often visit one another in the evenings. Lucien goes down to answer the door. Soon, male voices and laughter accompany two sets of footsteps clomping up the stairs.

Dag saunters across the room, his blue eyes roaming over me as I dry a plate. "Well hello there, Evan." A seductive smile crosses his face, revealing a set of dimples. He might be attractive, with his wavy blond hair and square jaw, if he wasn't so skeevy.

Cyrus appears out of nowhere, grabs a towel, and helps me finish drying the dishes. The others are at the table readying for a game of poker by the time we're done.

Dag deals a couple of extra hands, one for Cyrus, and apparently one for me. "Now don't go runnin' off, darlin'. I dealt you in. Play a hand with us."

I glance at Cyrus who's taking a seat, his face set in a determined scowl. I weigh going outside or even up to my room, but as much as Dag creeps me out, I would rather be with my friends than alone.

Taking a seat, I toss my chip into the ante pile and make the mistake of glancing at Dag. His eyes linger on my lips before sliding down to my chest. "So, Evan, how'd you end up here with these losers?"

I open my mouth to answer, but Lucien interrupts before I get a word out. "You hear anything about a shipment of scotch? I want to make sure I'm there when it arrives. Don't want to chance missing out."

Dag turns his attention to Lucien. "Yeah, next week some time."

I sort the cards in my hand while they talk about scotch, tuning them out. Sonia lets out a loud laugh and knocks over a glass of water, spilling it on my shorts.

"Oh, I'm so sorry." She hops up, pulling me with her and drags me up to her room.

"You did that on purpose, didn't you?"

"Yes. You can't trust Dag. Don't tell him you're from the Union. Make something up. Anything."

I search her face for answers but she's busy finding a clean pair of shorts for me. After I change, we return to the game. With the first lull in the conversation, Dag jumps back in. "So, Evan, you never did say how you ended up here."

I think about Ally's story from this morning and manage to conjure up a couple of tears. "I'd rather not talk about it."

"Oh, hey, darlin', I'm sorry."

I've had enough of Dag for one night and excuse myself. As I get up, Dag says, "Darlin', I'm real sorry. I didn't mean to upset you."

Plopping down on my bed with a satisfied smirk, I grab a book from the pile and read for a while. I'm just starting to doze off when Sonia comes in.

"You were amazing, Evan."

"What?"

"With Dag. The crying thing, what you said, it was perfect. He apologized a couple more times."

"I've met some real douchebags in my life, but he's right up there with the worst of them."

She sighs. "I wish he was just some creep, but I have some serious doubts about why he's really here."

22

Upping the Ante

*A*fter breakfast, Cyrus corners me in the kitchen. "Come on, I want to show you something."

Intrigued, I trail him outside where he slings a pack over his shoulder and leads the way behind the house. Stuffing down my nervous excitement, I remind myself he and Lucy spent yesterday together.

We follow the tree line before he makes a sharp turn into the wooded area. Leaves crunch beneath our boots as we plod along, our feet kicking up the rich, dark soil, creating a musty, earthy odor with each step. Curiosity swells, filling me until I'm ready to burst. I resist the urge to ask where we're going, only for fear of spoiling the surprise.

Bird songs and the percussion of our footfalls are soon joined by the gentle notes of flowing water. Off to the left is a steep drop into a ravine where the stream runs through this part of the valley. We skirt the edge a short distance before Cyrus descends, reaching back to take my hand. I know the gesture is only meant to steady me, but someone needs to clue in my heart which thumps harder at his touch.

A structure built about halfway down the sloped sides hovers over the water, stopping me in my tracks. Even from here I can tell it's well-crafted and oddly familiar, although I know I've never been here. The ground has been leveled on either side of the ravine supporting a concrete and rock foundation. Thick wooden beams traverse the gorge, and additional uprights embedded in the foundation hold up and support a hut-like dwelling.

I take a few steps closer and can make out an upper deck with a bench, table, and a ladder leading down to a suspended area below, about ten feet above the stream.

"What is this?" I ask, awe clinging to my words.

"A place where I come when I need to get away."

I tear my eyes away from the hut to stare at him. "This is yours?"

He shrugs and leads the way to the entrance. When I step onto the floor, I realize why it feels familiar. The same materials and craftsmanship that went into their house are evident throughout.

"Did you build it?"

He grips the back of his neck. "Yeah. I started not long after we arrived, taking the leftovers from the house. It took almost a year to finish." He's quiet for a moment before his gaze slides to me. "I've never brought anyone here."

I find that hard to believe. This must be where he brings girls when he wants to be alone with them. Where he brings Lucy. "No one?" I eye him with suspicion.

"You're the first."

The desire to kiss him overtakes me again, and this time it's impossible to resist. All the feelings I've been trying to deny bubble to the surface. I take a step toward him, drawn to the heat of his body. Without thinking through the wisdom of my actions I reach up and touch my lips to his soft, full bottom lip.

He responds immediately, his mouth softening against mine. Something intense and wonderful wends through me like tiny vines of heat and happiness. Then, for whatever reason, Lucy's face flashes behind my eyes, unwanted and intrusive.

I place my hands on his chest and push away from him, my breathing ragged, guilt scorching my face. "I'm…I'm sorry."

"What for?" he asks.

"For that… I don't…I'm not…" I'm not what? A boyfriend kisser? I think I've proven that I am. Shit, I have to get out of here. I spin and head toward the steps.

"Evan, wait."

I pause, but don't turn around. Things are going to be all kinds of awkward at the house now because of my actions. I need to fix this. With a deep breath, I press my lips firmly together and pivot to face him.

His golden eyes bore into mine, genuine confusion lacing his features. "Did I do something wrong?"

"God, no. I shouldn't have kissed you. I know you and Lucy—"

"Lucy?"

"Yeah, Lucy. The blonde?"

"I know *who* she is, but why are we talking about her?"

"Because, you…the two of you…on the way home yesterday you stopped to talk to her. For a *long* time."

The corners of his mouth tip up in an infuriating smirk. Then he shakes his head and his smile grows. "I only talked to her for a couple minutes before going back to the trading post."

"What? You went back to the… So, that was you?" He was the one who put the hair balm in my room. He went all the way back in that god-awful heat. *For me.* Between that sweet gesture and the realization he didn't spend all afternoon with Lucy, my heart melts into a puddle of goo.

He takes two strides toward me, until his face is inches from mine, his breath warm and inviting, dancing across my lips. With a soft sigh, his mouth is on mine in an unhurried, sensuous kiss, that sends heat pulsing through my veins.

He pulls me closer, kissing me deliberately, perfectly, turning my bones to mush. His hands slide to cup my face, his thumbs gliding over my cheeks.

My fingers push through his hair and I inhale his intoxicating scent. Union guys mask their odor with aftershaves and cologne, but Cyrus always smells earthy and natural.

The kiss is unending, a slow dance of tongues and lips, and heavy breaths, until he finally pulls back, pressing his lips to my forehead.

Holy crap, what did I just do? I'm already torn up enough over going home, and kissing Cyrus isn't going to help. But I can't deny that being with him like this feels more right than anything I've ever known.

"We should get back," he says. "We're supposed to be checking snares."

He takes my hand, lacing our fingers and leads me out of the hut. We walk in silence, but I'm hyper aware of the heat from his hand sending little jolts of electricity through me.

We take a diagonal path away from the ravine before he stops and smiles. "Looks like we have dinner."

I follow his gaze to a large wild rabbit hanging from a tree. Below it are two sticks driven into the ground parallel to one another. Cyrus retrieves the dead animal, stuffs it in the pack, and we head to the next snare. All in all, we have three rabbits.

As we trek back to the house, I want to end the somewhat awkward silence between us. "Cyrus?"

"Hmm?"

"What did you need to get away from?"

"What?"

"You said you built your hut thing because you needed to get away. Get away from what?"

He gives me a sexy half smile, that sends my heart skipping. "When we first got here, it was just Lucien and Draya, Marcus and Sonia...and me. Being the fifth wheel got old pretty fast. I had to get away from all of that cozy...coupleness."

When we reach the outer edge of the clearing where the house sits, Cyrus abruptly stops and tugs me to him. He wraps a hand around my waist and kisses me until I can't think straight. An easy smile lights up his face when he pulls back, making my blood run slow and warm.

He takes my hand and leads the way into the house where Ally and Marcus are at the dining room table pouring wax into candle molds. Marcus glances at us, his eyes zeroing in on my hand in Cyrus's. A grin blooms across his face and he nods at Cyrus.

Cyrus leans over and kisses my temple, his whiskers grazing my cheek, before opening the pack to pull out the rabbits.

Then I get my first lesson in skinning and cleaning a rabbit and find myself longing for the days I only had to clean fish.

23

Cozy Coupleness

*A*fter all the kissing Cyrus and I did that morning, an uncomfortable air settled between us like an annoying relative trying to monopolize the conversation. More than once I wondered if he regretted what happened between us or if he was sorry he'd showed me his secret place.

We sat far apart during dinner, and I caught Marcus shooting Cyrus questioning glances, but no one else seemed to notice the big cloud of awkward hovering over the table. After finishing the dishes, I went outside to escape the weird vibe as much as to relax and cool off.

Even though I hoped Cyrus would join me, I wasn't sure what to say to him if he did. Everything changed between us after our lips locked, and the comfortable compatibility we'd had was replaced by an electrifying intensity I wasn't sure how to handle.

He came outside a few minutes later and climbed up next to me. We sat beside each other for a long time, his warm, taut body pulling at me like a magnet to steel.

Then he started talking. About walking for weeks before they found this piece of land and how they just knew this was where they'd build their house. I got lost in his words, forgetting to be uneasy around him. When he reached over and took my hand, weaving his fingers between mine, things felt...right, like they had before only better in the best possible way.

Once we got past the initial post-kissing weirdness, things have been great, although we never seem to have enough time for each other. We're so busy during the days and in the evenings there's dinner, reading, and socializing with everyone. As much as I want to be alone with Cyrus, the others demand our involvement in card games and group discussions, as if nothing has changed. Most nights we're lucky if we can find even an hour to ourselves.

Tonight, as soon as we finish the dishes, Cyrus takes my hand and pulls me through the living room, past everyone sitting down to play cards and the boys holding out a book for me to read. "Not tonight. Tonight, she's all mine," he says with a smile that sends anticipation zinging through my veins.

We head out the front door, but instead of leading me to the rock, he pulls me to the side porch where a hammock is suspended between two posts. He rolls in, reaching out a hand to help me in beside him.

I lay next to him as we talk about nothing in particular, my head on his shoulder, his hand resting on my hip. While telling me about the first time he went hunting, he lifts my chin, tipping my face up. His words trail off as he lowers his head, his eyes roaming over my face before slipping closed as his lips find mine.

A wave of heat pulses through me as his kiss deepens. When his mouth demands more, I willingly respond. He lets out a soft groan, sending me tumbling into a heady, delicious fog.

He makes no further attempts at conversation, his lips only leave mine to nuzzle my neck or glide across my jaw on their way to my ear. His hands remain respectful, never straying to inappropriate places, even when my body would like a little less respect.

I come up for air, my face flushed, and try to gather my thoughts, which is nearly impossible when he kisses my collar bone. "One of us should probably go to bed."

His lips trail up my neck, making me forget what I was saying.

His voice is husky next to my ear. "Then it's going to have to be you, because I'm not leaving."

With one phrase, he renders me speechless. The way he kisses me like he can't get enough, the way my body responds to his touch...I can't make sense of what's happening with us. It's both powerful and scary as hell.

And then there's the annoying voice in my head that reminds me the closer we get, the harder it's going to be when I leave. I hate that voice. It tries to force me to think things through and make logical decisions, but what I'm feeling is intoxicating and explosive—anything *but* logical.

I give a fleeting thought to going inside, but he pulls me closer and the idea pops like a bubble on a summer breeze. I breathe in his masculine scent, and let myself drift off on a dreamy cloud of avoidance.

It's hotter than hell on a mid-summer day. So hot, that even those who've lived here for years aren't immune. To survive, we get up before dawn to get as much done as possible before the heat beats us into submission. Then we pack a bag and hike to a large pool of water to cool off. It's always crowded; everyone else from the area seems to have the same idea.

Last week, Sonia and I went shopping at the trading post for swimwear. It was something straight out of the ninth circle of hell, but I found something that fits and isn't hideous. It's just a basic navy and white striped bikini, but I'm mostly happy with it and it covers more skin than some of the girls around here.

While lying on a rock drying off, I feel the burning rays of Lucy's heated glare from across the pool. Cyrus says they weren't together, so I don't know what her problem is, but after three days of this, it's getting old.

I push up and walk over to where she's sitting with her family.

If she's surprised I'm confronting her, she doesn't give anything away.

"Hey," I say.

"You're just the shiny new thing. I know you're not from around here, so I'll clue you in. He burns through girls faster than a wildfire during a wind storm"

Ohhh-kay, maybe I didn't need to know that. "I don't want to fight with you over Cyrus. We don't need to be friends, but could you dial back the animosity some?"

She flicks her long blond hair over her shoulder and glances across the water to where Cyrus is messing around with Lucien, Marcus, and Will with pure longing. After schooling her features, she turns back to me. "Whatever. You can have him. I was done with him anyway."

I roll my eyes and walk back to my towel, pissed I let her get to me. With a renewed determination to just ignore her, I close my eyes and soak up the rays, but her words play on repeat in my head. The boy kisses like he's a freaking expert in the fine art of lip-locking, so he's either a natural or he's had a lot of experience.

A shadow passes over me and I open my eyes to find Dag grinning down at me, his eyes raking over my body.

"Well, hello there, beautiful."

Shielding my eyes with my hand, I meet his gaze. "Dag." He drops down next to me, and I sit up so we're eye level. Several long moments of silence pass before I ask, "What do you want?"

He directs a blinding smile my way. "I wanted to find out if you're free for dinner."

"Oh. Thanks, but I'm going to pass."

His grin only grows wider. "Can't blame a guy for trying. If you change your mind, you know where to find me."

"Fat chance," I mutter as he saunters off.

Sudden water droplets on the rock dry almost instantly, and I glance up to find Cyrus glaring after Dag, his jaw ticking. "What did he want?"

"A date."

His hands ball into fists at his side, then he drops down beside me and kisses me. Hard and possessive. I put my hands on his shoulders and shove him back. "What the hell?"

He grumbles something under his breath and jumps back into the pool, swimming back to the others leaving me to wonder how I'm the one who just screwed things up. I wade into the cool water and make my way over to Sonia, Ally, and Draya.

"What was that all about?" Sonia asks when I reach them.

"I don't know, some possessive pissing contest between Cyrus and Dag."

"What happened?" Ally asks.

"Dag invited me to dinner. I said no. Cyrus licked my tonsils to prove a point. I asked him what his problem was and now he's pissed at me."

Draya snorts. "You're unbelievable."

I turn to face her, ready for her to enlighten me as only she can.

"We may not have modern technology, but we're not cavemen. Cy wasn't marking his territory. Dag is mighty interested in you and where you came from, and he won't stop sniffing around until he gets some answers."

"The current rumor is that you came back with us from Summer Fest," Sonia says. "The timing is right. Plus, couples meet and fall in love at the festivals all the time. Since people travel so far to attend, relationships can't continue unless one of them is willing to move. We aren't discouraging the rumors." She rubs my shoulder. "The last time Dag saw you and Cy, it was before you were together. He's probably testing to find out if the rumors are true."

"Cyrus was trying to protect you but not in the way you thought," Draya says.

"How the hell was I supposed to know any of this? You get your hackles up when I assume wrongly, but you don't tell me shit unless I happen to ask the right questions."

"Sorry, Evan, sometimes I forget how different things are from what you're used to," Sonia says.

"So, what should I do now?"

"Go talk to him," Draya says.

I watch Cyrus with his brother and friends, noting the playful expression from earlier is gone. With a deep breath, I wade over to him.

"Can we talk?"

He doesn't answer but he does follow me to the center of the pool where a large rock juts out of the water. I hoist myself onto it, dangling my legs over the edge. "I'm sorry. I jumped to conclusions earlier, and...I'm sorry."

"You do that a lot."

"What?"

"Jump to conclusions."

I start to argue, but I can't come up with anything because he's right. But it's not all on me. "Okay. But if you don't tell me what's going on, I'm going to try to make sense of it on my own. And I'm not always going to reach the right conclusion."

He reaches up and places his hands on either side of me, penning me in. "Okay."

"Yeah?"

"Yeah." My favorite smile breaks across his face.

I push myself forward and slide off the rock, wrapping my arms around his neck. His fingers press into my hips as I reach up to kiss him, and this time I don't care who's watching.

24

Destiny

The moon is almost full in the darkening sky by the time Cyrus and I head outside for some alone time. We've both been so busy over the past few days we've barely seen each other. Tonight, we agreed to make us a priority. Cyrus sits, tugging me in front of him and wraps his arms around my waist. I lean my head against his solid chest while we talk late into the night.

Occasionally his lips stray to the side of my neck, destroying my ability to focus. When he stops and my head clears, our conversation resumes. This time I stay awake as he tells me about growing up with his parents and siblings. He openly shares about the tornado that ripped his world apart and what it was like to leave the only home he'd ever known with his brother and friends.

He asks about my family and I tell him about my mom and Joe, Katie and Rachel, and about Eddie and Liam and Quinn, the siblings I have yet to meet. Something shifts inside me as I talk. Words fall from my mouth and things I thought I'd never share suddenly come with ease.

I tell him about Bryce and the beating by Alivia and her friends the next day, and how I needed to decide whether to stay and go to a trial or agree to the deal and move on. This requires a bit of background on how our justice system works and the way politics came into play.

"They got off with just some community service. It was my word against theirs, three against one, so it would've been harder for me to make my case. Plus, I would've had to stay put until after the trial. With Alivia's dad being the mayor and my uncle the governor, a trial was the last thing either of them wanted, anyway. Sometimes I think my uncle pushed me into the deal."

Cyrus stiffens behind me. "What did you say?"

I shrug. "I didn't want to testify, but sometimes I wonder if my uncle pushed me harder than he needed to—"

"Not that. Your uncle's a governor?"

"Technically he's my step uncle..."

"I'll be right back. Stay here." He unwraps his arms from me and jumps down before heading into the house.

What the hell? I wait a few minutes before curiosity gets the best of me and follow him inside. As soon as I open the door, loud, angry voices filter down.

"She's going to get us all killed," Draya yells.

"That's a bit extreme," Cyrus says.

"No, it's not, and if you start using the brain between your ears for a change, you'll realize I'm right. You've been a pathetic love-sick puppy since we found her, but now your lack of judgment regarding her isn't just stupid, it's dangerous."

"That's enough Dray." Lucien's voice is low, but there's no mistaking the authority in his tone.

I make my way up the stairs and stand on the top step. They're all in the kitchen, unaware of my presence.

Draya's harsh expression softens a little. "I'm sorry, Cyrus, but she needs to go back."

Marcus says something too quiet for me to make out, then Sonia says, "He's right, Cy."

They continue to converse in tones too low for me to overhear.

"I'll talk to her," Cyrus says, staring at the floor.

He turns toward the door and pauses when he sees me, his face drawn. A hole bores itself deep in my gut, making breathing difficult. He's sending me home. Anger and pain twist through me as I turn and rush down the stairs.

"Evan, wait," Cyrus calls after me.

I slam the front door behind me and walk to the back of the house, my heart pounding. I can't decide if I'm more pissed at him for making me care or at myself for falling for another guy I barely know.

"Damnit, Evan, wait!" He throws a few more choice words in for good measure.

Not a chance. He can't talk his way out of this. Whatever I thought was going on with us was just as Lucy said, another fling, destined to end sooner rather than later.

Balling my fists, I stomp away from the house toward the wooded area. If he follows me, my fist might just connect with that perfect face of his. I glance over my shoulder to see him turning back to the house. Tears fill my eyes against my will and I shove them away, but more rush in to take their place, blurring my vision.

I trip over a log, falling hands first to the ground, tearing open the skin on my palms. That hurts a lot less then my heart, though. I told myself I wasn't that far gone, but it was a lie because I'm in deep for that boy.

Something moving through the tangled vegetation stops my thoughts as unease takes over. I stand and peer into the darkness, straining to see. Low-growing plants rustle only seconds before a mountain lion comes into view, its eyes reflecting the moonlight like two glowing orbs.

Fear immobilizes me as I lock gazes with a giant predatory cat.

The beast lowers its front end, it's back still up, tail swishing.

My mind struggles with what to do next as panic crawls through me like vines in an untended garden, choking off rational thought.

If I give into panic, I'm dead. Somehow, instinct kicks in, and I take a slow, careful step back, keeping my eyes on the lion. My pulse races, making my limbs unsteady, as I move back another step.

The lion's tail twitches.

My foot catches and fall back, landing on my ass with a thud.

My head whips up in time to catch the lion running toward me, it's powerful legs readying for a leap. I turn my head and squeeze my eyes shut, holding my breath.

A sharp sound, like the crack of a bat, startles me. My eyes fly open, zeroing in on the lion crumpled in a heap two yards away.

I stand and spin around. Cyrus is holding a still smoking rifle, Lucien, Marcus, and Sonia pulling to a stop behind him. In an instant Cyrus is at my side, pulling me to him. I forget my anger and dig my fingers into his shoulders, trying to get closer.

He kisses the top of my head as my body trembles against him. He hands his rifle to Sonia and cradles me against his chest, whispering soft words as he guides me back to the house.

I can't stop shaking or form any thoughts except of the lion lunging at me. Cyrus deposits me on the couch and drapes a blanket over my shoulders. I open my mouth to say something, but nothing comes out because I don't know what to say, there are too many emotions rolling through me — fear, gratitude, love, heartbreak, guilt.

"I'll be right back," he says and heads into the kitchen behind me. Voices converse in whispered tones, too low for me to make out, until Cyrus snaps, "Not tonight, Draya."

He returns to my side and lies down, tugging me next to him. I snuggle back into his warmth, pushing away all the ugliness from tonight and allow myself to surrender to the fatigue hell-bent on dragging me under.

25

Surrender

I let out a groan and stretch, opening my eyes to unfamiliar surroundings. Right, I slept on the couch. The events of last night come flooding back. Cyrus left at some point, but I never felt him get up.

After a solid sleep, I'm resigned to leaving, but it doesn't hurt any less. I started to believe I belong here because of Cyrus or because I felt needed, or maybe a little of both. I get up and fold the blanket, draping it over the arm.

Cyrus approaches from the kitchen with two mugs of tea. God, I'd kill for just one cup of coffee. He hands one to me and inclines his head toward the front door. "Come on, we need to talk."

With a sinking heart, I follow him outside where he climbs up on the rock. He reaches down to take my tea and pulls me up next to him. His eyes have a determined edge to them and the sting of betrayal is as fresh as when I first realized he was sending me home.

"Evan..." He sighs, raking a hand through his hair. "You are the most frustrating girl I've ever met."

Tears threaten, but I blink them back and swallow hard, refusing to cry in front of him. "It's fine. Really. I get it."

"What? What do you get? I haven't said anything yet."

"You...you..." my bottom lip trembles and I clamp my top teeth down on it to still it.

"What you overheard last night...it's not what you think."

"No? Somehow I doubt that." My eyes are glued to my drink, watching the water turn a darker brown as the leaves steep.

He blows out a long, frustrated breath. "Your uncle's position in the Union poses a very real danger."

"What?" My head jerks up. "What kind of danger? He doesn't even know anyone exists out here."

Another heavy sigh. "Trust me, he knows. But more importantly, your family isn't going to give up looking for you until you're found."

A new wave of guilt gnaws at my stomach and I set my cup down "I don't get how that's dangerous for you?"

"Not just me, everyone in the Ruins, Evan. The Union knows we're here, whether you believe it or not. When they don't find you in the Union, they'll search out here, and they won't care who gets hurt in the process. They wrote us off a hundred years ago, we have no value to them."

"That's not true. That's not how—"

"We've seen it before."

A dirt cloud billowing in the distance draws my attention over his shoulder. Cyrus follows my gaze, and his body tenses. He jumps down and reaches for my hand, pulling me with him.

"I need you to go inside and stay there." He grabs my shoulders and turns me to face him. "I'll explain everything later, but for once, listen to me." As I turn and run toward the house, I hear him yell, "Lucien, we've got company."

Pacing the living room, I try not to overthink things, but this can't be good. Outside, the crunching of rocks and twigs is followed by silence. Bits of conversation float in through the open window, but I can't make out what's being said. The voices get louder, and I recognize Lucien's and then Cyrus's. A third voice, one I'm far too familiar with, makes my heart slam to a halt. *Walker*.

How did he find me? I fly upstairs and shut my door, pushing the dresser over to block it. Panic grows, overtaking my thoughts. I move the chair under the window and climb up, sliding out the narrow opening.

My breaths come fast and my hands shake as I twist around and grip the sill with my fingers. Taking a deep breath, I squeeze my eyes shut and let go. Wind rushes through my hair before I hit the ground hard, jarring my hips and knees.

Leaves and dry grass crunch beneath my feet as I cross the yard toward the wooded area, careful to keep the house between me and the group out front. Once I'm safely camouflaged by the trees, I break out into a run, not bothering to look back.

My lungs are ready to burst by the time I slow my pace, unsure where I'm heading. Except maybe I do. Maybe I've known all along where I'm going. All I need to do is follow the stream until I reach Cyrus's hideaway. I glance back over my shoulder to make sure no one's following me, then inch my way down the steep side into the ravine.

My boot slides on a loose rock, and I slide on my ass several feet before my right foot catches on a root, twisting me around. A sharp pain shoots through my ankle as I come to a halt, dangling upside down.

Blood rushes to my head as I repeatedly jerk my leg trying to untangle myself. With one final tug, it comes free, and I tumble down the remaining distance, landing in the water.

Dripping from soaked head to sodden boots, I crawl to the bank and assess my injuries. A few tender spots on my shins and a couple of scrapes seem to be the worst of it. Until I stand and realize my ankle won't support my weight.

Hobbling along the shore is painstaking and it takes me close to an hour before I see the structure up ahead. And there's only one way to reach it. With slow and painful movements, I haul myself up the side of the ravine, grabbing roots and clawing the dirt with my good foot, slipping and swearing. I'm drenched in sweat, dirt, and weeds by the time I drag myself onto the main floor.

After lying on my back long enough to catch my breath, I take off my boot and examine my ankle. Deep purple patches cover swollen tissue. My stomach rumbles, reminding me I haven't eaten since dinner last night. I wonder if Cyrus has any food stashed in here.

Using one of the posts, I pull myself up and poke around the bench and cubbies, but come up empty. I hobble across the floor and find a rifle and a box of bullets beside a set of built-in shelves. Standing on the toes of my left foot, I reach up to the top shelf and my hand brushes against something cool and hard — a knife. A fishing pole and some matches are in the corner and there's a stream full of fish below me. Guess I'm better equipped at surviving out here than Walker gave me credit for.

After a frustrating day of not catching anything, I drag myself back to the hideaway hungry and defeated. I climb down the ladder into the suspended sleeping area with the knife and a rifle that may or may not be loaded — I'm not sure how to tell.

Shaking out the blankets to make sure nothing of the eight-legged variety is waiting to crawl on me, I settle down on the sleeping cushions, trying to relax. The knife tucked under my pillow and the rifle under my arm, I'm not far from sleep when a rustling in the leaves above startles me. My pulse quickens and I sit upright, straining my ears, unsure if it's the wind, an animal, or worse.

The rustling comes closer, and I freeze, my breaths increasing, as I realize I'm basically trapped down here.

It's not the wind or an animal, unless the animal wears boots. Fear coats my skin in an icy layer as heavy footsteps move across the floor above me. I grip the knife tighter with my right hand and balance the rifle in my left.

The footsteps head toward to the ladder and I scoot back until I'm against the far wall.

The boots descend, landing on the top rung and I drop the knife to grab the gun with both hands, my finger shaking violently on the trigger. I let out a small cry when I recognize Cyrus and throw myself at him. He sighs and buries his face in my hair, circling his arms around my waist.

He leans back and tucks a piece of hair behind my ear, then his lips land on mine. He kisses me like he hasn't seen me in weeks instead of hours.

My doubts about his feelings for me melt beneath his scorching kiss. He pulls back, his mouth still close enough that we breathe the same air. "I'm glad you're here."

"I know you told me to stay inside, but I couldn't. Not when..." An involuntary shudder rolls through me.

"Not when what?"

My chest tightens. "Not with Walker out front. What did he want?"

He shakes his head and takes a seat on the cushion. "He was looking for you."

I drop own beside him, and pick a leaf out of the blanket. "He's the leader of the pack of guys who kidnapped me. How did he find me?"

He runs a hand through his hair, looking in the direction of the house. "He said he was trying to find his missing niece and heard we had someone staying with us who fit her description. If this Walker is a smuggler, it wouldn't take much to connect the dots. Especially with Dag being tight with them."

"So what happened? Is he gone?"

"Yeah. Lucien told him you'd moved on, saying you had to get home."

"Do you think he bought it?"

"I wasn't sure at first, but he eventually left. That's why I waited until dark to come out here. He seems pretty motivated to find you. He'll probably watch the house until he's convinced you're gone and then try to figure out where you went."

Cyrus pulls me closer and I rest my head on his shoulder. We sit quietly for a few moments, avoiding the big topics of conversation and all the unsaid words between us.

I'm too tired to get into anything else tonight, so when he lies down, tugging me with him, I let myself succumb to the bone weary exhaustion crawling through me.

26

Doubts

*M*orning light peeks between the slats, casting long shadows. I roll over looking for Cyrus, but he's not here. Based on the position of the sun, I've slept later than normal.

Bruises in several delightful shades of purple and black populate my skin. My ankle looks as if it tried to swallow a grapefruit. I stand, and the second I put any weight on my right foot, dark spots swim across my vision. I hop to the ladder and drag myself up with my arms.

No Cyrus here either. I plop down on the bench to wait for him. Before I have too my time to dwell on my empty stomach, whistling comes through the trees. A tune I'm not familiar with. Moments later Cyrus steps into the hideaway and stomps dirt and leaves from his boots. He spots me waiting and a smile blossoms on his face.

"Good morning. Hope you're hungry."

"Famished."

He hands me a foil packet of freshly cooked fish and sets two thermoses of tea on the table. He sips his tea while I devour my breakfast. When I'm done, I sit back, satisfied.

"Let me have a look at that ankle."

I move over to make room. He lifts my foot to his lap and examines it, but doesn't touch it, for which I'm grateful. Then he reaches over and pulls some bandaging strips from his bag and begins to wrap my ankle, starting just above my toes.

"Where did you go this morning?" I ask. "You're even more prepared than usual."

"Back to the house. We should hang out here for a few days, so I grabbed some supplies." He pulls the last of the strip tight and clips it with two metal prongs. "And I wanted to talk something over with Lucien." He places my foot back on the seat cushion "This is serious, Ev, we need a plan, and I think we've got one."

I lift my eyes to meet his. The way he called me, Ev, is warm and intimate. I reach over, my lips scraping against rough stubble on their way to his mouth.

He leans, drawing my legs up to his lap. The pads of his fingertips trail up my shin, sending tingles of excitement racing through me.

I recline, tugging him with me, and my hands roam the firm muscles in his shoulders and chest. His fingers glide over my hip before sliding under my shirt and across the bare skin of my abdomen, making me gasp. He nips at my bottom lip and deepens the kiss, filling me with a desire that drowns out everything else, including rational thought.

I grasp his arms to steady myself before coming up for air, Pulling back, I try to clear my head. He studies me, brow furrowed.

"I'm sorry. I just...I need..." I have no idea what I need.

Space, definitely some space.

Away from him.

So I can think.

Yesterday I was sure he was sending me home, now I'm seconds away from getting naked and horizontal with him. That's not the best way to sort out what I want.

His gaze falls from mine. "Okay." With his tousled hair, he

appears vulnerable, more boy than man as his face morphs into an unreadable mask.

There's too much bouncing around in my head right now, and whatever's going on with us is just one more thing I need to figure out.

Cyrus took off after I put the brakes, and he's been gone all morning, giving me plenty of time to think. Unfortunately, I haven't figured out much yet. Instead, I'm worried I screwed things up between us.

When he finally returns, I search his face for anything to indicate he's still upset about earlier, but he's either over it or he's hiding it well. He parks himself on the bench beside me.

"We need to talk about something, and you're not going to like it."

Or maybe not.

He reaches into his pack and takes out a pair of scissors and a box of hair bleach. "We have to change your appearance."

"Um..." I touch the back of my head, and while I may not love my hair, I'm sort of attached to it. "Okay, but not *too* short."

He turns me so my back is to him and tugs down a long curl before cutting it. I turn to glance over my shoulder and he's holding more than twelve inches of hair. I suck in a breath and reach back to feel what's left. With all the weight gone, it's even curlier, and it springs up just below my shoulders.

Cyrus sets down the scissors and fistful of hair to cup my cheek. "This isn't easy for me either, but as sexy as your hair is, we need you to blend in."

He thinks I'm sexy? I shift my gaze from the pile of hair to his warm eyes, little jolts of electricity humming through me. I lean forward to kiss him again, but stop short, memories of this morning flooding back.

"Talk to me, Ev. What's wrong?"

Shit. Is there any easy way to tell a guy you're still a card-carrying member of Club V? "I'm not...you're..." I sigh and chew my lip. "I'm a consequence of two people who rushed into something without..."

The smile that takes over his face tell me he understands. Thank god, because I'm not sure I can continue. He leans forward, pressing his forehead to mine.

"I'll never push you to do anything you're not ready for."

"I didn't think you would, I just...wanted you to know." And if what Lucy said is true, he's a lot more experienced than me. I don't want to disappoint him.

He kisses my head, turns me back, and resumes cutting my hair. When he's finished, he ties a band around the jumble of red curls and stuffs the whole mess in his bag. Then he helps me down to the creek and applies the bleach. We sit on the bank while we wait for the chemicals to do their job.

"Where did you get the hair color?"

"Sonia. She went blond a few years ago. Marcus hated it so there was some left over. No one can connect a recent purchase of hair color with the hot new blonde living with us."

A warm flush rises up my chest, but a heavy dose of reality sets in when I remember why we're doing this. I need to tell him the rest of my story.

He sits quietly, watching me as I share the events from my kidnapping up until they found me in the desert.

"Tell me again what they said about Bryce."

"Uhh...'he's sticking his nose where it doesn't belong,' something like that." I shake my head. "Like Bryce was butting into Walker's business. At the time, I didn't understand what that meant, but now...Do you think Bryce is a smuggler?"

He stares at the ground for several long moments before lifting his head to meet my gaze. "Maybe. If products are going into the Union, they need people on the inside. Bryce could be smuggling into the Union or even out of it. Or a little of both. Anything's possible."

"What do you think they wanted with me?"

"I don't know. Kidnapping a Uni seems extreme if he wasn't living up to his end of the bargain. That's a big risk. Why not just take him out?"

"Yesterday, what did you mean when you said 'it' happened before?"

"The Union coming out here to retrieve one of their people."

"When?"

"A couple years ago. A Uni kid was found out here. A Teen. A family stumbled across him and nursed him back to health. He said he ran away from an abusive home." He blows out a slow breath. "The kid's family had government connections and sent a search party into the Ruins for him."

He pauses for a long time but, there must to be more to the story. "And?" I prod.

"They found him. The family had two boys of their own. The search party killed both parents in front of all three boys, and said the same would happen to the other boys if the Uni kid talked about where he'd been or what he'd seen out here."

My stomach rolls at this latest revelation. "What happened to the other boys?" I whisper.

"We found them on our way to the Summer Festival not long after. They've been living with us ever since."

Will and Ben.

"Time's up," Cyrus says, holding out a hand to help me back to the stream as if he didn't just tell me a horrific tale about two people I love.

We rinse my hair and climb back up to the hideaway where Cyrus hands me a set of clean clothes from the house along with a couple of books. He drops a light kiss on my lips before going to check the snares.

While he's gone, I change and toss my dirty clothes into the bag to go back to the house. I pick up a book and sit on the bench to read, but I can't focus. All I can think about is Will and Ben. I don't understand how my government could do this. Does my uncle know?

Something about all of this isn't sitting right with me. The Union doesn't kill people. Maybe the smugglers were behind it. I mean, they have a vested interest in keeping the Ruins a secret, because if Unionites found out, they'd demand something be done. That would make smuggling irrelevant. But if everyone in the Union knew, that would mean people demanding action, the Union opening itself to everyone in the Ruins, the end to our way of life. Maybe they don't want anyone to know either.

Cyrus whistles as he approaches and his face lights up when he spots me, making my heart do somersaults in my chest. He sets down the rabbits he's holding and takes my hand, pulling me off the bench.

"I didn't think it was possible, but you may be even more beautiful as a blonde." He kisses me deeply, stealing my breath, then releases me and gets to work on dinner as if he didn't just plunder my senses.

After dinner, we sit beside a fire outside the hideaway. Cyrus wraps his arms around me, tugging me against his chest, and we talk late into the night. During a lull in the conversation, my thoughts return to yesterday morning again.

"You said you weren't going to send me back to the Union, but I heard you say you'd talk to me right after Draya said I had to go."

He sighs, his hot breath fanning across my now mostly bare neck causing me to shiver despite the warm night. "Marcus said you had a right to know how much danger we're in. That I had to let you make your decision based on all the facts. I was afraid you might leave once you knew." Then he kisses the back of my head and tells me the plan he and Lucien came up with. It's just crazy enough, it might actually work.

27

Crazy Plans

*L*ast night's conversation is front and center when I wake from a fitful sleep. My brain is like a blender of whirling thoughts, too jumbled to put any of it in perspective. I hobble over to the ladder and climb up to find Cyrus at the table nursing a thermos of tea.

He hands me a second thermos and brushes his lips against mine. "How's the ankle this morning?"

"Better, I should be able to walk more today."

"Good." He pauses, his features pulled tight. "Before we do this, I want to make sure it's what you want. There's no point in going through with this if you're leaving."

This is it.

The moment of truth.

I always believed I'd go home someday, but he asked me to stay and I need to decide. Closing my eyes and weigh my choices. My family and friends in the Union. My life and friends here. Cyrus.

Both sides tear at me like a cruel game of tug-of-war. In the end, one side tugs harder, yanking me over the center line. The desire to stay with him is a desperation, rivaling hunger or thirst. I open my eyes and nod.

The creases in his forehead relax and a smile spreads from the corners of his mouth to his whole face. He stands and wraps his arms around me, lifting me off the bench with him. "Then we've got our work cut out for us."

I eat the oatmeal he brought for me and then we head out, where Cyrus teaches me how to choose appropriate sticks and carve supports for a snare. I practice setting them until I get it right. After a short break for lunch, he teaches me how to clean, load, and shoot the rifle.

"This is a basic lever-action rifle. It's accurate and simple to shoot. Slide the cartridges in the tube like this." He demonstrates then lets me try. When I get the hang of loading, he shows me how to cock, aim, and fire. The intense bang startles me, the butt of the rifle kicking against my shoulder as it spits out the casing.

I empty the gun without hitting much. He has me reload and try again, and I have a bit more success.

"Don't pull the trigger. You need to squeeze with a constant, increasing pressure until it fires."

He continues to hurl directions at me on sighting, my stance, my breathing, until I give up in frustration.

"That's enough for today." He takes the rifle back from me and picks up my hand as we return to the hideaway.

We're both quiet as we sit beside each other on the bench, our dinner dishes scraped clean. I pull my knees up and wrap my arms around them as I stare into nothingness, the consequences of putting the plan Lucien and Cyrus came up with into action wreaking havoc with my conscious.

"What are you thinking about?" Cyrus asks.

I shake my head, not wanting to talk about it. In desperate need of a distraction, I lean over and kiss him. My lips capture his bottom one, the stubble beneath scratching me, rough and masculine. I sigh and unwrap my arms from my legs and wrap them around him. The gentle motion of his mouth against mine slows my thoughts and heats my blood.

He pushes me back until I'm reclined as his soft, warm kisses engulf me. I lose myself in him, in breathing him, touching him, absorbing him, until there's no room to think about anything else. Our breaths increase as our mouths devour each other's.

His hands slide beneath my shirt, hot and course against bare skin, making me feel alive. I need to feel alive. He trails his lips down my neck, sending shivers of desire through me.

I slip my hands under the hem of his shirt and run across the firm muscles of his chest. He separates from me to peel off his shirt, giving me an unobstructed view of his perfect six-pack abs v-ing into the waistband of his shorts.

He quickly returns his mouth to mine, rolling to his side and pulling me with him so he can grasp the edge of my shirt and lift it over my head. This is the farthest I've ever gone with a guy. At nearly eighteen, I never made it past first base, but I'm completely at ease with this. At least until Cyrus's eyes travel over my body, both heating my skin and making me blush.

His lips crash back to mine, his hand snaking around my back to unhook my bra in one smooth, practiced move, sliding the straps down my shoulders. This is definitely not his first trip to the rodeo.

He kisses me harder while his hands explore with gentle determination. His calloused palms against sensitive flesh causes goose bumps to rise over every inch of my skin. I'm ready to go even further, no longer worried about the consequences. If I'm old enough to make serious, life-altering decisions about my future, I'm old enough to have sex.

Just as I decide I want more, Cyrus abruptly pulls away from me and runs a hand through his hair, making it jut out at crazy angles. His eyes smolder then his gaze falls from mine. He stands and grabs his shirt, thrusting it over his head.

"Uh...what's wrong?" I hate the way my voice sounds insecure and hurt and it hits me that he's fully dressed and I'm still half-naked. I grab my top from where he discarded it and clutch it to my chest.

His fingers rake through his hair again, leaving it even wilder. "I can't believe I'm saying this, but...we can't do this." He sighs and closes his eyes. "God, I love you."

My eyes widen at his confession. I've had two boys tell me they love me, and both times they seemed conflicted about it. "Cyrus..."

"I want you more than I've ever wanted anyone, but not like this." He turns and walks out of the hideaway, leaving me alone, rejected, and embarrassed.

After pulling my shirt back on, I lean against the post and process what just happened. Warmth billows in my heart as I replay his words over and over. He loves me. And I don't need to ask myself if I love him, too, because I already know that I do.

My parents huddle together on a cliff overlooking the Ruins. Mom sobs as Joe consoles her. I peer over the edge, curious what's captured their attention. It's a body. A girl with long curly red hair, legs and arms splayed at unnatural angles. Tears stain my mom's cheeks, her beautiful green eyes puffy.

The scene morphs into an L-Train platform. Katie and Rachel stand with Eddie who's holding two little hands. Dark circles burrow under Eddie's eyes, his skin pale and drawn.

The train transforms into a gurney with my twisted body, gliding down the track. Mom lets out an anguished cry, trying to follow while Joe holds her back. I scream at them to look at me, that I'm alive, but they only see their own pain.

"Shhhhh, you're dreaming." Cyrus whispers while stroking my hair.

I sit up, the nightmare still fresh, and a sob escapes my throat.

"Hey, hey, you're okay." He pushes a curl away from my sweaty face.

I take a shaky breath and tell him my dream.

"Are you having second thoughts?"

"No. Maybe. I don't know."

"It's not too late," he murmurs. "You can still go home."

But I *am* home. Being in the Ruins, being with Cyrus, centers me. The sense of purpose I have here, the peace that curls into every corner of my body, can't be denied.

He lies back down, pulling me with him and kisses my forehead. "I can't pretend I know what you're going through. I want you to stay, but this is a choice you need to make for yourself."

"I know."

His arms tighten around me, but he doesn't say anything more. There's nothing else he can say. I made my decision and the consequences of my actions can't be soothed with words. I close my eyes, but sleep evades me. Soon his breathing becomes deep and even, leaving me alone with my thoughts.

I'm about to destroy my family. They'll never stop looking for me unless they think I'm dead. And I can never go back. Cyrus said the Union will hunt down everyone involved in the deception if they find out. I believe him, I guess. But what if he's wrong?

It doesn't escape me how twisted it is that my parents spent twelve years pretending Eddie was dead to protect me, and here I am about to pretend I'm dead to protect the Ruins. And yet, I don't feel any sense of satisfaction in this. Only gut-wrenching guilt. I shudder at what I'm planning to do to them.

I can't put my family through hell until I'm sure it's absolutely necessary. I need to see the evidence for myself. Proof of what the Union has done out here.

28

Tough Choices

 y head is lighter without all my hair weighing it down, but it's also a reminder of the reasons I needed to change my appearance. No matter how many distractions I tried to throw in their path, my fears found me last night.

I climb up to the main floor and see Cyrus heading back this way with Sonia and Marcus. Sonia raves about the hideaway. "You built this? Sneaking off while we were working on the house?"

Cyrus shrugs and grips the back of his neck. "Whenever you guys started making out, I took the leftover materials and hiked out here."

A dark stain colors Sonia's caramel-colored cheeks and she turns away.

Marcus steps inside and runs his hands along the side posts, glancing up at the thatched roof. "I can't believe you did this by yourself. How'd you get up there?"

"Took a while," Cyrus says, handing me a bowl of oatmeal with fresh berries and a thermos of tea, avoiding eye contact.

After Cyrus and Marcus head off to hunt, Sonia examines my ankle. She removes the wrappings and presses firmly, feeling my bones. "It's not broken. You should be able to put your boot back on in a couple of days."

She hands me a fresh set of clothes and helps me down to the creek to bathe. The water is cold and getting cleaned up is awkward. I miss showering at the falls. How crazy is that? I'm longing to take a shower in the Ruins.

After I dress, Sonia steps back and studies me. "I like your hair. The color suits you." She smiles, her eyes crinkling at the corners. "It's nice to see Cyrus so happy. You're good for him."

My smile joins hers. "Can I ask you something personal?"

"Sure."

"I mean something *really* personal."

"Okaaaay..."

"Have you and Marcus ever...you know...?"

She laughs. "Of course. Why do you ask? You and Cy?"

I blush a deep shade of scarlet and shake my head. "No. We came close last night. I thought I was ready, but...Cyrus stopped things before it got that far. I'm not ready to be a parent, and I'm pretty sure he isn't either, but after last night, I'm not even sure where things stand with us now."

She stifles a laugh. "Evan, I realize we live differently here than you did in the Union, but we *do* have condoms. It's not the 1800s even if it seems that way to you."

Oh, god. "Right, right, of course...I mean, I saw them at the trading post. And obviously neither you nor Draya have a baby. Please shoot me now," I mumble.

This time there is no stifling the laugh as she hugs me. "Oh, Evan, maybe he just didn't have one with him last night."

The way she says it makes me feel about ten years old. We're chronologically close in age, but she seems so much older and wiser sometimes. My lack of knowledge of Ruins birth control is just another reminder of how completely clueless I am about the choice I've made. What happens if we break up? Where will I live? What if I'm making a huge mistake?

"He's crazy about you, you know. If you don't feel the same, be careful. You have the power to really hurt him."

"What about all the other girls? Lucy said—"

"Lucy's jealous. I don't know what she said, but I can guess. Forget about her."

She stands and offers me her hand to help me back up the side of the ravine, effectively ending our conversation. It doesn't escape me that she didn't answer my question, but I should really be talking to Cyrus about this.

After lunch of fresh fish Sonia and I caught and some apples Cyrus picked yesterday, we head out so I can practice with the rifle. I'm getting better, but shooting targets is one thing, I'm not sure I can shoot a living, breathing thing.

Dinner is roasted pheasant, then we around the fire to talk. Cyrus and I sit beside one another, but the gap between us seems much wider than the foot of space separating us. Things have been awkward since he walked out on me last night.

Cyrus and Marcus explain the plan in detail. "We'll time it right to make sure Dag sees the body in the water. We just need him to believe it's you," Cyrus says.

"Dag knows what I look like, though."

"Ally will be face down wearing a hat with your hair sewn inside. He's not going to touch her. Hell he won't even get close enough to notice she's still breathing. Dag is freaked out by the dead," Marcus says.

"Will Walker just take his word for it? Won't he want proof?"

"He'd probably be happier with a body he can take back to the Union, but we only need to convince Dag. He's gotta be Walker's source, the one who told him you were staying with us."

Cyrus leans back against the log, propping his elbows up on it. "Walker wants the Union off his back. If he can't return you alive, knowing you're dead will be enough."

"How can Walker convince the Union I'm dead without a body?"

"He's probably working with someone inside the Union. They can help him with a death certificate."

My death certificate. I shudder, realizing what a big deal this is and how much is at stake if we're not successful. "I can't let everyone risk themselves for no reason. I have to be a hundred percent sure before I end that part of my life for good."

Cyrus nods with a resigned expression, then turns to Marcus and Sonia. "I'll take her to the old Madera Mesa power station."

"You two shouldn't go alone," Marcus says.

"And you shouldn't be walking that far on your ankle yet," Sonia adds. "We can go in a few days." The finality of her tone leaves no room for argument.

The low rumble of thunder rolls above us, something I haven't heard since leaving home in June. We walk to the edge of the tree line and look east. A single massive cloud swells up to an astronomic height. Every minute or two, it snaps a brilliant pink and yellow, as if thousands of lights inside are going off at once.

"And so begins monsoon season," Marcus says.

"Monsoon season?"

"Yep. We get most of our rain this time of year in the form of daily thunderstorms. It can come down hard enough to cause flooding, but stops as fast as it starts."

Standing here watching nature's light show, I don't think I've ever witnessed anything more beautiful.

Sonia and Marcus went back to the house after breakfast with promises of returning in a few days. Cyrus and I spend the morning at target practice. He's amazingly patient with me, but I'm ready to scream in frustration. I can line the shot up, but when I shoot, I still miss.

"You're too keyed up, Evan. Relax and focus on your breathing."

I doubt my breathing is the problem, but I'm willing to try

anything at this point. I swipe my hair from my face with the back of my arm as he stands dangerously close, the heat from his body distracting me.

"Rest the butt against your shoulder, like this." He positions the rifle for me, wrapping his hands around mine. This is the first time he's touched me since the other night and this isn't doing anything to help me relax or focus. "Take in a deep breath and steady the rifle. Keep your breath even and gently squeeze the trigger. Don't pull it."

I try, but miss again and tell him I'm hungry so I don't need to admit I want to quit.

We've managed to stay busy since Sonia and Marcus left, but the knot of tension hovering above us is a reminder of what happened the other night, or rather what *didn't* happen.

After dinner, we sit by the fire as it snaps, sending sparks up into the cobalt sky, filling the awkward lapses in conversation until I reach my tipping point.

"Cyrus?"

"Yeah?"

"Can we talk about the other night?"

He turns to face me, his eyes intense on mine.

"I hate this..." I move my hand in a sweeping motion between us. "...awkwardness. I want things to be the way they were before."

He reaches for my hand and tugs closer, wrapping his arms around me. "Nothing's changed, I promise, but I'm worried about you. About what you're giving up to stay here."

I swallow around the lump in my throat. I guess we're finally going to address the giant elephant in the Ruins. I'm acutely aware of what this decision is doing to me, I just didn't realize he knew it, too. Plus, I need to make sure he's really thought about what this means, what kind of commitment this is. "Are you sure this is what *you* want?"

He sighs and leans his forehead into mine. "Yes. I'm sure."

"Okay," I whisper.

"Sonia told me you heard some things about me, but that was before...before I fell in love with you."

I search his eyes and find only certainty. That's all I need. "Okay," I whisper again.

He reaches out and tucks a curl behind my ear. "I don't want you to realize in six months, or a year, or even two years that you made a mistake." He pauses and closes his eyes. "If you stay, there will be plenty of time to pick the right time and place, but if you don't..." He shakes his head. "I don't want you to regret it."

I close my eyes and nod. "That's why I have to see the evidence for myself. If I'm never going back...I have stay for the right reasons."

He kisses my temple. "I know this his hard, Ev, but I'll do whatever I can to make it easier for you."

I sigh and relax against him, wishing I knew what that was.

29

The Right Reasons

We wait on the bench for Sonia and Marcus to return. I lean into Cyrus and let the boy I love and the beauty of a Ruins morning fill me with happiness. Both of us are quiet, listening to the sounds of the wind rustling the leaves around us and the trickling of the stream below.

I've told him my whole story, start to finish, but I'm still missing a piece of it myself. How they came upon me. I twist to face him. "Tell me about the day you found me out here."

He blows out a slow breath while I settle back against him. "We were almost at the end of our three-day hike home, tired and short-tempered. I was looking forward to sleeping in my own bed."

I smile. "Didn't get to do that, did you?"

"No, but I'm not complaining." His voice hints at his own smile.

My grin grows broader and I reach out to lace my fingers with his.

"The boys ran ahead, excited to get home. Ben was so far in front, we couldn't even see him until we crested a hill. He was still, just staring at the ground. When we got closer, I saw something red near his feet and thought it was a fox. Knowing Ben, he'd try to pet it, so I dropped my bag and ran after him. Somewhere in those first few steps, I realized it wasn't an animal, but a person. I thought you were dead, but Sonia found a pulse. So, I picked you up and carried you to the house. We had no idea you were from the Union until Sonia took off your socks and saw your painted toenails, uncallused hands, and your strange lack of body hair."

"I'm glad it was you and not someone else." I tilt my head back and he bends down to press his lips to mine. It's the first real kiss we've shared since the "night nothing happened," as I now refer to it. He deepens it, sliding his tongue into my mouth, and I wrap my hand around the back of his neck before twisting to face him, straddling his lap.

My pulse quickens, and his heart stampedes under my palm. I love that I have the same effect on him he has on me.

"Hey, you guys ready?" Sonia calls out.

Cyrus nips my bottom lip and smiles. "Guess it's time to go."

We hop up and walk out to greet them. Sonia hands me a backpack. "How's the ankle?"

"Good to go."

Marcus hands a rifle to Cyrus and Cyrus offers me the one I've been practicing with. A look passes between the them, and Marcus raises an eyebrow. Cyrus nods, the corners of his mouth tipping up.

"Are you going to accidentally shoot one of us with that thing?" Sonia is much less subtle.

I shrug. "I hope not. But if shooting breaks out, you might want to get out of my way."

We head northwest, deeper into the wooded area, over ground thick with leaves and underbrush that crunches beneath our boots.

The power station is fifteen miles away, so we should arrive by nightfall. The trees thin and the dense groundcover gives way to boulders and low-growing scrubby plants as we approach the western edge of the woods.

Once we clear the tree line, the sun beats down, scorching the air around us. The landscape sprawls like an endless sea of dirt and rocks, splattered with weeds, and cactus. Hills rise in the distance, brown and lifeless, and ripples on the horizon remind me for all of the lushness behind us, we are in a desert.

Closer to the hills, the carcass of a long-dead city bakes in the unrelenting heat. We approach a wide road, forty to fifty yards across, with a short crumbling concrete wall in the center. Grass and weeds grow through the mangled pavement where the road buckled from extreme temperatures.

Beyond the road are miles of buildings. Some stand tall, but years of neglect left most in ruins. Scattered rubble gives no indication of its former glory. We skirt the outside of the abandoned city, avoiding the wreckage.

"The cities are occupied by scavengers these days," Marcus explains when he catches me staring at the destroyed city. "They harvest building materials and furniture, but they're a rough bunch, so it's best to avoid them."

More buildings occupy the eastern side, some in slightly better condition. Sadness settles over me as I try to imagine life here before the war, the heat, the bombs, and the droughts took their toll. I picture children playing in yards covered in grass instead. It's hard to believe these were once the mighty cities of the old United States.

"We'll take the next turn off on the left," Cyrus says, leading us across the road, up and over the crumbling center half wall, to a smaller street veering off.

We pick our way over a large pile of rubble.

"This used to be a bridge," Sonia says. "See those." She points at thick rods poking out of the ground. "That's where it connected on the other side."

The sun sets over the hills to the west as we make our way down the wreckage. "It's not much farther," Marcus says.

Dusk brings long shadows and looming darkness, so we search for a suitable place to make camp for the night. We come across a small group of outbuildings that provide adequate cover and pitch our tents.

Cyrus and I take the first sentry duty while Sonia and Marcus get some sleep. Sitting outside the tents, we keep an eye on our surroundings, listening for anything out of place. We're about halfway through our shift when boredom sets in.

"What do you miss most from the Union?" Cyrus asks. "Besides your family and friends."

"What about my dog?"

He smiles. "I'm assuming your dog is part of your family."

"Okay." I pause and think for a moment. "Coffee."

"What's so great about coffee?"

"Oh wow, where do I start? Coffee's dark and rich, and the smell...oh my god, it's like it enters your nose and winds its tendrils into your brain hugging it with warmth."

He grunts, but the corners of his mouth give away his amusement. "What else?"

"Hot showers. Sushi."

"Soo-shee?"

"Sushi. It's Japanese. Raw fish and rice."

His eyebrow notches up. "You miss eating raw fish?"

I laugh. "Not *any* raw fish. Only specific kinds prepared a certain way. It's kind of hard to explain, but it's so fresh, it melts in your mouth." A few moments of silence follow before I query him. "What's your favorite childhood memory?"

"Hmmm." He thinks for a moment before a smile tugs at his lips. "The first time I went to a Summer Festival. I was ten. Our whole town went together as a group. We had to walk five days to get there. That's probably why we'd never gone before, the distance would've been too much for the younger kids."

His smile reaches his voice as he continues. "Tents, booths, musicians — everything you could ever want was for sale or trade. More people in one place than I'd ever seen. They had these games pitting families and towns against one another for bragging rights. That's all it took for everyone to compete like their lives depended on it."

The animated tone in his voice reaches deep inside and touches me, making me wish I'd known him before heartbreak and loss stole his playful side.

Suddenly, his body tenses and he locks eyes with mine. Confused, I start to say something, but he puts a finger to his lips. I strain to hear what set him on alert and freeze. Distant voices grow louder and more raucous as they near.

"Stay put," Cyrus whispers before moving to the edge of one of the buildings to peer around the corner.

I'm supposed to be on sentry duty, too so I creep over to another building. A group of four men pass by about fifty yards away, oblivious to our presence. I slink behind the building, my heart racing before taking another look. They're stomping along, talking over each other, passing around a bottle of something.

All four are armed with wicked looking weapons — long guns, like rifles, but with two barrels, one above the other. They're made of some sort of black metal with scopes and molded hand grips.

The men are loud enough I can easily make out what they're saying. "...and then, boom! No more Unis. It's going to be historic. Future generations will study us."

"The plan's not to destroy the Union, we're just gonna take down the government, you moron."

"But those weapons, they're huge. Those are gonna do some serious damage."

"You're both idiots. This isn't about us killing as many Unis as possible. It's about taking back our country. Getting back to the good ol' U. S. of A."

"Whatever. I've got a weapon, and I plan on taking as many of them lazy commie bastards as I can."

Whooping and hand slapping follows before fading away as they move out of range. Icy fingers twist in my gut, and I slump to the ground. Cyrus finds me and his eyes tell me he heard the same thing I did.

"Do you know what that was about?" I whisper.

He shakes his head and takes my hand, pulling me up and leading me back to our spot in front of the tents.

"They were kidding, right? I mean, they're drunk."

"I don't know. Yeah, they're drunk, but—"

"But they have wicked looking weapons," I finish. "Have you seen anything like those before?"

"No."

My hands shake as I replay the conversation, but there's also a surrealness to all of this, as if what I saw was all a dream. We spend the rest of our shift in silence before waking up Marcus and Sonia to take over.

Cyrus briefly explains what we overheard so they're aware of what to watch for.

"That's some messed up shit," Marcus says. "Should we move camp?"

Cyrus narrows his eyes and glances around before shaking his head. "We're probably safer staying put. We can reevaluate in the morning."

We crawl into the tent, and Cyrus wraps me in his arms, pressing his lips to my forehead. "Whatever that was, we'll figure it out."

I'm exhausted from the day's activities, so even though I'm keyed up, my eyelids soon become heavy. When Marcus wakes us, it feels as if I've slept only minutes, but the sky is already dawning with a hint of color from the sun's first rays.

30

Figuring It Out

"How'd it go after we went to bed?" Cyrus asks over breakfast.

"Good. Nice and quiet," Marcus responds.

"Who do you think those guys were?" I ask Cyrus.

He blows out a breath. "I don't know. They could've been scavengers from the city."

"But where'd they get those guns?"

He shakes his head. "I don't know."

I ask a dozen more questions trying to kick-start a discussion, but they all end the same. No one knows anything and they can't even guess. They're clueless and they've lived here forever. How am I supposed to figure this out as a recent transplant?

Cyrus takes my hand to shut me up or to calm me down, not sure which. "We don't know any more than you. We'll ask around at the trading post. Find out what Dag knows."

"So, we're not going to do anything?"

"No one is suggesting that, Ev. But until we figure out what we're dealing with, there's not much we can do."

My insides feel like they're fighting to get out, and I hop on the balls of my feet while I wait for them to finish eating. Maybe I don't know what those guys are up to, but I can at least do what we came here for — convince myself that faking my death is the only way.

When they're finally done, we head out. We don't walk far before coming upon the devastated remains of ... something ... stretching out in front of us. The damage is so complete I would've never been able to guess what used to be here. Charred rubble becomes larger and closer together as we approach a blackened crater surrounded by huge chunks of concrete. Steel rebar pokes up like broken bones. The crumbling towers marching away from the abyss are the only indication this was once a power plant.

I make my way to the edge and peer down at the utter devastation, wondering what type of weapon could result in this much damage. This happened fifty or even seventy-five years ago, but the murder of Will and Ben's parents was recent. The atrocities aren't ancient history. A piece of me, one I don't want to acknowledge, understands the anger that leads to talk about attacking the Union.

With careful steps, I pick my way across rocks toward the towers. I'm not sure what I expect to find, but I move closer, trying to immerse myself in the destruction, be a part of it. My foot catches on something, sending me stumbling forward where I come face to face with a cord snaking out of a hatch nearly hidden in the rubble. The thick, heavy wire trails across the ground before connecting to several large solar panels concealed in the ruins.

The hair on the back of my neck stands on end. Sonia told me how much these cost out here. I can't imagine any good reason they'd be here. Based on the efforts taken to conceal them, I doubt they'll be happy to find out I stumbled onto them.

Turning back, my heart pounds as I rush to rejoin my friends, holding a finger to my lips.

"What's wrong?" Cyrus asks.

"Let's go."

I take off at a run, anxious to put as much distance as possible between us and that underground bunker. The others catch up to me, Cyrus glancing over his shoulder, likely trying to figure out what spooked me.

When we're far enough away for my comfort, I slow.

"Ev, what's going on?" Cyrus asks.

I tell them about the solar panels and cord. "The power plant is close enough to where we camped last night, that those guys could've been heading there. Maybe it's some sort of base camp for their revolution."

"Maybe," Cyrus says, scratching an eyebrow with his thumbnail.

"This is bigger than I thought, then, this is real. I have to go back."

"Go back where?" Marcus asks.

"To the power nt. If it's their headquarters, we need to find out what they're planning. I have to warn the Union."

Cyrus grabs my arm. "What? Hold on. Let's talk this through."

I jerk free. "My family is there."

Marcus's calm reason breaks through my rising panic. "Your first instinct was to get the hell out of there. Trust your gut."

Fear envelopes his words, obscuring them, stifling rational thought.

"Ev, listen to me," Cyrus says. "You can't go storming back there demanding answers. You need a plan."

"You can't be serious, Cy," Sonia says. "She can't go back there, *period*."

He sighs and scratches the back of his head. "If you insist on doing this, I'm going with you."

"You can't just waltz up, knock on the door, and start asking questions," Marcus says.

"Yeah, I realize that." *Now*.

Sonia shakes her head and mumbles, "You're all crazy."

"That's just it, Sonia, we're not the crazy ones," I say. "Something weird is going on. They were talking about massive weapons and *blowing up* the Union. It would be easy to dismiss it as just talk, because they were drunk. But you didn't see their guns, and now that underground bunker..."

"I've never seen anything like those rifles. They were..." Cyrus shakes his head and describes them to Sonia and Marcus.

"The people of the Union are unarmed. If they're attacked, it'll be a slaughter," I say.

We're all quiet for a few minutes before Sonia asks, "How many solar panels were there?"

"I'm not sure. Ten or so. It was hard to tell, because they're trying to hide them."

"Okay," Sonia sighs, the stiffness in her shoulders releasing as she rolls her neck. "That's not a big enough base to take down the Union, no matter how deep underground it goes. It might be one of many, or just the first step in early planning of something months or years away."

The logical part of my brain knows this makes sense, and it helps settle the irrational half.

Cyrus takes my hand, his voice soft. "We need a plan, a good one. Nothing's going to happen today. Let's go back to the house and talk to Lucien and Draya. We'll figure something out. Okay?"

I nod and he lets out an audible sigh. Once again, the emotional Union girl acted without thinking, putting everyone on edge. By the time darkness falls, we're still several hours from home. Cyrus doesn't want to arrive at night, so Sonia and Marcus will go ahead of us in the morning to scope things out before I return to the house.

We set up our tents in the woods about a two-hour walk from the house. Sonia and Marcus turn in as soon as they finish dinner. Cyrus and I stay by the fire, sipping tea as thunder in the distance reminds me monsoon season is still in full swing. I lean against his churning through the events of the past twenty-four hours in my head.

"You're going back, aren't you?" He asks, and something about the tone in his voice rips through my heart.

I don't know that I'd come to that conclusion yet, but now that he's voiced it, I know it's true. "I have to. I can't just let innocent people be massacred. I have to at least try to warn them," I whisper, choking back the heartache shredding my soul as I realize this means I'm leaving him.

My universe tips as pain and loss twist together, battling with fear and responsibility. And then words fall from my mouth before they have a chance to enter my brain. "Come with me."

His eyes rest on mine and time stops. Something flashes in his whiskey-colored eyes, giving me hope. As much as I want to persuade him, I need him to come with me for his own reasons.

He sighs and pulls me to his chest, wrapping his arms around me. I inhale his scent, the natural, earthy smell mixed with sunshine that is his alone. Pressing his lips to my temple, he says quietly, "You're my world, Ev. Where you go, I go."

31

Where You Go, I Go

*S*onia and Marcus are gone when we wake. After a quick breakfast, we pack up and hike to the hideaway to wait for them. They arrive soon after and tell us the coast is clear.

Butterflies scramble in my stomach as we near the house. I didn't realize how much I missed my Ruins family. Everyone is out back waiting for us, and Ben runs up to hug me. Ty leaps into my arms the second Ben lets me go, while Lucien wraps his brother in a bear hug.

"I love your hair!" Ally squeals. "I almost didn't recognize you."

I'm floored when Draya embraces me. "I can't believe I'm saying this, but I actually missed your ass."

After hauling our gear inside, we sit in the dining room to talk. Lucien glances across the table at me, his ebony eyes meeting mine. "A group came by looking for you, Evan."

A chill trickles down my spine. "What did they say?"

"That you were a friend and they were concerned for your safety."

"At least they're getting more creative," Draya says. "They sent a bunch of teens this time, including a girl."

My head snaps around. "What did they look like?"

"A black guy, a blond guy and his girlfriend, and a tall kid," Will says.

My pulse quickens. "Ummm...the black guy..."

"Totally hot? Oh yeah," Draya says before I can ask if he has gray eyes.

"Wicked hot," Ally says under her breath.

"What about the girl?"

"She was a little taller than you, blond, cute," Will says.

It's gotta be my friends, and I get why Bryce and Jack are looking for me out here, but why are Lisa and with them? Maybe they kidnapped them and forced them to come.

I'm vaguely aware of Cyrus filling the others in on what we overheard near the power station and about what I discovered. Wrapped up in a fog, trying to process my Union friends being out here, I don't realize Lucien's talking to me until he calls my name.

I turn to him. "Huh? Sorry."

"Describe what you saw. What do you remember?"

I tell him about the cord coming out of the ground and the solar panels, being as descriptive as possible, but I'm still preoccupied. "What did you tell them," I ask.

"Tell who what?" Lucien asks.

"The group that came looking for me. What did you tell them?"

"We told them the same story we told Walker. If they're working together, the stories will match."

"What did they say?"

Lucien locks eyes with me. "What's going on, Evan?"

"I think those were my friends, I think they were telling you the truth."

His gaze darts to Cyrus then back to me. "They seemed genuinely concerned for you. But they also seemed to believe us and left not long after."

"I don't get what they're doing out here," I say. "It doesn't make any sense."

"It makes sense to me," Cyrus says, low enough that only I can hear, before he gets up and heads outside.

The domed ceiling is bathed in moonlight and dark shadows reach across the walls like fingers. I let out a long sigh, missing Cyrus's arms around me after spending the past week with him. My head rides a carousel of thoughts before I give up on sleep and make my way outside.

Cyrus is sitting on the rock, and my mind calms at the sight of him. The rain stopped hours ago and the sky is crystal clear, making it appear as if the heavens are touching the ground. Cyrus scoots over to make room for me, but doesn't offer me a hand up.

I sit next to him, hugging my knees. "Can't sleep?"

"No. You?"

I lean my head against his shoulder and close my eyes. A sudden thought of what might explain his recent aloofness sends unease skipping through me. "Are you having second thoughts about coming with me?"

"No." He takes a slow breath. "Are you having second thoughts about asking me to come?"

I lift my head and gape at him "Of course not. How can you even ask that?"

"Things are different now."

A mixture of confusion, anger, fear, and sadness blasts through me. I stiffen and try to calm my racing heart. I don't know what to say in response. After a few minutes of thick silence, I ask, "Different how?"

He shifts next to me but doesn't respond. We sit quietly for a long time as I refuse to give in to the impulse to go back in the house, slamming the door behind me. I'm trying to be the new me, the less impulsive me.

"Different *how*?" I ask again, fighting the incredible hurt building inside me. His continued silence is deafening, until it's too much. "Do you not want to be with me anymore?"

He turns and takes my face in his hands, kissing me with a soft desperation. When he pulls back, he leans his forehead against mine. I can tell he wants to say something and the fact that he's holding back is freaking me out.

He cups my face, his thumbs gliding over my cheeks. "I'm barely hanging on here, Ev, waiting for you to disappear out of my life as suddenly as you landed in it."

His tone rips straight through me and my soul aches for him. I'm touched that he's allowed me to see even this smallest hint of vulnerability. When I lift my eyes to meet his, I see my own fears reflected in his eyes, but I'm not sure how to respond. I want to reassure him, but I can't because I'm going back with or without him.

He kisses me again, harder this time, pouring all the emotion I just saw in his eyes into the kiss. When we go back inside, I pull him up the stairs and into my room, falling asleep in his arms, where I belong.

We sit around the table after breakfast, sipping tea and brainstorming. We don't have a plan for warning the residents of the Union without risking everyone in the Ruins, nor do we have any ideas for finding out more about an attack on the Union. Since we aren't making any headway on those, I try to tackle one of the easier problems.

"We need forged Union credentials for Cyrus. How do we get those?"

Lucien looks up from the rim of his mug he's been circling with his finger. "I hate to say it, but if your friend is a smuggler, he's our best bet."

Cyrus bristles next to me. "I don't think it's a good idea."

"What if someone out here wanted a Union ID and money was no object, who would they go to?"

Marcus's face lights up, a huge smile spreading across his face. He leans back in his chair and puts his hands behind his head. "Dag."

My stomach curdles. "I don't trust him."

"No one trusts him, but if you want someone who's connected, he's your guy," Marcus says.

"I prefer Lucien's idea. Plus, we need Bryce and Jack anyway."

Lucien's gaze flicks from Cyrus back to me. "What for?"

"I have to tell my family something when I go back. I have an idea, but I need my friends to be on board with it. I'm still not sure what's going on there, though. Bryce and Jack need me back in the Union as much as Walker does, but I don't get why they dragged Lisa and Colin along."

"I thought the blond guy and the girl were together," Ally says, twisting the tag of her tea bag.

"What do you mean 'together'?"

"Well, he was holding her hand when they first got here and had his arm around her later." She shrugs. "I just assumed."

"I can't believe my two best friends would willingly go along with a couple of smugglers. They must not know. Or maybe Jack and Bryce are using Lisa and Colin somehow." I shake my head. "It doesn't matter, I guess, since it doesn't change what we need to do."

"What do you have in mind?" Lucien asks.

"We could say I met Cyrus on the train and then went sailing off the Southeastern Peninsula." I pause, realizing this plan has a big flaw, well, four actually. "My friends know that's not true, though. I was with Bryce on the train, and since the four of them are still together..."

"She's got a point, Cy," Marcus says.

"Is this Bryce guy going to go all jealous boyfriend and rat Cyrus out?" Draya asks.

"I...we weren't involved all that long, but..." Tension rolls off

Cyrus in waves next to me "I don't really know him. I thought I did, but clearly I didn't, so I have no idea what he will or won't do."

"That's not even our biggest problem," Draya says. "I still don't understand what you're hoping to accomplish in the Union. You can't warn the government. The only sure way to prevent an attack is to bomb us to hell and back. If you tell them, we're as good as dead. So, what's your plan?"

"I don't know." I let out a long frustrated sigh. "Union citizens are unarmed and totally unprepared for any kind of an attack. You can't make me choose between the people I love here and back home. That's a choice I won't make."

The smell of wet earth pervades the warm evening air and humidity hangs heavy around me. The stars blink to life as I stare up at the twilight sky, trying to figure out a way to make this all work without involving Bryce, but I'm coming up empty.

On top of that, I need a way to warn the people of the Union without risking everyone in the Ruins. The situation is impossible, and I blow out a puff of air. I'm about to go to bed when an idea sparks inside, taking hold. While I can't control any of this, maybe I can find a way to work within the natural order of things.

Excitement builds and I want to talk it over with Cyrus, have him help me flesh it out, but he disappeared after dinner. His crappy attitude about Bryce is wearing thin and I'm not sure I want to deal with it anymore tonight.

Disappointed and feeling more isolated than I have in a while, I go up to my room and climb into my bed, alone.

32

The Spark of an Idea

*T*his morning I'm more hopeful than last night, and after dressing, I head out in search of Cyrus. He's not in the house, so I wander outside, checking the chicken coop before heading to the barn. Lucien's finishing up milking as I enter.

"Morning. Have you seen Cyrus?"

Lucien glances up and smiles before picking up a rake. "He went to the trading post."

"Oh." I pick up the other rake and work silently next to Lucien, grateful for a return to our normal routine. I didn't realize how much I missed the rhythm of my days here.

"He loves you, Evan, but he's never been in love before." He stops and directs his dark gaze my way. "Cy was only fourteen when the tornado ripped his life apart and turned it upside down. Then you landed in our lives out of nowhere and turned his world upside down again. His life tends to change suddenly — it's what he knows but also what he fears."

I study Lucien's handsome face that looks so much like his brother's. "What can I do to convince him he's not going to lose me?"

Lucien places his hands atop the rake handle, resting his chin on them. "Give him some time, he'll come around."

"We don't have a lot of time."

He scratches the back of his neck and studies me with a thoughtful expression. "He'll do what he needs to when it needs to be done. The rest will work itself out." Lucien sets his rake against the side of the barn and puts his arm around my shoulder. "You're a part of this family now, part of *my* family, and the people in my family work things out. No matter how long it takes."

"Thanks, Lucien. I'll try to talk to him when he gets back."

He kisses the side of my head and we finish cleaning the barn before heading in for breakfast.

After cleaning up the kitchen, I head back out to pick berries. It's already beyond hot, and soon sweat is running into my eyes. I stand to swipe my forearm across my face, and someone grabs me from behind. Terror crawls up my spine as I look for something to fend off my attacker with.

Before I can formulate a defensive plan, soft lips nuzzle my neck and rough stubble grazes my shoulder. Hot breath fanning my skin and firm hands on my waist do nothing to calm my pounding heart. I twist around and Cyrus's mouth finds mine.

He breaks the kiss and rests his forehead against mine. "I'm sorry."

Relieved that he's not avoiding me anymore, I can't wipe the dopey grin off my face. "You didn't say goodbye this morning."

"I know. I left before you woke. I went to the trading post to put out the word that you're back. Hopefully that'll draw your friends back to us."

His resigned expression pulls at my heart and I want to reassure him. "I know you don't like Bryce being here, but if it wasn't for him, I never would've met you. He's the one who convinced me to leave home and not to settle for a life I didn't want. I'd still be in the Union working for my stepdad if he hadn't. And if he didn't care for me, Walker wouldn't have kidnapped me."

He doesn't respond, but his faraway gaze and clenched jaw tell me he's processing my words. I return to picking, my fingers turning dark from the juices of the blackberries, forming burgundy rivers where it settles into scratches from the thorns.

When my bucket is full, I turn to see Cyrus watching me, his eyes intense. "I'm sorry for everything you went through, Ev, but I'll never be sorry I met you."

Something deep passes between us, an understanding of what we found in each other. I lean over and kiss his cheek. I've been through a lot in the past few months, but I found my second family, the boy I love, and quite possibly my purpose in life.

Cyrus and I prepare for our trip to the Union while we wait for my friends to circle back around to us. A hole the size of a basketball bores its way through my chest whenever I think about leaving. Lucien, Draya, Marcus, and Sonia are trying to find out what they can about a planned attack on the Union, but details are sketchy. Rumors flourish at the trading post, but weeding the facts from the garden of myths is difficult, especially with the myths growing exponentially every day.

"They're looking for recruits," Lucien says. "We might be able to get more info if we join up."

"What? No, you can't. What if they discover what you're up to?"

"They won't," Lucien assures me. "No one out here loves the Union, if they don't outright hate it, they're at least indifferent."

Indifference and hatred are the two opposing views. My life raft of hope just took a major hit. I stare at the table, tracing the scratches in the worn wood with my finger before looking up at Lucien. "Then warning the citizens of the Union is the only way."

"I still don't like it," Draya says, glancing from me to Lucien. "But I'll admit we don't have anything better."

"I have a bit of an idea," I say. "I was thinking of a grassroots movement, like the Underground Railroad that helped free slaves in the 1800s or the Peace Patrols that sprung up in the late 2000s to help broker a cease fire. We just need to figure out who we can trust."

"How do you do that?" Sonia asks.

"I haven't figured that part out yet, but I can start with my uncle."

"No way!" Draya jumps up from the table, her arms flying like crazed windmills. "He's a government official."

"But I trust him."

She shakes her head with exaggerated force. "No. You...you just can't."

Wild fear colors her blue eyes, and while I understand it, he's my uncle and he'd never betray my confidence. "I'd never do anything to put you all in danger, you have to know that. Yes, my uncle is a governor, but he always puts family first."

Draya stares me down, and this time I'm the first one to look away. I don't know what to say to make her understand. After everything I've learned out here, I don't know if he's really the man I believe him to be, but my gut tells me he is.

I turn back to the others. "I'm going to tell you a story, and then if you still think I'm crazy to trust him, I won't."

They exchange glances before Draya nods at me.

"My uncle and I have always been close. Not long after he and his wife lost their infant daughter, they divorced and he moved in with us while he got his life back together. After my twin sisters were born, I spent a lot of time with him. He took me to school in the mornings and picked me up after to help my parents out."

My hands twist in my lap as I ready myself to share this next part. "When I was twelve, my life was turned upside down. It was nothing like what you all have gone through, but in my short pampered Union life..." I throw a smile at Draya and she gives me a small smile one return, "...it was the absolute worst thing that'd happened and I wasn't equipped to deal with it.

"My mom and stepdad told me a few days before the news became public that the biological father I always thought was dead was not only alive, but was Eddie McIntrye, lead singer of Epic Vinyl. I know that doesn't mean anything to you, but he's kind of a big deal in the Union. At the time, Eddie was at the top of his career and a pretty notorious bad-boy rocker."

Talking about this is more difficult than I expected, and I get up, walking over to lean against the back of the couch. "What made the story of Eddie having an illegitimate daughter even more salacious was the fact that he'd always known about me. It was a tabloid dream come true, the stories practically wrote themselves. And if that wasn't bad enough, my Uncle David had just launched his campaign for Governor of the Eastern Province. What should have been just another juicy story became something with political implications.

"I stopped going to school once the press got wind of it. They set up camp outside our apartment and I couldn't leave without passing them. The night the story hit, my uncle stormed through our front door, slamming it against the roar of shouted questions behind him. I was curled up on the couch, trying to disappear into myself. I'll never forget the look on his face. He was pissed as hell, but the moment his eyes met mine, all of that anger just sort of diffused and the sadness that replaced it told me he didn't have any more of a clue than I did.

"I'd never seen the two brothers fight, they barely even argued, but my uncle lit into my stepdad and I was scared he was going to punch him. Joe said, 'I'm not proud of myself but it wasn't my secret to tell. This is between Christine, Eddie and Evan.' Then my uncle said, 'Except Evan was never a part of it. You all made the decision for her.' Joe accused him of putting politics ahead of my needs and that the only reason this story was so hot was because of his run for Governor. I was in the other room and I doubt they thought I could hear, but I'm pretty sure the whole neighborhood heard."

I know there's a 'poor little rich girl' vibe to this story, but it's not about me, it's about my uncle. "Then my uncle said he was quitting the race. Even at that age, I knew that would only make it worse. Sure, Eddie's secret daughter was big news, but the girl who undid a governor's campaign? Yeah, that would've sucked about a hundred times more.

"So, when my uncle went to leave, I told him he couldn't quit. He sat next to me on the couch, put his arm around me, and said he couldn't make things worse for me and that he'd run in another four years. We talked for a long time, and I finally convinced him to stay in the race. That night I realized he understood me better than anyone else in my life."

When my eyes meet Cyrus's, I can't read him. He knew some of this, but not the part with my uncle. I drop my gaze, take a deep breath, and continue. "He was willing to sacrifice a lot on my behalf. And I know that even if he's knee-deep in stuff he shouldn't be, if I go to him for help, he'll do whatever he can for me." I lift my head and glance at each of their faces, and can see I'm at least making them think.

Draya collapses onto the bench, her arms drooping like a beaten scarecrow, shaking her head in defeat. "I don't like it, but if you trust him that much, I'm willing to take a chance. But only because we're out of other options."

My life has come full circle as Cyrus and I sort through stacks of clothes and supplies piled on my bed. Not long ago, I was packing to leave home in search of a purpose for my life. Now I'm packing to go back with the purpose I was seeking — to save the world. There's some pressure for you.

I toss the same pair of socks I keep moving from pile to pile into the corner. "Cyrus?"

"Hmmm?"

"Are you scared?"

He stops and turns to face me, a canteen in one hand and a bottle of water in the other. "Some, but it's gonna be okay."

"What if it's not?"

He sets both items down and reaches out to pull me against his chest. "You're right, it might not, but sitting around doing nothing isn't really a plan."

I was hoping for reassurance, and he's giving me brutal honesty. He never bullshits me. That might be one of the biggest reasons I love him. I lean into him, letting his warmth comfort me. He smells so good I consider kissing the side of his neck and sliding my hands up his chest. I could use a distraction right now, a short escape from reality. But it's just that, a distraction, so instead I burrow my face into his shirt. "I'm not sure I can do this."

He puts his hands on my shoulders and gently pushes me back. "Hey." He lifts my chin, forcing my eyes to meet his. "Where's the feisty redhead who threw me out of my own room the first time she met me?"

A shaky laugh escapes my throat. "I don't know." I run my fingers through my now blond hair. "I think she's gone."

He presses his lips to my forehead. "As soon as you say you can't, you've already lost."

"I'm terrified of doing it all wrong and getting everyone killed. How can I live with myself if that happens?"

"I don't know, Ev, but the girl I had to hold back from running into an underground bunker is one I'll follow anywhere."

33

Doing It All Wrong

*T*he sun peeks over the horizon, striking the dew and making it sparkle. The crisp morning air holds the barest hint of the approaching end of summer.

Lucien resets a snare for another catch while Cyrus stuffs a rabbit in his bag. The two of them banter, sending warm ribbons of happiness through me. I've never had a relationship with my siblings like they have, and I'd be jealous if I didn't love them both so much. The early light glints off the golden highlights in Cyrus's hair as he says something to Lucien and they laugh.

Cyrus is in an exceptionally good mood. On the way out here, he said he planned something special for dinner tonight, just the two of us. The sexy smile that graced his lips with the invitation sent shivers racing across my skin.

"Hey, Evan," Lucien calls out to me, with a broad grin.

Cyrus shoots him a look.

"Yeah..."

"Cy says—"

Cyrus grabs his brother around the waist and the two go down, Lucien laughing.

A twig snaps behind me followed by a sharp metallic click. I turn and my breath catches. Hopp and Dantel are standing at the edge of the clearing, Hopp pointing a gun at Cyrus and Lucien.

"We'll take the girl," Hopp says.

Fear cuts straight through me like ice water flushing through my veins.

"There's no need for that." Lucien stands slowly, his voice steady. "We're taking her back ourselves. She'll be in the Union in a few days."

"That's not gonna work for us," Hopp says.

Dantel closes in on me and grabs my arm, pulling a large hunting knife out of his waistband. He buries his nose in my hair, inhaling. "I've always had a thing for blondes."

I try to jerk away as Cyrus takes a step toward us, but Hopp waves the gun at him, stopping Cyrus in his tracks.

"My wife needs surgery," Hopp says. "She gets the operation in exchange for returning the princess."

Dread coils inside me, and I make another attempt to get away from Dantel, but he yanks me closer, wrapping an arm around my waist. Revulsion scorches through me like acid.

"Tell us what Evan needs to do so your wife can get her surgery." Lucien says, freakishly calm.

"I'm not taking any chances," Hopp says. "I'll personally deliver her."

"Then let Cyrus go with you. We need to make sure she's safe and treated properly."

"Nah," Dantel says with a tone that makes my stomach heave. "The princess and I have some unfinished business."

He tightens his hold on me and leans in to kiss me. I curl my lips back and scrunch my nose. At my reaction, he grabs my hair, yanking my head back before jamming his tongue in my mouth.

I twist my head to break the kiss, but he only holds on tighter. My blood boils and anger rages through me. When he lets me go, I wipe my mouth with the back of my hand and spit at him. He lifts a hand to slap me, and in that split second, Lucien tackles Hopp as Cyrus covers the distance between us, throwing Dantel to the dirt.

"Evan, go," Cyrus yells.

I spin around to take off toward the house to get help, but halt mid-stride. The two of them are fighting for their lives. I turn back to see Cyrus dodging multiple knife strikes by Dantel, the last one only narrowly missing his side.

Cyrus twists and connects his elbow with Dantel's jaw. Dantel recovers and swings the knife at Cyrus again just as a loud grunt behind me tears my attention away. I swivel to see Hopp go down, doubled over, but still waving the gun at Lucien.

Fear paralyzes me as Lucien dodges the path of the muzzle and kicks Hopp's hand, knocking the gun to the side. They both dive for it, but Hopp is closer.

Lucien tackles Hopp, throwing him to the ground.

The two struggle before Hopp throws a punch that connects with Lucien's face, snapping me out of my stupor. I have to get the gun before Hopp does.

I only take two steps before Cyrus swears loudly before groaning. When I turn back to him, he's holding his right biceps, blood pouring out between his fingers.

"Evan get out of here," he yells again, but I refuse to abandon them.

Dantel takes advantage of Cyrus's weakened state and swings the knife. I suck in my breath as the blade just misses his neck.

My heart beats in my throat as the events unfold before me, feeling helpless to stop them, but I know I need to act now. A jolt of adrenaline propels me into action, and I make a move toward Dantel, hoping a surprise attack from behind will give Cyrus some momentum. He's younger and in better shape, but his injured arm evened things up.

A gunshot behind me stops me cold. I whirl around and see Lucien lying face down, Hopp next to him.

Horror coats my insides, and I hear someone screaming before realizing it's me. I launch myself at Lucien, my hands shaking as I flip him over. He's still breathing.

Hopp wraps his arm around my waist and lifts me up. "Dantel, let's get outta here."

My heartbeat pummels my ribcage, but I can't give up. I drive the heel of my boot into his shin, he swears, dropping me.

I crawl over to Lucien. A dark red stain spreads across his midsection. I lift the edge of his shirt and notice the gun wedged beneath him.

There's too much blood, I need to stop the bleeding. I turn back to Cyrus for help, but he's lying on the ground, not moving.

My heart trips in my chest as Dantel straddles Cyrus, bringing the knife up to plunge it into Cyrus.

Everything happens so fast, yet seems to unfold in slow motion. Without thinking, I grab the gun, warm and sticky with Lucien's blood, and point it at Dantel. My right hand shakes so much I have to support it with my left. I aim at Dantel and squeeze the trigger the way Cyrus taught me. The gun fires and recoils as two more shots follow in rapid succession. One of the bullets hits Dantel in the back and he falls forward onto Cyrus.

I rush to Cyrus, where he lies unmoving. He lets out a faint grunt and it's the sweetest thing I've ever heard. Relief ebbs out some of the terror and I lie back for a few seconds to catch my breath before hurrying back to Lucien. It's only now I realize Hopp is gone. My head swivels, looking for him, but he's nowhere.

Blood pools from Lucien's wound and I drop to my knees, frantically searching for a way to stop it. Huge waves of panic rise up and crash into me. I need help, this is so far beyond what I know how to deal with.

Cyrus throws Dantel's body off him and scrambles to get up.

"Go get Sonia," I yell to him.

He turns to me with grief-stricken eyes but doesn't move.

"Get Sonia," I scream as hysteria fills me, overflows, and spills on the ground around me.

Cyrus only stares at his feet as I yell at him over and over.

"What the hell is wrong with you? We need help!" A sob chokes me before escaping my throat.

He slowly approaches me, taking the gun from my trembling hand and dropping it to the ground. I stare at him trying to understand why he's not doing anything. When I turn back to Lucien, he's no longer breathing.

My own breaths come rapid and shallow, and I try to remember the CPR steps, the ABCs. A is for airway. I tilt his head back. Blood pours from his mouth.

I realize what Cyrus has known all along. It's too late.

Shouts behind us pull me from a blanket of darkness. I stand, wiping my bloody hands on my shorts, and move beside Cyrus, wrapping my arms around his waist. He drapes his good arm across my shoulder and I burrow into his chest, watching the others absorb the nightmare before them.

Draya halts, letting out a guttural, animalistic wail and crumples. Marcus catches her before she hits the ground and holds her as she screams.

Everyone processes the scene with varying levels of emotion, from screaming, to crying, to horrified silence. Ben drops Will's hand when he sees me and launches himself into my waiting arms.

Marcus releases Draya and she stumbles over to Lucien, dropping to her knees beside him, placing her hands on his chest. Her body wracks with silent sobs as grief overcomes her, and the remaining fragments of my already broken heart shatter completely for her.

Cyrus fills them in on what happened. When he's finished, Marcus turns and walks back toward the house. Draya stretches out beside Lucien, resting her head on his shoulder and hooks her leg over his. It looks as if they're sleeping except for the giant red stain on his shirt that continues to bloom.

Sonia, finally realizing Cyrus is hurt, comes over to check on him. "Take off your shirt, Cy." She tears it into strips and binds the wound to stop the bleeding. "I'll have to stitch this up when we get back to the house."

Marcus approaches with two wooden poles and a large blanket. He lifts Draya and guides her to Sonia, who pulls her in, wrapping her arms around her, holding her together.

Will and Marcus construct a makeshift stretcher by tri-folding the blanket over the poles. They place Lucien on top, Will taking the front and Marcus the back. I rush to take one of the poles from Will, and Ally takes one from Marcus. The four of us walk Lucien's body back to the house while the others.

The only sounds are intermittent sniffles and an occasional hiccup to accompany our footfalls as we make our somber journey. It's not a long walk, but the distance feels overwhelming.

34

Overwhelming

*W*e set the stretcher down behind the house, and Marcus heads off toward the barn. My knees buckle as I watch him go, realizing I'll never work next to Lucien in there again, never talk to him, hug him. *Lucien.*

Marcus returns with a shovel and begins digging. A grave. I hadn't even thought about the customs here for burying loved ones. In the Union, everyone is cremated.

Draya snaps out of her trance and the hatred she directs my way scrambles my insides. She closes the distance between us and slaps my face so hard my head jerks to the side. The sting radiates from my cheek into my jaw, bringing tears to my eyes. My mouth drops open and I stare at her.

"This is your fault." Her words drip with enough venom to stop my heart for a second. "I told Lucien you were trouble the minute we discovered you were a Uni." She turns her anger on Cyrus. "I warned you letting her stay was a mistake, and now your brother is dead. I hope she's worth it."

"Lucien loved you, Dray. More than anything," Cyrus says with a calm that is almost as frightening as Draya's anger. "But if you think he would have kicked Evan out or taken her back against her will, you didn't know him at all."

Regardless of what Cyrus says, Draya's right, this *is* my fault. If I hadn't been here, none of this would've happened. I should've gone home weeks ago.

"If she stays, I'm outta here." The coldness in her voice cuts me like knife blades, inflicting pain as sharp as the slap she just delivered.

"Draya..." Cyrus starts but doesn't finish.

Draya whirls around and stalks into the house.

"But I'm leaving, so she doesn't have to go." They just lost Lucien because of me they can't lose Draya, too.

Cyrus's eyes are fixed on Draya's receding form, but he doesn't answer.

Sonia approaches him. "I need to check your arm now."

I start to follow, but Sonia shakes her head. A few minutes later, I find out why. A steady stream of obscenities flows from the house as she cleans and stitches the gash in his biceps.

Ally walks toward us, from the direction of the creek, with an armload of wildflowers. Sonia and Cyrus return at the same time Marcus and Will finish digging the grave. Draya exits the house in fresh clothes, a bulging pack slung over her shoulder.

Ally hands each of us a single wildflower then offers the rest to Draya. The air is punctuated by a blend of freshly dug earth and wildflowers that is oddly fitting.

Draya bends down to place a soft kiss on Lucien's lips before setting the flowers on his chest. She stands, squaring her shoulders and walks off without a glance back.

Will and Marcus each grab a side of the blanket and lower Lucien into the ground. Cyrus stares down into the grave, watching the last remaining member of his family being lowered. I stifle a sob as Lucien's body disappears. Sonia wipes several tears before tossing her flower onto his body. The rest of us toss ours before taking turns shoveling dirt on top.

When we're finished, deafening silence engulfs me as a cold

emptiness rips through my heart, making it nearly impossible to breathe.

Pivoting, I walk away from the house. When I reach the creek, I break into a run, pushing faster and harder than I ever have. Even faster than when I was outrunning Dantel the night I escaped. It feels good to run — the sharp pain in my still healing ankle, the burning in my lungs, the earth pounding beneath my feet jarring my shins, every muscle straining — I relish it. It's good to feel something because when I finally stop, I feel nothing at all.

———

The atmosphere is thick, pressing down on me as clouds billow up for an afternoon storm. The air is heavier than in days past, as if the weather is aware of the horrible, unspeakable events of today.

I sit beside the creek, trying to push back against the all-consuming emptiness inside me while scrubbing my bloody hands with a rock until my skin is raw. It won't all come off, and Lucien's blood on my hands is a constant reminder of *everything*.

I don't know how to survive this. The others have sustained incredible losses before today and still managed to keep going. I wish I had their strength. The grows with an explosive sadness that both rips me apart and deadens me.

The first drops of rain spill from the sky, alerting me to how late it is. I push up and trudge back to the house, the oppressive air penetrating me and occupying the emptiness in my soul, weighing me down. The rain falls harder, and thunder rumbles in the distance.

Cyrus is pacing the edge of the property as I approach. His shoulders drop when he sees me, some of the tension in his body releasing. I didn't think he'd even notice I was gone with everything else on his mind.

I run the last few yards into his warmth. He wraps me in his arms, holding me tightly to him with his uninjured left arm. I press my head into his chest and inhale his scent, a mixture of soap, sweat, and rain. My fingers grab his shirt as I try to get closer to him, climb inside him, become a part of him.

Sweet relief fills me, edging out some of the ugliness. Things could have been even worse this morning, and I'm grateful he's still here with me. Maybe gratitude is what keeps people going after tragic loss — appreciating what they still have.

"I'm so sorry," I whisper, winding my arms around his torso and kissing the side of his neck, the taste of rain trailing down his skin coating my tongue.

He curls his fingers behind my neck and lifts my face. His thumb glides across my jaw as he brings his lips to mine, kissing me tenderly. The rawness and heartache are momentarily replaced by us and this moment.

He draws back. "We should go inside."

Taking my hand, he leads me into the house where a flurry of activity explodes around us. Packs stuffed to the brim are lined up next to the door.

Sonia turns when she hears us. "You two go put on dry clothes and grab rain gear. We need to leave."

My mind blanks for a moment. "Leave? Now?"

"They'll be back," Cyrus says. "We can't stay here."

"Where are we going?"

"North for now, and after that, we'll figure it out."

"But my friends...they'll come here. Dantel is dead. Hopp will tell them what happened. They won't come back now."

Something flickers in his eyes and I realize he's no longer coming with me. A new wave of grief rolls through me at the thought of losing him, too.

"Wait, just...wait." I need to think. When my friends get here, I can tell them what's going on and let them figure out a way to stop the attack. That way I can stay here. At least for now.

"This is about Hopp and his wife," Cyrus says. "He won't stop until he has you."

"How do you know that?"

"It's what I'd do."

From across the room, Marcus says, "Me too."

I shake my head. "There was no girl in that house, wife or otherwise."

"We don't have time to argue. We need to go," Cyrus says.

"No!" Panic pushes to the surface as too many things are spiraling out of my control. "Can't we talk about this?"

Cyrus turns to Sonia and thrusts a hand through his hair. "You talk to her. I'm going to take the cows up to the Grahams'." He heads downstairs and out the front door, leaving me to watch his retreating form.

I spin around to face Sonia, ready to fight her on this, but she merely sighs and says, "We're going. Come with us. Or don't. We're not staying, though. I won't risk anyone else." Then she turns and heads upstairs.

Her words hit me more forcefully than Draya's slap and everything slides into place. They also blame me for what happened, and they're leaving, with or without me.

Up in my room, I strip off my wet clothes covered in Lucien's blood, unsure what to do with them. Finally, I stuff them into a drawer and pack up my room. It's not much — the stack of books, my hair balm, a handful of outfits.

The numbness, prevalent over the past hour, gives way to a jittery tension pulsing across my skin. Does Cyrus blame me, too? I'm faced with returning to the Union without Cyrus, or staying here, knowing I'm the cause of all this heartache.

The sound of someone crying spills up the stairs, pulling me from my thoughts. I walk down the short flight to find Ty on his bunk, his body wracked with heaving sobs. As screwed up and confused as I am, the younger kids are even less equipped to cope with today's events.

Ty rolls over when he hears me approach, his big blue eyes brimming with tears. He wipes his nose with the back of his arm and sniffs. I sit down next to him, ducking my head under the top bunk and pulling him against me.

"Hey, buddy."

He burrows into me. "We can't leave," he whimpers. "What if Draya comes back? She won't know where we are."

"She's not coming back," Cyrus says. I startle and glance over my shoulder to see him standing outside the room, water dripping from his bright yellow rain gear, puddling on the rough-hewn wood floor. "The only thing keeping her here was Lucien."

Ty's cries become hysterical, and I pull him tighter to me. He gulps in deep breaths and lifts his head. "C-c-come with us, E-e-van. You c-can't go away, too."

My chest tightens. I glance at Cyrus, but his expression is indiscernible. Not knowing what he wants, I'm not sure how to answer Ty, so I say nothing.

"Y-you have to p-p-promise me."

He's demanding, not asking, and I realize this is about more than what Cyrus or I want. Other people need to be considered.

Despite the gut twisting pain it causes, I force myself to think about what Lucien would want me to do. He'd want me to do right by his family, by my family, even though they're not making it easy. You don't walk out on family just because everything turns to shit. I know that better than anyone. But I can't give Ty the answer he wants either, I have to be honest with him.

"I can't make that promise, Ty. What I *can* promise is that I'll stay with you for now. And when I do leave, I'll tell you before I go so we can talk about it first. Okay?"

He blinks, taking in another stuttering breath, and two large tears roll down his full cheeks. "Okay."

I peek at Cyrus to gauge his reaction. One eyebrow is arched in silent question. I nod and the barest hint of a smile tips up the corners of his mouth. It might not be the same as him telling me he wants me to stay, but on today of all days, it's enough.

*R*ain beats down on the roof creating a deafening barrage as I tie the hood of my yellow poncho over a baseball cap. Sonia paces the living room and urges us to hurry. When we're ready, she ushers everyone down the stairs and out the front door. The downpour pounds the earth, carving tiny rivers in the mud, carrying leaves and debris through the yard.

Our feet slosh in puddles and muck as we head north into the trees. Marcus and Sonia lead the way with me and Cyrus bringing up the rear, keeping the rest in between.

Cyrus reaches down to take my hand as we walk, threading his fingers with mine. I still don't know how he feels about my role in his brother's death, but this small gesture is a much-needed reassurance.

The creek resembles a raging river, and the level has nearly reached the bottom of a weathered footbridge. Wooden planks are thatched together with fraying ropes, and more ropes at the four corners anchor the bridge to trees on either side.

Marcus takes a tentative step, and when it holds without complaint, he takes a few more, grabbing the side rope handrails.

Sonia follows Marcus across then the kids go, one by one. They continue on, disappearing into the foliage.

Cyrus turns to me. "Go, I'll be right behind you."

The wood creaks under my foot and sinks lower, the water rushing beneath the lowest slats in the center. I grab the rough side ropes and work my way across, shifting my hands as I go. When I hit the muddy bank on the other side, I wait for Cyrus, holding my breath as he crosses. It feels like forever before he finally joins me, and I let out an audible sigh.

As we turn to join up with the others, I hear voices over my shoulder and pause. In this bright yellow rain gear, we'll be easy to spot. I reach for the rifle strapped to my back when the ropes catch my eye. No one will be able to follow us if I sever them. The turbulent creek is impassible without the bridge.

Pulling out my knife, I kneel at the water's edge and start to make the first cut. Someone calls my name and I freeze. Shock and fear curl through me, turning my insides cold. Another voice joins the fray and then another.

"Evan?"

I lift my gaze to meet Lisa's across the creek.

Relief colors her features with recognition. "She's here!" she yells over her shoulder.

Colin, Bryce, and Jack appear through the trees, joining her.

Cyrus takes my hand and pulls me up and around to face him, his golden eyes dark and serious. "You have to go with them."

My heart trips in my chest. "No," I whisper.

"You have to, Ev. You can do this."

"No, I can't, not without you."

He presses his palm against my cheek, searching my eyes. "You can."

I start to object, but he puts his finger to my mouth, quieting me. He slides it down and traces my bottom lip, his eyes shifting lower as an incredible sadness settles into them. "You're the *only* one who can, because you're the only one who cares enough about both the Union and the Ruins."

Even if he's right, that doesn't mean I have to go. I can tell Lisa and Colin what's happening and they can figure out what to do. Rising fear pulls at my thoughts and I can't think beyond what he's asking — for me to leave him.

He places his hands on my shoulders, holding me back when all I want to do is burrow into his chest and cling to him. "This is what you're meant to do."

"Come with me, then," I plead.

He closes his eyes and swallows hard. "I wish I could."

"No, no, no..." My voice gives way to a hoarse croak on the last one.

He folds me into his arms and kisses me, softly at first before deepening it. I don't know this kiss, there's too much emotion, then it hits me — he's kissing me goodbye. A lump builds in my throat, strangling my breath. I press closer to him, grabbing the front of his jacket so he won't let me go.

But he does.

He comes up for air and murmurs my name against my lips before tucking my head under his chin. His voice is barely above a choked whisper. "I love you, Ev, and I believe in you. Believe in yourself." He releases me roughly and starts to walk away.

"Cyrus..." I call after him, my throat clogged with tears. He stops and turns back to me. I want to tell him I love him and I can't imagine my life without him, but the words won't come. As if saying them will somehow mean goodbye and I can't accept this is the end. Instead I ask, "How will I find you?"

A shadow crosses his features, and he opens his mouth to say something before shaking his head. My heart stops as he turns and disappears into the thicket, tearing my soul into a million tiny pieces.

I watch the spot where I last saw him long after he's gone. Every part of me aches to run after him, and yet I don't. Maybe because deep down, I know he's right.

I gradually become aware Lisa and Colin are calling me and pull my gaze away from the trees. In the short time since Cyrus walked out of my life, the water has risen even higher, cresting the middle of the bridge. If I'm going back, it has to be now. I take a cleansing breath and start across.

When I reach the halfway point, a rope behind me breaks free, making the bridge lurch and my feet slip out from under me. I grasp the ropes tighter as the violent creek threatens to drag me in. The rough handholds dig into my palms as I grip them even tighter and haul myself forward.

My heart beats a staccato rhythm while the free corner twists at my back like a crazed animal. A slat pulls away beneath my foot and goes careening off with the current. Lisa and Colin yell at me to hang on, but I'm already holding so tightly my fingers tingle with loss of feeling.

"Evan, take off the backpack," Jack yells. "It's weighing you down."

I can't. I lost everyone I care for in the Ruins. All that's left of my life out here is inside the backpack.

The other corner behind me pulls free, whipping my body. I scream and gulp in a ragged breath, hanging on with all my strength, my muscles quivering with the strain. What's left of the bridge is only connected by the two ropes in front of me and twists violently with the rushing water.

The powerful current drags me beneath the surface. My lungs burn with the need for oxygen as I struggle to get oriented. Panic rolls through me like a dark wave, and I flail, searching for something to grab onto.

My hand brushes a rope, and I grip it with both hands, pulling myself up, coughing out a mouthful of water.

Bryce kneels on the edge of the bank and reaches out his hand to me, I stretch, but he's too far. The rushing water pulls me under again, and I wrap my legs around the rope, squeezing my ankles together.

My energy is drained from the effort and I resign myself to dumping the backpack. I wiggle my left arm out of the strap. The raging creek grabs the pack, nearly taking me too.

I free my other hand and release the pack. The moment I do, I'm lighter, and scramble up the next two slats before my boot slips and catches on something. I try to jerk my foot loose, but it's stuck.

The force of the rushing creek prevents me from getting a grasp on whatever I'm tangled in. As I struggle to free myself, the water level continues to rise along with my level of hysteria. I don't want to die this way.

Swallowing back some of the panic, I regain a small amount of control over my fear and yell to Bryce, "My boot is caught on something."

Using my other foot, I attempt to pry it off, but the fit is too snug. The only way out of this is to untie my laces. I inch my hands down the ropes, hanging on with one arm and reaching for my laces with the other.

Ducking under water, I fumble with the double-knotted shoelace, unable to loosen it. When my lungs are about to burst, I surface and gulp in air. Shaking my head at Bryce, I take a deep breath and dive down to try again.

The next time I come up, Bryce is tying a rope around his waist. Jack wraps a length around his forearms and gives the end to Colin. Bryce jams a knife into his waistband and jumps in. He dives down and gets to work cutting my shoestring.

On the shore, Jack and Colin struggle to hold the rope. If they drop it, Bryce will be washed away. I silently beg him to hurry. Finally, my boot loosens.

Bryce comes up, grabbing on to the bridge. "Go!" he shouts.

I grab the closest slat with my left arm and the rope with my right, pushing my boot off with my other foot, and pull myself up one slat at a time.

Bryce calls up to Jack and Colin, "I'm fine, grab Evan."

Jack leans down, reaching for me. I stretch, my fingers only inches from his. A slat breaks off under my foot and a scream tears from my throat before I slip under, water filling my mouth. Murky water that is impossible to see through impedes my ability to see the rope. My hands thrash until they make contact. I thrust my head to the surface, gulping in air and coughing out water.

My muscles burn as I climb, inching closer to Jack. I let go, reaching for him. He grabs me below my wrist and hauls me up. My feet scramble, knocking the top two slats loose, sending them downstream.

Safely ashore, I turn, searching for Bryce. I find him barely hanging on to what's left of the bridge.

"Grab the end," I yell.

Jack reaches for it, but Bryce slips under, taking the length of the rope with him before Jack can get a hand on it. The little air remaining in my lungs exits in a wheeze. I stare at the spot where he vanished, seconds feeling like hours, pass before he reappears, panting.

Another slat rips away and Bryce disappears beneath the water again. Oh *hell* no, he is not going to die trying to rescue me. I have plans to be royally pissed at him for the rest of my life, and he is not going to ruin this for me.

I tie another rope around my waist and yell over the roar of the raging creek. "I'm going back in. Hang on to that end."

Jack, Lisa, and Colin voice their objections, but I move closer to the edge before they can stop me. They grasp the rope winding it around themselves as I climb down what's left of the bridge. Somehow the current is even stronger than it was mere moments ago.

My heart pounds a violent beat, and my eyes dart frantically, searching for Bryce. He bursts to the surface, choking and clinging to the remains of the footbridge, exhaustion etched into his features.

I inch my way over to him, operating on pure adrenaline. "Grab onto me," I yell. He wraps his arms around me and I twist until I get the rope wound around both of us. "Okay, pull," I call up to the others.

Bryce and I cling to each other as we're hoisted up, gripping the roots when we reach the bank to keep from slipping back in, until we're pulled over the side to solid ground.

We sit on the shore, muddy, soaked, and out of breath. When I meet Bryce's gaze, relief mixed with regret are threaded through his gray eyes.

"Thank you," I say to him then look up at the others. "You all risked a lot to come find me."

Lisa smiles and bends down, wrapping her arms around my shoulders and squeezing. When she releases me, Colin reaches a hand down to pull me up and bear hugs me until I can't breathe.

36

Trust

I blindly follow the others back to the house, incapable of thinking for myself. Lisa bombards me with questions but I shake them off, in no mood to answer. I'm too busy fighting the desire to run after Cyrus.

Colin chats with Bryce as if everything is just fine. I grab Lisa's arm and pull her back so we're separated from everyone else. "Lis, what's up with Bryce and Jack?"

"What do you mean?"

"I mean, why are you with *them*? What are you doing out here?"

She opens her mouth to say something but the back of the house comes into view. My eyes lock on Lucien's fresh grave and my legs give out. I stumble before Lisa reaches out to catch me.

"Are you okay?" she asks.

No, and I'll never be okay again, but I mumble, "Yeah."

A dark blue pickup truck, similar to ones that run around on the ground level of the Union, is parked in front of the house.

I halt, scanning the area for any sign of Walker or Hopp.

"What's wrong?" Bryce asks.

"Is this your truck? We need to get out of here, like now, before your friends come back."

He furrows his brow and parts his lips, like he's going to say something, but only shakes his head.

"No, it's not your truck?"

Jack moves to the cab and climbs behind the wheel, essentially answering my question. Bryce holds the passenger door open for me, but there's no way I'm sitting up front with either of them. I hoist myself into the back. Lisa glances at the front, but ends up climbing in next to me followed by Colin, leaving Bryce to sit with Jack.

I crawl to the cab and lean back, stretching my legs out in front of me, Lisa and Colin on either side of me like human bookends. I close my eyes as the truck pulls away from the house, bouncing across the mud and rocks. We move further from what has been my home for...I don't know how long.

"What's the date?" I ask.

Lisa pauses, counting on her fingers.

"It's August 30, I think," Colin says.

I've only been here a few months, but I'm having a hard time remembering my life in the Union. This is home now. Or it was. I'm not sure where I belong anymore.

"Who were those people you were with?" Lisa asks.

"They saved me." In more ways than one. I'm not comfortable revealing anything else until I have a better grip on what the hell is going on. I want to ask how much they know about Walker and my kidnapping, but I'm too drained to even open my mouth. Bone aching weariness settles over me, and I give into it, nodding off.

A dramatic change in speed drags me from a dreamless sleep. I open my eyes and wait for the fog to clear. The air is warm and dry — enough that Lisa and Colin are no longer even damp.

We pull to a stop at the Union's back wall. Jack and Bryce get out as Lisa, Colin, and I jump down from the back. A man approaches Jack, his dark hair overflowing beneath a red baseball cap, hands stuffed into the front pockets of his jeans.

"Throw your rain gear in the back," Jack says to me.

I take off my remaining boot and both socks, tossing them into the truck bed before doing the same with the pants. Finally, I flip back my hood.

Lisa gasps. "Evan! Your hair..." I toss the jacket and ball cap and run my hand through my still damp hair.

"Damn. You're hot as a blonde." Colin gives me a crooked smile.

Jack exchanges a few words with the man before the guy climbs into the cab and drives off. Jack walks up to the Union wall, running his hands along the surface and pulls something. I stare in amazement as a door seems to magically appear.

Unlike the dark narrow corridors I was taken through on my way out, these are clean and well lit. We head down a long hallway, my friends' boots clopping on the concrete floor in contrast to the slap of my bare feet. Jack leads us to a service elevator, motioning for us to climb in before pushing the button for the ninety-fifth floor.

We exit into a corridor that leads to a crowded sidewalk alive with nighttime activity. The glaring lights, shrill noises, and deep thump of the bass set my teeth on edge. Bryce places himself between me and the busy evening activities, careful not to touch me, as he guides me to a door a couple of buildings down.

We enter a hotel lobby where Lisa leads the way to another elevator and up three more floors. Lack of food, overwhelming emotions, and too many things to process all occupy a space inside me, duking it out for the top spot.

Lisa tugs me down the hall and opens a door on the left. "See you in the morning," she calls out before pulling me in and closing the door behind us.

Chaos gives way to numbness as I take in my surroundings. The room is large with dark wood flooring and a wall of nothing but windows. Two king-sized beds with crisp white sheets and soft mustard-colored blankets occupy the bulk of the space. My bag from the train sits on the one closest to the windows.

When I turn to Lisa, she's smiling, her apple cheeks glowing. "How..." I start.

"It's a long story, but once we figured out you'd been taken into the Ruins, Colin grabbed our stuff. We ended up in the Southwestern Province and checked into this hotel. We've been living out of here when we're not in the Ruins."

"Wow." The bed sinks beneath me, soft and decadent. "I said it before, Lis, but thanks."

Her eyes glisten as she steps toward me, wrapping her arms around my shoulders. "You've lost weight. I feel like I'm going to break you."

"I'm okay."

She releases me. "I didn't think you were going to come back with us."

"I wasn't sure I was going to either." I get up and walk over to the windows where the bright craziness of Union nightlife glows three floors below.

"That guy you were with..."

"Cyrus."

"Did you love him?"

I turn to face her. "I do." The ease with which I can express my feelings about him with Lisa contrasts with my inability to tell him how I felt. The hollowness returns, building momentum. I can't talk about Cyrus now, so I change the subject. "So, you and Jack, eh?"

She smiles at the floor. "Yeah."

"How did that happen?"

"After you went missing, he told us that he and Bryce are undercover detectives." Time stops and my eyes freeze open. "Did you know that? No, I guess you couldn't. Anyway, that's how Colin got into your room to get your stuff. Bryce just flashed his credentials and they opened the door for us."

"Wait, back up a sec." The words bounce around inside my head like a rubber ball, but they don't make any sense.

Lisa lets out a soft laugh, but her voice is laced with awe. "Yeah. I was shocked, too. They're investigating smuggling or something. They can tell you more. But anyway, he just took charge of the situation, and it was kinda hot."

I shake my head, trying to get the pieces to tumble into the right boxes. This is the exact opposite of what I thought I'd so cleverly deduced. How can they be detectives? I was in school with Bryce mere months ago.

"I...I need to clean up," I mumble, grabbing my pajamas out of my bag and heading into the bathroom to take my first decent shower in forever. Setting the water temp to a perfect 105 degrees, I step into the stall and let the heat and steam envelope me as my mind goes blank. I stand for a few minutes after turning off the water, enjoying the sensation of the warm drops trickling down my skin before drying off.

When I catch my reflection in the mirror, I almost don't recognize myself and it's not just my hair. My face is thinner, all the baby fat I used to hate is gone, but it's my eyes that are the most different. Besides the deep shadows beneath them, they're tight, bold... stricken. No amount of makeup can cover up what's in my eyes.

Lisa's in bed reading when I re-enter the room. I climb into the other bed and lay on my back. It's like sleeping on a cloud compared to my recent accommodations. A sudden stab of guilt pierces my core thinking about my friends sleeping on the hard ground. I get out of bed and lie on the floor but I do take the pillow and a blanket with me. I'm not a complete martyr.

"What are you doing?" Lisa asks.

"The bed's too soft." I meet her gaze. "I know we need to talk, but I can't, not right now."

I close my eyes and somehow manage to sleep. Not a restful, regenerative sleep, but a fitful one, overflowing with disturbing images of pain, death, and unbearable loss.

37

Disturbing Images

*T*he sun angles through the window, stretching across the floor when I wake. Lisa's not in her bed, nor in the bathroom.

"Lis..." I call out, but get no response.

Getting up, I toss my blanket and pillow on the bed and get ready. I dig around in my bag for something to wear, and my hand brushes my tablet. I pull it out to several text messages from my mom. I sigh and lean against the counter. What am I going to say to her? The unvarnished truth will only land me on the next train home, not to mention the shitstorm that'll follow if I tell her everything I learned in the Ruins. This particular drama is going to need to wait.

I get dressed in a pair of shorts and T-shirt and grab my flip-flops, the footwear that used to be a staple in my wardrobe. They're yet another reminder of the stark contrast between my two lives.

The door opens and Lisa waltzes in with a paper bag and a steaming cup of...oh my god, is that coffee?

"Good, you're up." Lisa says, handing me the bag and cup. "It's your favorite — cappuccino with a drizzle of caramel."

"I think I love you," I say, taking the coffee from her and inhaling the aroma, letting it wrap around my brain. Inside the bag are a blueberry muffin and a banana. My shorts slip down to my hips when I move. "Hey, Lis, can I borrow a belt?"

She rummages in her duffle and tosses me a brown leather belt. I thread it through the loops and tighten it as Lisa's brow furrows, but when her eyes lock onto my biceps with their new definition, she keeps whatever she's thinking to herself.

I take a sip of my drink, savoring the creamy rich goodness before turning to stare at my tablet, contemplating my next move.

"What's wrong?" Lisa asks.

"My mom. She texted me. I'm not sure what to tell her."

"She just wants an update on your latest adventure. When we went into the Ruins this last time, I told her we were going sailing. I've been texting her as you every week since you...disappeared. Oh, and she's been bugging me, er you, to call, so you should call her. Soon."

Warmth fills the space that had been occupied by cold dread and I smile. "I don't know what to say... I keep saying that, but it's true."

She shrugs. "I always knew we'd find you and I didn't want her to worry."

While Lisa takes a shower, I pick eat my banana, trying to determine my next move. A knock interrupts my thoughts, and I set down the muffin to open the door.

Bryce stands on the other side, hands shoved into the front pockets of his jeans, rocking back on his heels. "Hey, Evansville."

I cringe at the nickname, no longer finding it cute. "Hey."

"Are you hungry? Do you want to get breakfast?"

"Um, no. Lisa brought something for me."

"Oh." He glances past me and shifts his feet. "I thought maybe we could talk. With Jack and me, I mean. Would you mind?"

Wow, he's not wasting any time. "Do I have a choice, *detective*?"

His head snaps back and his mouth drops open. "Of course, you do."

Might as well get it over with. "Fine." I grab my coffee and follow him down the hall to a room on the right. He presses his finger to the scanner and opens the door for me.

Jack sits at a table studying something on his tablet. He glances up and smiles, indicating the chair across from him.

I take a seat, Bryce dropping into the chair on my right.

"How are you this morning?" Jack asks.

"Okay, I guess." No doubt they have a fair number of questions, but I want to get my mine out of the way first. "So, Lisa tells me you two are detectives." I turn to Bryce. "Was anything you told me true?"

He rolls in his bottom lip and glances at Jack, but doesn't answer.

Jack shifts in his chair, as if he's about as comfortable with this as I am, and folds his hands on the desk. "Can you tell us what happened?"

Something about this whole scene is a little too much like those cop dramas my mom loves so much. These people are supposed to be my friends, not giving me the third degree. "Is this an interrogation?"

"No," Jack says. "We're just trying to piece together what happened."

I narrow my eyes. "If you want to hear what happened to me, start by telling me what you know. Then I'll decide if I can trust you. Because right now? I wouldn't trust either one of you to watch my coffee."

Bryce's eyes blaze with sudden anger. "The last time I saw you, I told you I loved you. The next time I see you, you're kissing some other guy."

A burning sensation claws up my chest. "Oh, no you don't. You do *not* get to be the injured party. I was kidnapped, nearly raped, and would've died if it wasn't for that *other guy*. All you ever did was lie to me."

Bryce's shoulders slump and he lets out a long breath before lifting his head to look at me. "I'm sorry, Evan. More sorry than you'll ever know."

It's a little too little, way too late. "Up until last night when Lisa clued me in, I believed you were smugglers in a territory dispute, and I was caught in the middle."

He lifts his brows. "A smuggler?"

"What was I supposed to think? You lied to me about your name..." I shrug. "I figured everything else was bullshit, too."

He sits back hard against the chair, his head falling forward before he and Jack do that whole silent communication thing again, and Jack leaves the room.

I walk over to the window and stare at the horizon, trying not to think about my friends in the Ruins, but I can't stop myself. The ache deep inside me would dull some in Cyrus's arms. I blink back tears knowing that will never happen again, so dwelling on it will only prolong the heartache.

My gaze drifts closer, to the Union's neat rows of buildings, manicured patches of grass, perfectly sculpted potted plants. It's hard not to compare it to the Ruins. The Union is so clean, so orderly, so...unnatural.

Jack returns a few minutes later with Lisa and Colin.

Colin throws me a crooked grin. "Hey, EvTay, how're you doing?"

I give him a small smile in return, realizing how much I've missed my friends. "Hanging in there."

Bryce takes a deep breath and begins a long and winding tale filled with characters, drama, and intrigue even more fantastic than the story I made up in my mind.

38

Drama and Intrigue

"I grew up in the Western Province," Bryce starts. "The youngest in of four and the only boy. My mom's an artist, my dad a detective, or at least he was up until five years ago." He pauses, taking a deep breath. "Before he disappeared, he'd be gone for long stretches at a time, and when he was home, he was edgy. The last time, he just never came back. Weeks turned into months, and months into years."

He moves to the window and stands with his back to it, hands stuffed into his front pockets. "I wanted to be a writer for as long as I can remember. I was accepted at the Hemingway writing community in the Northwestern Province, but shortly before the end of my last year of school, two agents approached me, trying to recruit me. They knew about my plans, but kept at me, telling me I could help find out what happened to my dad."

The way his shoulders hunch and the vacant expression in his eyes makes him appear vulnerable, and some of the white hot anger I've been holding onto begins to cool. He's not a smuggler and I doubt he meant for any of this to happen.

"I wasn't sold, but they brought Jack in to close the deal. Our dad's had been partners and we'd been friends for years. Between that and a duty to my family to find the truth, I caved."

"What happened to Jack's dad?" I ask.

"He's our captain."

"Wait, what? You work for Jack's dad? What does he know about me?"

"Right now, nothing. But we don't report directly to the captain. We told our lieutenant we're following up on some leads, leaving out the details."

"Does anyone know I've been missing all this time?"

Bryce shakes his head. "No. Not through us, anyway."

I let out a small sigh of relief that the secret of the Ruins is safe for now. "Why were you posing as a student at our school?"

He blows air into one cheek and lets it back out. "After my internship ended, we were sent undercover to investigate a mayor in the Eastern Province."

"Alivia's dad." I say.

"Right. They thought it'd be easiest to get in with his teenage daughter."

"How old are you, anyway? I mean, you look like you're our age."

He scratches the back of his neck. "I'm only a couple of years older. I graduated two years ago, did my internship, and started undercover shortly after."

"So, Alivia was part of your cover?"

"Not exactly. I needed access to the apartment, and my relationship with her allowed me to do that."

"How do I fit into all this?"

He blows out a long, slow breath. "You weren't a part of any of this. I..."

"He shouldn't have gotten involved with you," Jack says. "We were under cover. Totally against every regulation."

So now I know what Jack's issue was. I turn back to Bryce. "Then, why did you?"

"Because I'm weak. I was intrigued by you the moment we

met, but Alivia was my assignment. Later, when I saw you on the train...I just...I don't know. I'm sorry." He drops his head into his hands. "Everything is my fault."

"So who were those guys who took me, then? Were you investigating them?"

Jack nods. "Yeah. While Bryce was keeping an eye on Benton, I was looking into weapons coming across the border into the Northeastern Province. We thought they were separate investigations, but we kept running into the same players. We're still not sure where the weapons are going, but they're using the Union's trains to move them. The L-Trains aren't as heavily scrutinized for cargo, so they thought no one would notice. That helped us because they got sloppy."

"A guy by the name of Walker's at the center of everything," Bryce says. "Benton is into all kinds of stuff, but it doesn't seem to be linked to the weapons smuggling, and that became more urgent, so they pulled me out and reassigned us to monitor the trains. We thought we had an iron-clad cover." He shakes his head. "I don't know how it got blown. But once Walker found out, he used you as leverage to get us to back off our investigation."

"The day you were taken, we were staking out a warehouse when we got a text," Jack says. "We'd thought it was the IT guys getting back to us with a hit on a facial recognition search we asked them to run. But it was a picture of you. Tied up and blindfolded."

The blood in my veins chills. Even though the events are in my past, hearing about them, knowing they took pictures of me, makes my skin feel as too tight for my body.

"When you didn't come back from the bathroom, I went looking for you." Lisa says. "Your flip-flop was just lying on the ground." She pauses and twists her hands. "I asked the waiter if he'd seen you, and he checked with the rest of the staff, but no one knew where you were. Colin went back to the train while I waited at the restaurant for you." Her voice drops. "None of it made any sense."

"After we got the text, Bryce took off, and I ran after him."

"I returned to the train." Bryce says, voice monotone. "To prove to myself the picture was fake, make sure you were okay. Then we could figure out who sent it and why."

"After an hour, I gave up and went back, too." Lisa stares at her coffee cup, folding down the corner of the paper sleeve. "When you weren't there either, I started to panic, but then I thought you must have run into Bryce or something and went off with him. I was so mad you left without telling us, but then Bryce came flying down the hall with Jack and not you..."

"She attacked me," Bryce says.

Lisa lets out a soft sigh. "I kinda went nuts. He was my last hope you were safe... So, we told them everything."

"While Lisa and Colin were filling us in, we got another text," Jack says. "This one said, 'We've got the girl. You want her alive, back off your investigation. Bring in anyone else and you'll get her back one piece at a time.'"

"They wouldn't tell us what the text said, though." Colin says. "But we knew it was bad, 'cause Bryce was freaking out. Lisa ran to her room to call the police."

"I went after her," Bryce says. "No way could I let her make that call."

"It took us a while to convince her that we *are* the police," Jack says. "We showed her our credentials, explained our investigation, and finally had to show her the text to get her to believe us."

Lisa picks up the pieces of her coffee sleeve and drops them into the trash. "It was like straight out of a movie or something."

"The whole time Jack was talking to Lis, Bryce totally flipping out," Colin says. "Kept mumbling shit and yanking on his hair."

"Then what?" I ask, glancing between Bryce and Jack. "Why drag Lisa and Colin out to the Ruins with you?"

"We figured they were probably already in danger and would be safer with us," Jack says.

I stare at Lisa and Colin, wondering how they just went along with all of this.

"It sounds a lot smoother now," Lisa says, as if reading my mind. "At the time, there was lots of yelling and I punched Bryce a few times."

"She wanted to call your parents and your uncle," Bryce says. "I finally convinced her that could put you in even more danger. Until Jack and I knew more, we needed to keep everyone else out of it."

"They always seemed to be one step of ahead of us." Jack stands and cracks his neck. "I was worried they were wired in somehow, monitoring our communications. Our best chance of getting you back alive was finding you ourselves."

"The clues kept leading to the Ruins," Colin says.

"We tracked video feed of your kidnapping and saw where they took you off the cargo train." Bryce says. "When we couldn't locate you in the Union, we suspected you might be in the Ruins."

"We were really scared," Lisa says. "I mean, everyone knows it's not safe out there."

Jack nods. "I'll admit, it was an obstacle we weren't sure how to overcome at first."

"How'd you figure out it wasn't toxic?"

"I met up with a buddy of mine to get some protective gear and he clued us in. Said he'd done some investigating out there and figured it out."

"And you just bought this? Because honestly, I thought I was going to die at any minute once they dragged me out there."

"It's not like he was going to send us out there if it was danger-ous. Plus, he had pictures of plants growing out there and animals."

"He geared us up with camping stuff, the truck, and showed us how to get out there," Colin says.

"Took us awhile to get a lead on you," Jack says. "Once we did, the place was already deserted."

"It was like slamming into a solid wall," Lisa says. "We'd been so close and suddenly you were farther away than ever."

"It was obvious they cleared out in a hurry, so we figured they couldn't have gone far," Bryce says. "Because if not, I was afraid we'd never find you."

"I have no idea how long they stayed in that house after I left, but I escaped the first night."

Lisa's mouth drops open. "You what?"

"I have a lot to tell you." After everything they risked to find me, I guess I need to trust them with the lives of my Ruins friends. I don't really have any a choice. Taking a seat on the bed, I launch into my story, only leaving out the extent of my relationship with Cyrus and the fact that I was about to fake my death.

As I relive the last few months of my life, things start to fall into place. "I think I know where the weapons are going." I describe the wicked looking guns I saw on the guys near the power station. "Maybe the solution to stopping the attack is nothing more than stopping the flow of weapons."

Bryce glances up from the floor and fixes his gaze on me. "Nothing is ever that simple."

39

Nothing Simple

*a*fter lunch, we climb the stairs to the gleaming white A-Train and grab seats in the second car. While not nearly as luxurious as the L-Train, it's a lot faster. Lisa and Jack snuggle together on one side of the aisle leaving the rest of us to sit on the other with me sandwiched between Colin and Bryce.

I decided to continue on to the Western Province instead of heading back east. Going home feels like giving up, and I can't do that. Lisa's internship starts next week and Colin needs to be in the Northwestern Province in two weeks, so everything is moving along as if nothing happened.

My mind drifts as I lay my head back against the seat. I called home and my parents were happy to hear we had fun on our adventure. I sent my mom pictures of my hair, which she claims to love, but says she likes the red better. I can't decide whether to stay blond. Red hair is an oddity in the Union. Something like three percent of the population of the former United States had red hair, but in the post-war Union, less than one percent of us are gingers. I never liked my hair color, it was always another thing that made me different.

My friends agreed to keep quiet about the Ruins and what I overheard about an attack on the Union. We're going to work together to figure something out. Hopefully four heads are better than one, because right now, I've got squat.

The trip to the Western Province only takes a few hours, but it feels more like days as the minutes crawl by. I'm cramped and confined on the train after spending so much time outdoors. When we finally approach the station, the Union sprawls out below us like colorful steps inching their way to the coast twenty-five miles west. For the first time in my life I see the Pacific Ocean, sparkling in the distance beneath a vivid blue sky.

The Western Province is so different from where I grew up in the east. Here, pastel stucco terraced buildings are adorned with radiant flowers.

We wait our turn to disembark then take the stairs down to the terminal, overflowing with passengers crisscrossing the tracks like scurrying ants. We walk the two blocks to catch a commuter train, Lisa, Colin, and Jack heading north to Lisa's new place.

Bryce and I follow them to the platform to say goodbye, and I pull Colin aside. "Are you sure you want to do this? Stay at Lisa's I mean? Won't it be awkward with her and Jack?"

He shakes his head, dark, shaggy hair falling into his eyes. "I never said anything to her. I'm heading north soon anyway, so this is better."

"I love you, Col." I kiss his cheek.

He presses his lips to the side of my head. "I love you too, EvTay."

Lisa walks over and clutches me to her, shedding a few tears before saying good-bye with promises of talking tomorrow. After watching them go, I grab my bag and check the map on my tablet to find the quickest way to Eddie's.

"Hey, can I walk you to your dad– er, Eddie's? I'd feel better knowing you got there."

I shrug. "Sure."

He takes my bag and slings it over his shoulder. We walk in

silence for the first few blocks, passing lively shops with eager customers before turning down an alley and up two flights to the top level. I can still hear the muted activity from down below, but the atmosphere here is quieter, as if we've entered a bubble of tranquility.

Bryce takes advantage of the lower noise level. "I'll probably say this every day for the rest of my life, but Evan, I'm really sorry about what happened to you."

"I know."

"We'll figure this out, I promise. I don't know how yet, but we will."

I nod. "Thanks, Bryce. That means a lot."

We make another turn and the level opens onto a broad expanse dotted with flowering plants, grass, and palm trees on one side and large, expensive sun-washed stucco and glass apartments on the other. Beyond the gardens is a breathtaking view of the sprawling Union.

I check the address again and locate the right apartment. A stone walkway winds from the sidewalk to the front door, lined with tall, spikey grass sprouting colorful flowers in orange, yellow and fuchsia, interspersed with low-growing plants covered in tiny white flowers. A redwood trellis over the porch, covered with pink bougainvillea is a colorful splash against the stark white building.

The arched door is a wooden behemoth with tall, narrow windows on either side. I take a shaky breath and reach out to press the doorbell. After a few seconds, the lock unlatches and the lever moves down, but nothing more happens at first. The lever moves again and the door cracks before finally opening. On the other side is a tiny princess, wearing a fluffy pink tutu and silver tiara. Pale blue eyes shine out from a porcelain face framed by bouncing red curls.

She narrows her eyes. "Who you?"

I squat down to her level. "You must be Quinn. I'm your sister, Evan."

She crosses her arms and shakes her head, whipping her curls across her face. "No. Eban has wed hair like me. You hab white hair."

I run my hand through my hair. "Oh, yeah. Well, it's usually red. I colored it."

Her eyes widen. "Why?"

"Oh, just for fun, I guess."

"I don't like it." She twirls around and skips into the other room, her tutu flouncing up and down as she goes.

Bryce chuckles behind me.

I turn to look at him. "What?"

"I think you've finally met your match." When I stand, he reaches out to touch my arm. I glance at his hand and he drops it to his side. "I'll call you tomorrow so we can figure out a time to get together and talk about...everything...before Colin leaves."

"Okay."

He gives me a small smile. "See you tomorrow, Evansville." He turns and disappears down the path.

Eddie approaches the entryway with Quinn and a blond curly-haired boy of about five. He stares at me with eyes the same mix of green and brown hazel as my own.

Deep worry lines on Eddie's face ease with each step in my direction. For the first time, I don't see my estranged father — the selfish rock star who traded his daughter for fame and fortune. Instead, I see a worried parent who's relieved his child arrived safely, albeit months after she said she would.

I let go of some of the anger and resentment. My time in the Ruins taught me the importance of family, even a flawed one. When Eddie wraps me in his arms, I don't stiffen the way I normally would, but allow him to hold me, even if I don't return the embrace. I'm willing to let go of *some* of my anger, but I'll keep plenty in reserve for future use. You never know when a heavy dose of parental guilt will come in handy.

"I'm so glad you're here, Evan." He steps back and eyes me at arms' length. My father's wavy cinnamon-colored hair reaches his shoulders now. He pulls me in for another hug, but doesn't ask where I've been. Maybe he believes the texts Lisa sent about us going sailing, or perhaps he doesn't think he has the right to ask after being absent most of my life.

When he releases me, my little brother peeks out from behind his father.

"Hello, you must be Liam."

He blinks at me a few times. "Wanna see my new boxcar?"

"Uh, sure."

I step into the foyer, paved with terracotta tiles polished to a shine. My flip-flops slap across them as I follow Liam into the back of the apartment. It opens into a great room with floor-to-ceiling windows that flood the room in warm, natural, late afternoon light and provide a view of a lush, private garden. Liam leads me over to his trains, pulling out and naming each car for me before setting them on the tracks.

Quinn plops down next to me on the floor where I'm sitting with my back against the lime green couch. She thrusts her tablet at me. "Wead to me, Eban."

I recognize *Night Night Lights* from when Katie and Rachel were little. Quinn lies on the white shag throw rug on the floor beside me, chin propped up on her little hands, as I begin reading.

Eddie enters, handing me a steaming mug of coffee.

I meet his gaze and give him a small smile. "Thank you."

He nods in response but I catch the light reflecting off the tears in his eyes. Perhaps I can give him a serious second chance. Maybe it took having two new children to make him realize what he missed out on with me, but I've changed, too. I'm no longer the unsure, bitter teen who left the Eastern Province. He'll never be able to make up for all the years he abandoned me, but we might be able to start fresh.

Sitting next to my half siblings, it occurs to me that Quinn and Liam are the future of the Union. I can't sacrifice the Union to save the Ruins any more than I could allow the slaughter of the innocent people in the Ruins to save the Union.

I look at these two little people, one with my hair, the other with eyes like mine, and I know I'll do whatever's necessary to protect them.

It is my destiny, and I embrace it with everything I am.

DEAR READER

Thank you for reading *The Union*. As an independent author, gaining exposure relies on readers spreading the word, so if you have the time and are so inclined, please consider leaving a short review on Goodreads or your favorite site for books.

To stay up to date on the latest releases and get access to exclusive content, including the story of *The Union* from Cyrus's point of view, be sure to sign up for my newsletter: http://thhernandez.com/newsletter.

ALSO BY T.H. HERNANDEZ

ACKNOWLEDGMENTS

This has been a long journey and so many people helped me along the way, so this is going to be long. Might want to use the bathroom and grab a beer.

First and foremost, a huge thanks goes to my long-suffering husband, Ernie, who not only participated in brainstorming sessions with me, but also countless rounds of edits to the "final" version of my manuscript (there were lots of final versions, for the record).

It was nearly four years ago when, recently laid off as a proposal writer, he asked me if I could do anything I wanted what would it be. When I told him I'd like to write a novel he asked me what was stopping me. Sometimes you just need to be hit upside the head with the obvious to truly get it.

Thanks to my family for never letting me give up. To my daughter, Mattea, for inviting her friends to read and provide feedback. To my sons, Noah and Grayson, for sharing the story with their classes at school. To my parents, Jim and Judy, for always encouraging my creativity.

A special thanks goes out to my beta readers, Cori Griswold, Elizabeth Parks, Elizabeth Shulok, Emily Kelton, Gen Curry, Judy

Trageser, Kat Wills, Kim Guarnaccia, Lia Trageser, Marcie Sheriff, Mattea Hernandez, Natalia Moorehead, Pam Richardson, and Ripal Patel. You all read early versions and provided invaluable feedback, which helped me realize that writing proposals and writing fiction are NOTHING alike.

Thanks to my fabulous critique group, Amanda, Cao, Jen and Sally. My story would suck without you.

Thanks to my wonderful editor, Barbara Trageser, you taught me self-control when it comes to comma usage and to never, ever go towards anything in the United States ever again.

To my fabulous cover artist, Mark Sgarbossa for creating a work of art that belongs on a wall and not just the cover of a book.

To the many wonderful young adult writers I met at Swoon-Reads, including Jennifer DiGiovanni, K.A. Cozzo, Sally White, Jenny Elliot, and Katie Van Ark. Getting to know other writers in my genre has been the best part of the journey.

And finally, to the best writer friends anyone could ask for, Jen, Karole, and Sally, for holding my hand through countless rejections, for pushing me to continue submitting, and finally for not telling me I'm batshit crazy for pursuing the indie route (although I might actually be).

BONUS MATERIAL

FOUND

FOUND is the story of The Union from Cyrus's point of view. To read the rest of this story, get access to exclusive content, and get advanced notification of upcoming releases, cover reveals, and ARCs, sign up for my **newsletter**.

Life in the Ruins is turbulent, and no one knows that better than Cyrus Matthews. After a tornado destroyed his hometown, killing most of his family, he needed a fresh start. Along with his older brother, Lucien, and a handful of friends, he migrated west to start a new life.

Now eighteen, Cyrus drifts through life, knowing he hasn't fully come to terms with the tragedy of his past. He finds plenty of consolation in the arms of the girls in the valley where he lives and at the annual Festival he attends with his brother and friends.

When a mysterious girl lands in their lives, seemingly out of nowhere, Cyrus's life is turned upside once again. He finds himself falling for the beautiful redhead with the incredible past and thinks maybe he's found what he hadn't even realized he'd been looking for.

But when tragedy strikes once again, he discovers that maybe what he's really found, is a reason to go on.

CHAPTER 1 - HERO

"When are you leaving?" Lucy asks, running her fingers through my hair.

"Tomorrow."

She slides her hand under my T-shirt, skimming my stomach.

"Then I guess we shouldn't waste any time."

"I like the way you think," I murmur, lowering my face and brushing my lips against hers. Lucy's hot, like seriously hot. I've been chasing after her for weeks, but she likes to play hard to get. We always seem to take two steps forward and one giant step back. She opens her mouth, inviting me in. Maybe today will be different. I test the waters, my fingers venturing beneath her shirt. When she doesn't push my hand away, I get more daring.

"This is the perfect way to say goodbye," she breathes. "Sealing our relationship before you go."

My hands stop their exploration and I pull back, staring at her. Her eyes are closed, pale lashes fanning rosy cheeks.

Her eyelids flutter open and brilliant blue eyes lock with mine.

"Knowing you're coming back to me will help get me through the long, lonely days without you."

I back away, putting some distance between us. "Luce...I like you and this has been fun, but..."

"Oh." She sits up, tugging her shirt down.

How did we go from messing around and making out to "sealing our relationship"? I stand and run a hand through my hair. "I ummm...I should get back, help with packing...and stuff."

She turns and begins jamming the leftovers into her picnic basket. I reach a hand down to pull her up, but she recoils from the gesture. She can't possibly think this is personal, I've never had a relationship with anyone.

"Let me walk you home"

"That's okay. I'm fine."

"Lucy..." I take the picnic basket from her hand. "Don't be mad. It's just...we're leaving tomorrow—"

"No, I get it. There'll be all kinds of girls at the Festival, and you don't want to be tied down."

"It's not that..." Except that's exactly it. Lucien's been whipped by Draya for as long as I can remember. And Marcus has only ever been with Sonia. I don't think he's even kissed another girl. I want to settle down someday. But someday when I'm a lot older.

Lucy's quiet as we walk. When we get to her house, she takes the picnic basket back from me. I weigh my options, wanting to apologize but not wanting to give her the wrong idea. I might not be the best guy in the valley, but I've never lied, never told a girl what she wants to hear so she'll sleep with me.

I'm still struggling with what to say when she suddenly throws an arm around my neck and kisses me. Before I even get a chance to react, a deep voice calls out, "Lucille!"

Shit, shit, shit. I bolt away from her, shoving my hands into my pockets.

"Hi, Daddy," she coos, giving me a knowing smirk over her shoulder before bouncing up the front steps, the picnic basket swinging on her arm.

Her father glares at me from the porch and I spin, heading home without a glance back. Soon, though, my feet are directing me past the house and toward my hideaway. I should go home and help the others pack, but the need for time and space to clear my head wins out.

A network of cobwebs greets me when I step onto the wood planks that make up the floor of my secret retreat. I built it four years ago when we first got here. It's the only place I can truly call my own. Based on the layers of dust and spider infestation, I guess it's been awhile since I was last here. After cleaning up some, I grab my fishing pole a head down into the ravine to the creek.

The water rushes past, blending with bird songs, creating a soothing harmony. While I wait for a bite, I replay my afternoon with Lucy, trying to figure out which signal I sent that made her believe I wanted to get serious.

My parents had this great relationship, the kind I want for myself. My fourteen-year-old self saw perfection, but my eighteen-year-old self sometimes wonders if I only saw what I wanted to see.

Jamming the end of the pole into the mud, I lie back against the grass, my hands behind my head and doze off. The sun hangs low when I wake groggy and disoriented. My fishing pole is in the water, caught between two rocks.

I grab the pole only to discover whatever dragged it down into the creek got away. With a heavy sigh, I trudge back up to put the pole away and head home.

"Where've you been?" Draya demands as I climb the steps from the front door up to the main floor.

"Out."

"Nice of you to finally join us. There's a lot left to do. Go find Lucien. I think he's out back."

I head outside, making my way around to the back of the house where my older brother is chopping firewood. My boots crunch against dead leaves and twigs. He glances up, wiping the sweat off his brow with the back of his arm.

"Hey," I say.

He nods, but doesn't say anything.

"Sorry," I say when he doesn't respond. "How can I help?"

He studies me for a moment and shakes his head. "I'm about finished. Check with Draya."

"She sent me out to you."

"Check with Ally, then, Cy." If I didn't know him so well, I'd miss the trace of annoyance in his voice. I guess he's got a right to be pissed, though.

I find Ally in the kitchen working on dinner. "What can I help with?"

She stares at me for a second like I just told her I discovered her secret super power. C'mon, I'm not that bad, am I?

"You...you, um, you..." she stammers. "You can make the salad." A rare smile graces her lips, making me feel for a moment as if I'm the one with a super power.

We work in companionable silence until Will enters. He glances between me to Ally, his eyes widening.

"Hey, I help out in the kitchen. Sometimes," I say.

"Whatever, dude," Will says before heading outside and returning with a bucket of water, placing it over the fire.

Over the past few months I've been spending less time here. I'm not sure why other than I'm restless. This is my family and my home, but it's like I've got an itch I can't isolate enough to scratch.

Once we clean up the post-dinner dishes, we pack all the crap we're taking with us and place the bags by the door. I say good-night to the others on my way up to my room, too excited to sleep. I love the festivals with all the new people to meet, foods to try, games to play.

Reminds me of the first one our whole family went to when I was a kid. They're bittersweet memories. It's not as hard to think about them now as it used to be. Sometimes I let myself remember small glimpses of my old life. Like now.

I smile thinking about how I carried Penelope on my shoulders into that first Summer Fest all those years ago. My hands were wrapped tightly around her shins as she wiggled and giggled, her little fingers laced under my chin in a death grip. In her three-year-old eyes, I was a hero. She might be the last person who ever looked at me that way.

CHAPTER 2 - WINGMAN

By the end of the second day of hiking, everyone is pissing and moaning about something. Everyone except Ben, that is. The kid is non-stop energy. Never complains about anything. I shift my pack to the other shoulder and stretch out my neck.

Ben walks beside me, a steady stream of words pouring out of his mouth. I gave up trying to keep up with the verbal diarrhea a long time ago, just making sure to nod and smile every now and then.

Tent tops appear on the horizon, and when the wind shifts direction, the sounds of music and voices carry to us along with the mouthwatering scent of grilled meats. My heart rate picks up in anticipation. No more hiking or grumbling, just good food, new friends, and lots of bullshitting. Ben takes off, and knowing him, he'll try to run all the way there.

"Ben, hang on. Wait for the rest of us," I call to him.

The others soon catch up to us. Sonia and Marcus bring up the rear, leading the calf we'll trade for supplies. He's been handy, carting most of our gear on the way here. Too bad we'll have to lug it all home ourselves.

"Hey, Cy," Draya calls from behind me.

I turn and glance at her over my shoulder. "Yeah?"

Lucien's arm is draped over her, their fingers twisted together. "Try not to sleep with everyone in camp this year, okay?"

I roll my eyes as Lucien whispers something in her ear.

"I'm just looking out for the family," she says with a laugh.

I think she's secretly thrilled I'm in no hurry to settle down. That would mean another body in our house, or worse, me moving out, leaving the rest of them to carry the workload I currently handle. Doesn't stop her from busting my balls every chance she gets. I may not have an older sister, but sometimes it sure feels like it.

"Don't listen to her, Cy," Marcus says. "We need to live vicariously through you single guys." Sonia elbows him in the ribs and he lets out a loud "Oof."

Will falls in step beside me, not saying anything at first, then clears his throat a few times. "So...do you think...maybe..." he stammers, his face beet red.

"Spit it out, Will."

He drops his gaze to his feet and mumbles something. Will and his younger brother, Ben, haven't been with us all that long. We found them on our way home from Summer Fest a couple years back, shortly after Union officials killed their parents. We brought them along, and they've been living with us ever since. But after two years he shouldn't still be this uncomfortable around me.

"Will you be my wingman? I mean, if I see someone I'm interested in?"

I throw my head back and laugh, draping my arm across his shoulder. He's started noticing girls but doesn't seem to know what to do about it yet. With Lucien and Marcus more or less married, I'd love to hang around with Will more. He's a few years younger, but he's cool. And he's got that lost puppy thing that girls eat up. This could be fun.

"Hell, yeah, I will."

He smiles and relaxes, the bright red stain on his cheeks fading.

"So, how do you do it? I mean, what do you say to a girl if you like her?"

I sigh and rub the back of my neck. "Depends on the girl."

"Cy doesn't need to do anything," Marcus says. "Girls just fall on the ground in front of him."

"That's not true. Just be yourself. Don't be Dag." Dag's a good enough looking guy, but he's got an edge to him that makes girls wary. "First, get a feel for the girl. If she's shy, find a way to compliment her. If she's outgoing, there's a number of ways you can approach her. But you can never go wrong with honest flattery."

"How do you know if she's interested?"

I shrug. "You just know."

Crazy is in full-swing by the time we make it to the edge of camp. Lucien checks us in and gets a location for our tents. As we make our way over to our designated plot, a girl catches my eye. Man, she's hot. My head swivels, not wanting to lose her in the crowd, and I slam into Marcus.

"Hey, watch where you're going." He must spot the girl because he says, "*Dayum...*" under his breath.

"Yeah."

Long brown hair brushes her bare shoulders which are tanned to perfection. Dark chocolate eyes turn my way and she smiles, revealing white teeth. The tiny shorts she's wearing barely cover her assets, and the little scrap of material she's got for a top looks like it's painted on.

"You guys are disgusting," Sonia says, walking off.

Marcus snaps out of his daze and chases after her. I dump my stuff on the ground and head toward the girl. Her smile broadens as I approach.

"Hi," I say.

"Hi. I'm Dru."

"Cyrus."

"Nice to meet you Cyrus." She glances over her shoulder at a dozen guys who are staring at her then turns back to me. "You looking for a partner for the three-legged race?"

"As a matter of fact, I am."

"Well then I'll be sure to look for you later." She walks back to join her group, swinging her hips with finesse.

This girl might just kill me.

After dumping my stuff and securing the calf, I head off in search of Dru. Thoughts of those long, perfect legs and super-short shorts play over and over in my mind. She's near the grove surrounded by no less than five guys. She turns her head and stares at me, as if she'd sensed me coming. The guys around her continue to talk, but she's no longer listening. Her eyes are fixed on me, and a small, triumphant smile tugs at my lips.

She leaves the other dudes behind without a word and walks over to me. "Hi," she says. "I thought maybe you forgot about me."

"Never."

She hooks her hand around my arm. "So, wanna join me for dinner?"

"Sure."

She leads me over to the mess area where we grab trays. I heap some food on my plate and follow Dru over to the picnic tables. I'm sure we'll be volunteering here tomorrow morning. Lucien likes to jump right in and get our work obligations out of the way quickly, giving us the rest of the festival to enjoy ourselves. I dig into my dinner, ravenous after two days of hiking. Plus, with the signals Dru is putting out, I'm likely to need the fuel for what I hope is a very long night.

"I need to go help out back at our campsite," I say when I'm done eating. "But I'll catch up with you later."

"I'll save you a seat at the bonfire," she says.

Tall trees surround our camp spot that allow only patches of sunlight to dance through the leaves. The dark velvety odor of freshly dug earth clings to the air as Ally grooms the dirt of our assigned plot with a rake.

Draya glances up from pounding the final stake in her tent. "Oh, glad you remembered where we're staying," her words are harsh, but her smile is playful.

I glance past her at my brother who doesn't appear amused at all. He doesn't say anything, but I can see the disappointment in his eyes. What the hell does he want from me? Shit, it's not like I slack off. I always do my share and then some. So what if I wanted to kick back and have some fun first? Shaking my head and muttering under my breath, I get busy, helping with the rest of the tents and take over the fire ring construction from the younger boys.

"We're going to get some dinner," Ally says to me. 'Coming?"

"I already ate. I'll finish up here and join you all at the bonfire."

"Okay..." She drags the word out, as if she wants to say more, but she doesn't.

After finishing up, I wander off looking for a place to clean up. I find a spot upstream without anyone around and strip to wash the sweat and grime from my body. When I'm dry, I dress and return to my tent, dropping off my dirty clothes before heading to the bonfire. For opening night, many of the families and sometimes whole towns put on sketches, sing songs, or provide other forms of entertainment that can last until late into the night.

The bonfire sits in the center of camp in a large clearing. Tree stumps and rocks provide an outer ring with people sitting on them, keeping a distance from the heat. It's plenty warm out without the fire, but it's tradition. Kids are jamming food onto the ends of sticks and pushing them into the flames. Sparks climb up into the speckled night sky, and wood and smoke mix with the smell of charred meat.

My family is sitting together near the picnic grove and I drop down next to Will. "See anyone interesting yet?"

Even though the sun set hours ago and the fire is throwing an orange glow on everyone, I swear he's blushing. "Maybe. I don't know. I guess not."

I laugh and nudge him with my shoulder. "If that changes, let me know."

Across the bonfire, Dru gives me a little finger wave, and I push up off the ground. "Well, I have, so I'm gonna go visit for a while. Catch you later."

I make my way around to Dru, reaching down a hand to pull her up. She wipes her palms on her shorts and inclines her head to the side. "Mom, Dad, this is Cyrus. We met this afternoon. Cyrus, these are my parents, Melody and Atherton."

Melody is an older version of her daughter, dark, exotic, beautiful. She reaches out a delicate hand to shake mine. Atherton looks as if he could tear my limbs off with his bare hands, but his smile seems genuine as he pumps my arm. Dru wraps her hand around my wrist and pulls me away from the bonfire. I reach down and take her hand, leading her to a picnic table outside the fire ring. I sit on top, pulling her next to me, our feet resting on the bench.

"So, where are you from, Cyrus?"

"A little valley two days from here. What about you?"

"North of here. This is our first trip to this Summer Fest. We went to one northeast of us last year."

"We always come to this one. It's close and we like it."

She trails one finger up my arm. "I'm glad we came to this one."

I drop my gaze to her hers, but she's staring at my mouth. She moves closer and kisses me, wasting no time taking the kiss to the next level. Before I know it, she's straddling my lap, running her fingers through my hair.

I reach up and take her hands, pulling them away from my head and setting her back on the table beside me. She gives me a sexy pout, but hell, we're only ten feet away from over a hundred people. That's not the kind of kissing you do in front of an audience, much less one made up of young kids.

Sliding off the table, I take her hand, pulling her with me back to my tent. Our camp site is deserted as I lead Dru inside. Even in the dark I can see her eyes shining. Yeah, this is going to be a good year.

THE RUINS

THE RUINS is book 2 in The Union series. The following are the first two chapters.

Heartbroken, grief-stricken, and wracked with guilt, seventeen-year-old Evan Taylor returned to the Union, leaving behind the boy she loved.

Now, she and her friends must find a way to do the impossible – warn the citizens of the Union about an impending rebel attack without alerting the government and risking retaliation against her friends in the Ruins.

When every move Evan makes is thwarted, it soon becomes clear she's being watched. Faced with a daily fight to stay one step ahead of her pursuers, she returns to the Ruins. But life in the Ruins has its own dangers, and soon she's fighting a different battle – to stay alive long enough to discover the truth.

THE RUINS is the second book in THE UNION series, a young adult romantic adventure set in the near future.

CHAPTER 1 - DESTINY

Grief, guilt, heartbreak, fear, loss, and abandonment all swirl in my head, creating a vortex of pain and confusion keeping me awake.

Three days ago I was planning a future with the boy I love. Cyrus was going to come back to the Union with me. We were going to figure out a way to warn the citizens here or stop the attack. Together. Now his brother is dead and Cyrus stayed behind, unwilling to abandon the rest of his family.

The scents of honeysuckle and fresh-cut grass float on a late summer night breeze. I stare up at the clouds from the chaise lounge on the balcony. A thick marine layer inched its way in from the coast hours ago, blanketing the sky and obscuring the stars I was hoping to see. With the moon hidden and the Union lights off for the night, darkness envelopes me.

Over the soft murmuring of desalinated ocean water burbling through the aqueduct, I hear the door slide open behind me and sit up. My bio-dad, Eddie, walks out and takes the spot beside me.

"Can't sleep?"

I shift to my right, giving him more room. "No. You?"

He shakes his head, his cinnamon-colored wavy hair sweeping

across his shoulders. "My grandmother used to say if you can't sleep, it means you're awake in someone else's dreams."

That's a comforting sentiment. Is Cyrus dreaming about me right now? Or is he like me, too afraid of the nightmares to close his eyes?

Eddie presses his lips together and studies me for several long seconds. "Are you ready to tell me where you've really been all summer?"

His question catches me off guard. I thought he bought my story, the one I told him when I came back. The one Lisa fed him while I was in the Ruins. Posing as me, she texted my mom and Eddie from my tablet with regular updates on our fake adventures sailing off the southeastern coast. When I first showed up here yesterday afternoon, he didn't seem to care where I'd been or what I'd been up to, only that I was here at all. I'm definitely not ready to have this conversation with him.

"I don't know, are you ready to tell me where you were for the first twelve years of my life?"

He shifts his weight on the chaise next to me and sighs. "I don't know how many times I can apologize."

"You think another 'I'm sorry' is going to fix everything?"

He rubs his palms on his thighs and stands. "You're welcome to stay here as long as you'd like, but you might want to ratchet the anger down a few notches." He moves toward the door before turning back. "You're going to have to forgive me some day."

I raise my head and turn toward his dark silhouette. "Why? You think sending me a ticket and letting me hang out with your new kids makes up for everything?"

"No," he says quietly, "because hanging on to all that anger and resentment isn't healthy." He walks back into the house, sliding the door closed behind him.

With a heavy sigh, I fall on my back and stare back up into the blackness. Seriously? After being nothing to me for three-quarters of my life, where does he get off being all parental right now?

My breaths come short and raspy, my arms pumping as my feet pound the earth. Lungs burning, I glance over my shoulder to make sure I'm out of arm's reach and trip over a tree root, falling to the ground. Lucien stares up at me with unseeing eyes, a bright red stain spreading across his midsection. I push myself up, spinning into Dantel's chest. He lurches back, blood pouring from his mouth as I shoot him over and over.

My own scream wakes me, my heart racing as fast as it was in my dream. A thin layer of moisture coats the lounge chair, as if it's broken out into a cold sweat, too. The chill is enough to send me back inside to burrow under the blankets. It still feels wrong to sleep in a bed while my friends in the Ruins are roughing it on hard ground. But sleeping on the floor out of guilt is something I'm not prepared to explain to Eddie.

The remnants of my nightmare continue to haunt my waking thoughts. It might've only been a dream, but it's wrapped in truth, tied with a bow of reality. Rolling to my side, I force my thoughts to something else, to a way to stop a group of unknown rebels in the Ruins from attacking the Union. Without any information on who's behind the plot, what their plans are, or when it'll happen, I'm second-guessing my decision to come home. Why did I think I could do this? I am no one. A spoiled Union princess who's had everything she's ever needed handed to her.

I punch my pillow and turn to my back, staring up at the ceiling and willing my mind to shut up. But it refuses. Crawling out of bed, I pad over to the window and slide it open before burrowing back under the blankets. Through the opening, I can hear the water gurgling past and finally drift off, lulled by the sweet song of fake nature.

A steady knocking pulls me from sleep, but I refuse to go without a fight. I burrow deeper under the comforter, trying to escape the relentless assault. When it's clear I can't win, I sit up and rub my eyes. "Come in," I croak, my voice adjusting to being used for the first time today.

Eddie pokes his head in. "You have a call."

With a sigh, I get up, shuffling down the stairs to the great room and pick up the phone. "Hello?"

"Morning, Evansville."

"Hey, Bryce. What's up?"

"We're meeting at Lisa's this morning. Want me to come get you?"

"No, that's okay. I need to shower and eat breakfast."

"Do you know where she lives?"

"Oh...no."

"I'll be by to get you in an hour," he says, a smile evident in his voice.

I take a quick shower and dress and startle at the stranger staring back at me from the mirror. My features are the same — wide-spaced hazel eyes that appear brown or green, depending on my mood or what I'm wearing, small nose, full lips — but the short blond hair is still foreign after seventeen years as a redhead. So are the muscles and tanned skin from spending my days working outside in the Ruins all summer.

I apply some product to my hair, trying to get my curls to behave and slip my feet into flip flops before bounding downstairs. It's too quiet in here, Eddie and the kids must have gone out. A plate of muffins sits next to a fresh pot of coffee. I pour myself a cup and grab a muffin. When I slide my finger along the edge of the counter, it lights up, displaying the central controls. I swipe a few times, selecting a music channel.

The front door opens, and two giggling children spill into the apartment, followed by Eddie.

"Eban!" Quinn, my almost two-year-old half-sister yells, running into the kitchen and shoving a fist full of crushed flowers into my hand. "For you." A smile splits her face, her pale blue eyes wide.

"Thank you." I say, scooping her up for a kiss.

Eddie reaches into the cabinet above the refrigerator and hands me a small glass vase. The tension hanging between us is heavy and ugly, but I don't know what to say or do to diffuse it. Our problems are not going to be fixed with a word or simple gesture. I put the flowers in the vase and add water, setting it on the counter for Quinn to see.

"Pwetty." She nods her head with enthusiasm, her red curls bouncing, which makes her nod harder until she giggles.

A knock at the door indicates my escort is here. I kiss the top of her head and high-five my half-brother, Liam, before heading to the door. "Be back later," I call over my shoulder, slipping out the door before Eddie can ask any questions.

CHAPTER 2 - PLAYING A PART

Bryce and I walk down the path from Eddie's apartment to the commuter station. The Western Province is so different from where I grew up in the East. Everything here is so pristine, new, white, clean, the only color coming from the flowers and plants. By contrast, the Eastern Province is dark and rich, like an old city with a storied past.

We cover the distance in silence. I'm still pissed at him for lying to me about everything from his name to his career. The fact that the smugglers he was investigating kidnapped me isn't something easily forgiven.

We hop a northbound train, grabbing seats in an enclosed area, giving us some privacy. Bryce stares out the window and I stare at his profile, trying to decide exactly how I feel about him today. I settle on still royally pissed off but no longer homicidal.

"How'd things go last night?" he asks with a lift of his brow after he catches me staring at him.

"Not well." I shift and twirl a piece of stitching that's pulled loose from the seat. "Eddie asked me where I'd been the past couple of months, and I lashed out, basically telling him he didn't even have the right to ask the question."

"Ouch."

"He can't just show up when I'm nearly grown and decide it's time to be a father."

Bryce grins, and I realize he was just teasing me.

"Lying doesn't come naturally to me." I shrug. "So, I lapsed into doing what I do best, antagonizing him. How do you do it?"

"Do what?"

"Lie to people so easily. About...*everything?*"

The grin slides off his face, and he becomes suddenly fascinated by his knuckles. "It's like playing a role. Were you ever in a school play?"

"Yeah, once. I played a toothbrush in an oral hygiene production."

He laughs. "Well, it's sort of like that. You become this other person and play a part."

"I guess."

"It's not easy, but you find ways to be as truthful as possible. Like embellishing or half-truths. Instead of telling your dad, I mean Eddie, you were kidnapped and taken into the Ruins, say you were exploring. It's both plausible and mostly true."

"It's okay to call him my dad, you know. I call him Eddie, but technically, he is my father."

The train slows, pulling into the station, and I stand to follow Bryce through the crowd as he guides us to the stairs. He leads me down a couple levels and out onto the main sidewalk. The structures here are concrete and glass, providing more of an urban grunge feel in stark contrast to the pristine white stucco where Eddie lives.

Bryce navigates an alley between rows of buildings, stopping at Lisa's place, which resembles a box with windows. She's in a bustling area of the borough with everything she could possibly want located within a few short blocks of her apartment.

Bryce knocks, and Lisa flings the door open seconds later, her blond hair tumbling past her shoulders. She squeals when she sees us and wraps her arm around my neck in a hug, her other hand gripping an oversized magenta coffee mug.

Still in pink flowered pajama pants and gray tank, she kicks the door open wider with her foot so we can enter. Her apartment is a cube of space with rustic wood floors and narrow windows set up high in bare concrete walls. A Japanese shoji screen sits in one corner hiding what I assume is her bed. A red fuzzy couch sits in the center of the space flanked by a pair of saffron colored armchairs with a cobalt acrylic coffee table in the middle. Along the side wall is a galley-style kitchen, and four teal padded barstools are pressed up against a narrow island, forming an eating area.

"This place is great, Lis," I say, looking around. "Like a box of crayons threw up in here."

"I know." Her dark eyes shine with obvious delight. "My parents surprised me with this as a graduation present. It's small, but it's mine."

Part of me is envious. I'd love to have a place of my own like this. And I guess I could've, if I'd figured out what to do with my life and applied for an internship somewhere. Instead, I'm stuck living with a man I barely know who just happens to have spawned me.

Colin saunters into the room from what must be the bathroom — the only door in the entire apartment other than the front door. He plops onto the couch and stretches out his lanky legs, propping his feet up on the coffee table. His dark messy hair is even wilder this morning, spilling into chocolate-colored eyes, tangling with bushy eyebrows.

I take a seat beside Colin and rest my head on his shoulder. He kisses the top of my head. "Morning, EvTay."

Bryce sits in one of the armchairs, which have bizarrely long seats, meaning either his legs will stick out straight in front of him, like Quinn when she sits on the couch, or he needs to slouch back so his feet can reach the floor. He chooses the latter.

"Hey," Lisa calls from the kitchen area. "How'd it go with Eddie last night?"

"I got into a fight with him," I mumble. She lifts an eyebrow, and I blow out a steady breath. "Yeah. He asked where I'd been over the summer and I asked where he'd been for most of my life. Not one of our better father-daughter bonding moments."

She studies me for a long moment before smoothly changing the subject. "Do you want some coffee?"

"Always," I say, taking the plum-colored ceramic mug.

The front door opens, and Jack sweeps in, carrying a bag of what I assume are baked goods based on their heavenly yeasty aroma. He gives Lisa a light kiss, but it's enough that Colin's jaw clenches in response. We swarm the island to find fresh bagels and cream cheese. Colin, Bryce, and I take ours back to the living area to eat.

"So, what's the plan?" Lisa asks around a mouthful of bagel.

"I've been thinking a lot about this," Jack says. "We need more information. There are still too many unknowns to come up with any kind of a plan yet."

I set my mug down and glance around the room at my friends. "So then what *do* we do?"

Jack runs a hand along his jaw. "Investigate. Find out everything we can."

"I might have an idea—"

"Give us a chance to sort through what we've already learned before you go off and do anything, okay?" Jack cuts me off. "These are dangerous people."

I narrow my eyes, pissed he didn't even let me finish. "How much time are we talking about?"

"Only a few days," Bryce says. "Just long enough to see what we can dig up. Then we'll regroup. The more information we have, the better plan we'll be able to develop."

Jack glances at Bryce. "We should get going. They'll send someone out to look for us if we don't show up for our debrief." He leans over to kiss Lisa before walking to the door.

Bryce pushes his plate across the coffee table and sets down his cup. He starts to follow Jack to the door but turns back to me, as if he's going to say something. Instead, he gives his head a slight shake and follows Jack outside without a word.

Once the door closes behind them, Lisa eyes me. "What's going on with you two anyway?"

I let out a long sigh. "Absolutely nothing."

After Lisa and Colin take turns showering and getting ready, we decide to kill time by exploring the neighborhood. Shopping isn't going to stop an attack on the Union, but it beats sitting around doing nothing while Jack and Bryce do their thing.

Outside, the early September morning is warm, promising to be hot by afternoon, but nowhere near as hot as it was out in the Ruins. Back-to-school shoppers swarm the sidewalks along with others who are trying to eke out the most of their last few days of summer vacation. Unfortunately, fresh air and mild exercise does nothing to ease my edginess at not doing anything productive.

"Why the scowl?" Lisa asks me.

I didn't even realize I was and work to relax my facial muscles. But rather than blow her off and give her some lame excuse for my mood, I go with the truth. "The reason I came back was to make something happen. Hell, if I knew we'd just be sitting around, I'd have stayed with Cyrus." Her jaw clenches and I realize how snarky that sounded.

"Jack and Bryce are cops, Evan. These guys...they're *really* dangerous."

"No shit. I know that better than anyone. They kidnapped *me*," I slap my chest with my hand. "They killed Lucien. You think I don't know what they're capable of?"

I've never yelled at Lisa before, and her stunned expression tells me maybe I've gone too far. She did come out to the Ruins to rescue me, even though I didn't actually need rescuing.

"I'm not saying that," she says. "But, well, it's...don't hate me for saying this, but you have a habit of acting first and thinking second. Jack deals with information, and he makes plans based on that information."

Colin shifts his feet, looking like he'd rather be anywhere

but here.

"He didn't even listen to my idea," I mumble, but I let it drop because arguing with her isn't going to accomplish anything. She won't really get it anyway. This is personal to me, it's my mission, or fate, or whatever, and I feel like it's being hijacked from me.

We walk in silence, a cloud of tension hanging over us until Lisa drags us into a clothing store. I pick up a few things then get an idea. "Let's find a salon. I want to color my hair."

"Your roots aren't showing yet," Lisa says.

"I'm gonna go back to red."

"I've never seen anyone with your color hair," she says. "Good luck finding it in a bottle."

"I know, but I want to at least try. For Quinn's sake."

She lifts an eyebrow.

"Quinn said I can't be her sister because her sister has red hair."

She nods as if she understands, and with two younger siblings who look like carbon copies of her, she probably does.

We stumble upon a salon a few blocks down with a sign saying they take walk-ins. I meet the colorist and explain what I want. Her eyebrows disappear into her bangs, but I pull up a picture on my tablet of me, Lisa, and Colin from last year to show her. She glances at the screen and excuses herself, returning with a stash of supplies. After checking the picture a couple more times as she mixes, she sits me down and applies the color to my hair. When she's done, even though it's still wet, I can tell it's close. As long as I'm here, I see a stylist who fixes the hatchet job Cyrus did on my hair. Glancing at my reflection with fresh eyes, the way I think Quinn will look at me, I decide I'm pleased with the results.

"I'm starving," Colin announces before we've taken more than a few steps outside the salon.

"Wow, it's been two whole hours since you ate something. I'm surprised you're still conscious," Lisa says.

Colin shoots her a look, then shrugs and leads the way to a bistro. We sit on the patio and people-watch while Colin inhales three sandwiches, Lisa picks at a salad, and I eat the first burger I've had in months. A boy about Quinn's age squats nearby and carries on an animated conversation with the pigeons camped out next to our table.

"So, do you want to talk more about what happened out there?" Lisa asks.

I glance up from the boy and meet Lisa's anxious gaze. I shake my head, and her shoulders drop. I know she's hurt, we used to talk about everything. "I'm sorry Lis, I'm just not ready."

She reaches out her hand, resting it on my arm and gives me a nod of understanding. Or at least I think that's what it is. I finish my burger and wad up the paper, tossing it onto my tray. Lisa abandons her salad, and we clear our table before heading out to do a little more shopping.

Lisa gets a few things for her apartment, and I pick out a pair of purple sparkly barrettes for Quinn and a T-shirt for Liam that says, "Don't blame me, I'm the middle child." Our last stop is the music store. When we walk in, my eyes are drawn to an enormous screen suspended from the ceiling, rotating through images of various performers. It's currently displaying a promotional image of Epic Vinyl with none other than Eddie McIntyre front and center. It's probably from ten years ago, he looks so young, definitely before I knew him. The picture must have been taken at the peak of their career.

I was such a huge fan before I knew Eddie was my dad. Their music was all about growing up, fitting in, finding your place in the world, and I could relate to the lyrics. But now I just see a hypocrite. All the time he was making his fortune off songs about finding himself, he walked away from his most important responsibility.

Lisa tugs on my arm. "Come on, we can go."

"No, it's okay. I mean it's not like I don't live in the guy's house. An image on a display is no big deal, just...*really* surreal."

ABOUT THE AUTHOR

T.H. Hernandez is the author of young adult books. The Union, a futuristic dystopian adventure, was a finalist in the 2015 San Diego book awards in the Young Adult Fiction category.

I love pumpkin spice lattes, Game of Thrones, Comic-Con, Star Wars, Doctor Who marathons, Bad Lip Reading videos, and all things young adult, especially the three young adults who share my home.

When not visiting the imaginary worlds inside her head, I live in usually sunny San Diego, California with my husband and three children, a couple of cats, and a dog who thinks he's a cat, affectionately referred to as "the puppycat."

To stay up to date on the latest releases and get access to exclusive content, including the story of *The Union* from Cyrus's point of view, be sure to sign up for my newsletter: http://thhernandez.com/newsletter.

You can find me online at:
thhernandez.com
thhernandezauthor@gmail.com

Made in United States
Troutdale, OR
03/28/2024

18765807R00181